A CHRISTM

"Miss Allen is heedless." ~~...~~ but there was no mirth in the sound. "Aren't most young people? But it is a condition we recover from and go on to change if we are lucky and are given the chance."

"Yes, change," Beatrice said, staring into the flames. "Like I did."

David moved imperceptibly closer to Beatrice. It was the first reference she had voluntarily made to her own life. He moved closer still and tried to take her into his arms again, finding he needed that more than brandy.

She pushed at his arms. "I do not need comforting. I shall be all right."

"Perhaps it is comfort that I need," he said.

She gazed steadily at him, and then moved into his arms. He enclosed her, feeling a budding hope swell and open, bursting into flower before he could quell it. He gained courage from that one simple movement. Something had changed with the night.

"Now," he said quietly, leaning back, holding her, "we must speak of something else, or we shall fret ourselves into illness. Tell me why you have gone around for a month with sadness in your beautiful eyes and a burden in your heart? I feel that it has something to do with me, and yet I do not know how that could be."

After a long pause, she sighed. "All right," she said, gazing up at him with fathomless blue eyes, the reflection of flames dancing there.

She reached up and touched his hair, smoothing the silvered temples and touching the corners of his eyes. He felt her soft form cradled against him and knew that this night was somehow going to change everything.

BOOKS BY DONNA SIMPSON

LORD ST. CLAIRE'S ANGEL

LADY DELAFONT'S DILEMMA

LADY MAY'S FOLLY

MISS TRUELOVE BECKONS

BELLE OF THE BALL

A RAKE'S REDEMPTION

A COUNTRY COURTSHIP

A MATCHMAKER'S CHRISTMAS

Published by Zebra Books

A MATCHMAKER'S CHRISTMAS

Donna Simpson

ZEBRA BOOKS
Kensington Publishing Corp.
http://www.kensingtonbooks.com

One

"It's been so mild today . . . almost too warm. But I have a feeling in my bones that the weather is about to change." Beatrice Copland sat back on her heels and gazed off into the distance and the sweeping expanse of the high Yorkshire moors. The warm colors of autumn painted the scrubby trees with a palette of rust and amber, cinnabar and salmon, underlaid with the color of old gold. "Soon all of this will change from gentle breezes and ripening harvests to frost and snow and icy blasts." With a sigh, she absently snipped a chrysanthemum too close to the bud.

She glanced swiftly up at her employer, aware suddenly that there had been no acerbic response to her musing, no sharp and acid rejoinder about the coming frosty weather or the idiocy of maundering on about it. But Lady Bournaud, well wrapped against any chill in her elegant Bath chair, was not sleeping. Her dark eyes were fixed on Beatrice, in fact, with a peculiar brightness.

"I snipped this one too close, my lady," Beatrice said, displaying her clumsy handiwork. Her ladyship had that look in her eye again, the one that unnerved her. Lately the old woman's gaze had rested on her companion for far too long and with too fixed a gleam.

"Doesn't matter," said the old woman. "Pick some more of the bronze, and then some of those yellow ones. Some Michaelmas daisies, too." She relaxed back in her chair and her gaze wandered to the distant moors, where the sinking sun would soon tuck itself to bed behind the misty hills.

With a sigh of relief Beatrice went back to her work, collecting the last buds and blooms from the south-facing flower garden. Dahlias and daisies joined the chrysanthemums in her heavily laden basket, where it rested on the flagstone walk. She sniffed the air appreciatively and said, "Squire Fellows must be burning some leaves or brush nearby." The squire rented from the Comtesse Bournaud all of the fields surrounding her gray stone manor, affectionately known as Chateau Bournaud, and farmed them, in addition to his own large acreage. He was a good tenant, caring for the land as if it were his own.

There was no answer from the comtesse, but Beatrice was used to long silences, since the old lady had never been one to talk for the sake of hearing her own voice. "I love that scent!"She sat back on her heels again, brushing her work-reddened hand over her plain gown of brown stuff. She never wore gloves, and saw the occasional blisters and calluses as honorable penance for so many old sins. "It reminds me of my childhood. Old Squire Gorpe did the same thing. He was such an interesting character, quite one of the old school; have I ever told you about Squire Gorpe?" Beatrice glanced up once more at Lady Bournaud and paused.

Her employer, the very English widow of the dashing Comte François Bournaud, was staring at her again.

"I don't believe you have, and I cannot say that I wish you to," Lady Bournaud said dryly. "Make sure the Parson's Pink," she said, naming one of her favorite roses, "is well protected before the frost tonight. It's going to be a long, cold winter. Been a miserable summer and it is not likely to get any better now."

Now that sounded more like her ladyship! Beatrice concealed a wide smile and went back to work, her hands getting colder and her knuckles reddening as she heaped coppery chrysanthemums alongside the bronze already collected. Squire Fellows and his good wife, Mary, were to come to luncheon on the morrow, and Lady Bournaud insisted on fresh-cut flowers as long as it was possible, and that no one should collect them but Beatrice.

It was work she loved. Nothing mattered when she was in the garden and could smell the rich scents of earth and foliage, the green juices of living plants staining her naked hands. She should hate the winter, for there was no such release during the long, dreary months when the ivy-covered manse was entombed in a thick layer of snow and crusted ice. But each season had its own sorrows and rewards, and she had learned long ago to take each day as it came; it was the only way for someone like her to advance through life. Looking ahead was too bleak and looking back unthinkable.

She cast a sideways glance at Lady Bournaud. The elderly woman had been even more broody lately than normal, and she was not a lighthearted lady in her best temper. But Beatrice was worried for her, and not only because with the old woman's death would come the end of her employment and certain penury. She had come to care for the crusty beldam and would miss her.

But still, she worked on in silence, directed by her employer's clipped phrases. With the help of Tidwell, the ancient butler, she moved her ladyship's Bath chair around to the west side of the manor house and began clearing the gardens there. But soon, as the sun glided toward the horizon, a chill wind drifted down from the moors, becoming more insistent as the shadows lengthened. It was almost time to go in.

"Beatrice, I have lived a selfish and grasping life."

Startled, Beatrice paused, a bunch of lily tubers in her dirt-crusted hands. "My lady?" she said, gazing at her employer.

"You heard me," Lady Bournaud said, pushing away the blankets that swathed her completely. "I have been selfish and grasping. What part of that phrase is incomprehensible?"

When Beatrice had first come as companion to the comtesse ten years before, the woman had been wont to pace when angry or agitated, which was often. Now, bound to a bath chair by her weakening legs, she looked like she longed for her old release from tension. But what was upsetting her this time? She had never heard her employer speak like this.

Her silence had been noted and interpreted.

The comtesse fixed her challenging stare on her companion. "You just don't know what to say in reply that is tactful. But it is true. I have been selfish and grasping and unpleasant." Each word of condemnation was punctuated by the beating of one large, gnarled hand on her blanket-covered knee. "I have outlived my usefulness." Her pink-rimmed eyes unfocused, her voice falling to normal tones, she continued. "I hate this present age of music I don't understand, prissy young folk allowed to marry wherever they wish, and a mad old king. Younger than me, the poor, sad fellow. And the war just over . . . It killed so many, wounded so many more. And riots in the countryside. Used to be men wanted to work for a living; now all they want is to break looms and riot for bread!"

Beatrice knew better than to join that particular argument. They had talked about it many times, but the old woman just did not seem to see that the times were changing so rapidly; swifter, more efficient looms had left many without employment. The work ethic had not declined, there just were no jobs. Without work, there was no bread for the children, and when men could not feed their children they became restive and violent. Lady Bournaud was not unsympathetic, but she was still living in her memory, a halcyon era when any man who wanted to could find work weaving or working the land. And so Beatrice, fearing her employer's agitation, stayed silent.

She dusted off her hands instead, rose stiffly, and came to kneel at the side of the Bath chair. She pulled the blankets around the old woman, feeling the chill herself now that she had stopped her work. She shivered. The light was dying. "Are you sure you are all right, my lady?"

"I am fine, Beatrice. Stop your incessant fussing." She pushed the younger woman's hands away, irritably. "You will make yourself old before your time if you start clucking like a broody old hen."

"My lady, in less than a year I will be forty. That is quite old enough."

"I am four score at Christmas. *That*, my dear Beatrice, is old enough." Her twisted hands plucked at the blue woolen blanket on her lap and her eyes misted. "If you are to live to my age you are only half done, child. Do not try to distract me. When François died twenty years ago, I buried myself here in Yorkshire as surely as I buried his cold, lifeless body in the cemetery behind the chapel. Since then I have done nothing but mourn." Her gaze sharpened and she looked down at Beatrice, still kneeling on the cold flagstone terrace. "And I forced you to immure yourself here, as well."

"You forced me to nothing, my lady. You were good enough to employ me." Beatrice smiled, taking the gnarled hands in hers and chafing them, feeling the cold, knobby joints stiffening. She massaged them; Lady Bournaud's joints were increasingly frozen into immobility. "I am a fortunate woman and I know it. You have been so very good to me. I have a roof over my head, a comfortable bed to sleep in, good food, and my work is not onerous. I know when I am fortunate."

"Stuff and nonsense," Lady Bournaud said vigorously. She gazed down at her companion curiously. What she had said to Beatrice was true. So selfish had she become that she had never given a second thought to what dreams or aspirations died when the young woman at her side became her companion ten years before. Surely Beatrice wanted more than this life, devoting every waking hour to an old woman's crotchets? A home of her own, a family, perhaps? And yet now, approaching forty, slim and youthful still, with only a couple of worry lines on her smooth forehead to show advancing age, she did seem content. Too content. She was still so young, if only she knew it. At Beatrice's age Lady Bournaud had only just met the dashing Comte François Bournaud. At Beatrice's age . . . The thought snagged in her mind like wool on a thorn bush. It would stay there she knew, for rumination later, when all was quiet and the household slept.

"Is that all it takes to make you happy?" Lady Bournaud asked. "Good food and a warm bed? I did not think you an idiot. Did you never wish to marry, Beatrice? I've never even asked you that, have I? Never bothered to ask if you wanted more from life than to cater to an old woman's whims."

"Now you are talking foolishness," Beatrice said, standing and stretching her limbs, hands on her hips as she arched her back. A chiffchaff hopped under a close-by gooseberry bush and she watched him with absent eyes, shivering and rubbing her arms against the breeze that was dancing over dried grass and dead flowers. Her gaze returned to her employer. "I can only think that this evening air is doing you harm. It is growing cooler and damper by the minute." She tried to inject some cheer in her voice, to conceal the melancholy wrought by Lady Bournaud's intrusive questions. "Let us go in and have a treat. Mulled spiced wine, mayhap, with those ginger biscuits Cook was baking this afternoon." With that, she kicked the brake lever on the rattan Bath chair and laboriously wheeled the comtesse up the winding flagstone path. She would have Tidwell send someone for the basket of blossoms she was leaving behind.

Despite Beatrice's brisk behavior, though, Lady Bournaud did not miss the fact that her companion had not answered the questions posed. And that the younger woman's eyes had shadowed with some old, remembered sadness. More food for thought later, in the still darkness, when she could not sleep.

Much later, after mulled wine and biscuits and a couple of hours of desultory conversation in the crimson saloon, near the fire, Beatrice sank gratefully into her snug bed and pulled the snowy counterpane up under her chin. Her prediction of a chilly night was coming true, but at least there was a banked fire in her room. Lady Bournaud's home was run along the most luxurious of lines, fires allowed even in the servant's quarters—though Beatrice was in the family wing so she could be close to the comtesse—and candles everywhere.

As she did every night, she said a silent prayer of thanks for her own good fortune and a wish for Lady Bournaud's health. "God, protect and keep her in Your hands," she whispered. "And grant me the strength to give her the good life she deserves for her many, *many* kindnesses." And then, as always, she ended with a supplication. "And please, *please* let me find forgiveness at last." She turned her face into the pillow as silent tears slid down her cheek.

As pearl-gray morning light peeked in, a tiny maid trotted into her ladyship's luxurious chamber, opening forest green curtains, stirring the fire against the pervasive chill, and offering steaming tea on a mahogany bedside tray. Lady Bournaud asked for her bed jacket and lap desk and set to work as she sipped her dark morning brew. As usual, she had slept very little, but out of the ordinary was the amount of time she had spent in the frozen darkness thinking of others. Most nights she would lose herself in old memories, happier memories. Memories of François.

François, her adored husband of almost twenty years, had been an extraordinary man, embracing English tradition and English customs as if they were his own. He had lost much of his family in the unrest in France, but England, he said, had welcomed him, and in return he loved it like he would an adopted mother who had taken him to her vast and tearstained bosom.

He was very Gallic, and tended to be florid in his praise. That he had chosen to wed the acerbic and sharp-tongued Lady Elizabeth, as she had been called until her marriage, had never failed to amaze folks who knew them both.

But it had been a happy marriage. Lady Bournaud paused as she sharpened her nib and considered the actions she was about to take. Yes, this was what she wanted. For twenty years she had mourned, but now she was approaching the time when she could expect to see François very soon, and what would he ask?

What had she been doing with her time on earth? Yes, certainly, that would be his first question, if he did not already know. Whom had she aided? Whom comforted? Could she face him and say, "Nothing and no one"? No. She would make of the end of her life some utility, some good. Selfishness had been her guide for twenty years, but now she felt urgently that she must make haste and do some good. She bent over her paper. It was only October. By December everything would be ready.

She was sanding a letter and consulting a list, almost illegible in her crabbed, spidery handwriting, when her companion entered. "Ah, Beatrice. Good of you to join me finally."

Beatrice paused just inside the door, but there was a humorous glint in the old woman's glacial eyes. She relaxed and moved toward the bed. "I, unlike yourself, Lady Bournaud, actually sleep at night."

"Ah, the benefits of youth and a clear conscience."

It was fortunate the old lady's eyes were cast down as she sealed a letter, dripping the wax onto the edge of the paper and waiting, then pushing the fleur-de-lis seal into the puddle of hardening blue, or she would have seen Beatrice's guilty start.

"I have made a decision," Lady Bournaud said, in her clarion voice.

Taking a deep breath and resuming her task, which was supplying her ladyship's table with fresh handkerchiefs, Beatrice steadied her nerves and said, in what she hoped was her normal voice, "Why do I have the feeling that this decision is going to mean more work for me?" After ten years, she was allowed more latitude in her behavior to the old woman, but always kept a close eye on the comtesse's uncertain temper. She appeared to be in a cheerful mood this morning, and indeed the autumn sun flooded the emerald chamber with glorious light.

"It could be that you are right," Lady Bournaud said, "but I think you will enjoy this, too. This great dungeon has been silent and cold for too long. When my husband was alive . . ." Her voice trailed off, and there was a note of pain. But she cleared her throat and continued. "When François was alive, this house echoed with music and laughter. He loved English tradition, and at no time of year was that more evident than Christmas. So this year we are going to have an old-fashioned English Christmas here, with the Yule log, and mistletoe, Christmas pudding, everything. And laughter and talk and music. We are going to invite company."

Every one of the past ten Christmases had been spent quietly, with Squire Fellows and his wife attending for dinner, and the exchange of small tokens of appreciation. Beatrice approached the bed and gazed down at her employer. "Does this mean you are inviting the St. Eustace children for Christmas? All seven of them? Oh, yes, and another on the way, if I remember right?"

Lady Bournaud shuddered. The St. Eustaces, her nearest relations and inheritors, by entail, of the estate and all of its furnishings, were not well beloved by her, being too numerous and too noisy for her aging sensibility. "No, most certainly not. They are quite happily at home in Cornwall. Traveling with that many children would be like gathering a band of Gypsies, and poor Rosetta could never do it, especially not in her current condition."

It made a convenient excuse, Beatrice thought, that the heir's wife was with child yet again. She looked down at the oak lap desk and tidied the mess of splotched ink and the sand that had been used to dry it.

"No, this is the guest list," the older woman said, handing her a sheet of paper covered in spidery writing.

Beatrice took the list and perused it, noting before she did the letters already addressed, piled on the lap desk. Lady Bournaud kept up a large and varied correspondence, and it was the one thing with which she required no help. She wrote and sealed all of her letters herself, and Tidwell took care of everything else, delivering them to the village with his own hand.

She scanned the list and her heart thumped and her stomach clenched. Her mouth was dry, as if it was wadded with cotton. But it was, perhaps, just a list of suggestions. It did not mean that Lady Bournaud had invited each and every one of them. "I . . . I've seen some of the names before, but I don't think I know any one of them."

"No, I don't suppose you do," the comtesse said, taking the list back and squinting at it. "And truthfully, I do not think all of them will come." She pointed her finger to three names and said, "These will not come, almost certainly. But I am hopeful of a few." Her smile was sly. "In fact, Beatrice, I must say I have made a special plea to those I truly wish to attend more than the others.

"Mark Rowland, for instance. He is the great-nephew of my oldest friend in the world, Mrs. Cordelia Selwyn. Delia is confined to her home in Bath right now—she suffers badly with gout—and for a time we did not correspond. Some idiotic tiff that we have now mended; I do not even remember the genesis nor the resolution of it. Mark will come because I may have—inadvertently, you understand—led him to believe in my letter to him that I wish more than anything to make amends, but need his personal attendance to help me frame my apology. Delia will know by advance warning and will back my story. Mark is a dear boy—taken holy orders, you know—and will do anything to make peace for his beloved aunt."

Diverted for a moment from her growing uneasiness, Beatrice said, "Lady Bournaud, that is diabolical! To lure the poor fellow all the way to Yorkshire in winter on a false mission is too bad of you. Why are you doing this?"

The woman pointed one thick fingernail at another name on the list. "This is my reason, my dear."

"Miss Verity Allen," Beatrice read out, leaning over the edge of the bed. She looked into the old woman's eyes. "I don't think I understand."

"Miss Verity Allen is the daughter of Fanny, my second cousin. They moved away to Upper Canada and make their home there now. But I received a letter in the summer that Fanny had sent her eldest daughter home to England. Verity refuses to marry appropriately." There was disapproval in the quavering voice. "Poor Fanny is at the end of her patience, and her brother, with whom Verity is staying while here, is resolute in sending her back to Canada. She is a bad influence, he fears, on his own daughters. Incorrigible, I am told! The girl is four-and-twenty, time and past that she was wed. And if Mark is to be a vicar, it is high time *he* wed."

Beatrice, appalled, said, "You cannot mean you intend to match these poor unsuspecting young people? A reverend and a hoyden?"

"Young Rowland is strong-minded. Just the influence to calm a disobedient girl."

If she wasn't so agitated over something else, Beatrice would have been amused. "My lady, it seems to me that you told me a story once of a young girl who refused resolutely to marry the man her father had matched her with. And she stayed unmarried until she found the mate of her heart."

The comtesse shifted awkwardly under her bedclothes and signaled for the desk to be removed. As Beatrice lifted it from her lap, she said, "That was different. That man was a bully and a coward, and I was right to refuse him. He died in a drunken duel the next year over some wager or other."

"And perhaps Miss Allen had similar justification."

"No, she has just refused to marry at all! It isn't natural."

Beatrice was speechless.

"There is another name on the list, another guest I am sure will come." The woman's tone was arch.

Beatrice placed the desk carefully on the table by the window. When she returned to her employer's bedside, Lady Bournaud held the list again and pointed out one name on it.

Sir David Chappell.

Beatrice felt a wave of sickness flood over her.

"He is my godson." Lady Bournaud traced the spidery

script with her fingernail. "Such a dear boy. Not really a boy, I suppose. Forty-seven, I think. Could he really be forty-seven? I suppose. If I remember correctly, the last time he paid me a visit you came down with that terrible summer grippe, and did not come out of your room the whole time he was here, so you have not met him yet."

Beatrice turned her face away and busied herself at the old woman's bedside table, filling her water glass and rearranging the vase of crimson bittersweet and rose hips. Her ladyship liked nature at her bedside now that she unable to get about herself to enjoy it. "Surely . . . surely such an important man will not wish to absent himself from London. . . . He will have other invitations. He will want to stay south."

"He will come," Lady Bournaud said.

"Why are you so insistent?" Beatrice said, trying to tamp down the desperation in her voice. But it was like banking a fire; covering it only made it burn brighter and hotter. "Why do you want him to visit?"

"I have my own reasons," she replied sharply. "I may need to accede to invasions of my privacy in a bodily sense, but my mind is my own, and my reasons are my own."

If she was not so desperate and so fearful, Beatrice would have heeded the warning in the sharpening tone of her ladyship's voice. "But Yorkshire, in *winter* . . ."

"Every person whom I wish to come, will come," Lady Bournaud said, in her tone an abrupt dismissal of the subject. "Now call Partridge. I wish to dress."

Beatrice retreated to the hallway on her mission to call her employer's maid. But outside the door she stopped and sagged against the wall, the tears she had been stifling flowing now, burning a trail down her cheeks. *Oh, Lord,* she prayed, scrubbing at her eyes. *Please do not let him come. Please. Have I not done my penance? Have I not paid the price? I can't bear to see him after all this time.* Please, *just let me have peace.*

Two

Sir David Chappell gazed out at the hard rain that drummed against the window of his library and fingered the letter in his hands. A steady stream of raindrops down the glass obscured the view of horses and carriages on the street and the black umbrellas that bobbed along the walk outside.

November. It was the dreariest month, or so he had been wont to think as a youth, the creeping darkness taking its toll on the spirits of the oversensitive child he had been. December had stolen that honor of most dread month after the awful events of twenty years before that forever changed for him the joyous Christmas season. The sorrow had abated somewhat when he was raising Alexander, the school holiday over the Christmas season being their opportunity to become the good and fast friends they were now, more so than was usual, perhaps, for most fathers and sons. Together they had created new meaning in the season, and he was grateful for his son, or the tragedy of that time in his life would have forever blighted Christmas.

But Alex was stationed in Paris with Lord Pelagar, one of Wellington's retinue, a diplomat in the service of the War Office. He would not be home for some months, perhaps, or even some years, the first time father and son would not spend at least Christmas Day together. The tiny babe who had been left so tragically motherless on that cold Boxing Day so many, *many* years before was now a fine young man, one whom his father was proud to call "son."

But a man. And no longer in need of his father at the coming season. He would have the gaiety of Paris, young ladies to flirt and dance with, companions of his own age.

Chappell looked down once more at the letter in his hands. It was a pathetically worded missive, and that was enough to make him frown over it. *I am going to be all alone at Christmas,* Lady Bournaud had written. The iron-willed lady of his memory would never have written a letter containing that plaintive phrase. Didn't she have a companion? Perhaps the old lady was sickening for something, or perhaps . . . He frowned at the paper and creased the corner absently. She *was* getting older. For all he knew it could be her last Christmas on earth.

His mind drifted back, past the last twenty years when Christmas had meant him and Alex spending it together in London, going to pantomimes and shops, or in visiting friends' country houses. Back farther, to the days of his own youth in Yorkshire.

Comte François Bournaud and his comtesse, the English Lady Bournaud, were his father's employers. Mr. Arthur Chappell was merely their estate manager. But childless, the aristocratic couple had lavished attention on the rather serious young boy David Chappell had been, and at no time more than at Christmas.

Christmas at Chateau Bournaud, as the comte had called his home in the wild North Riding of Yorkshire, had become, for the motherless boy, a time of joy: sledding, skating, riddles and forfeits, and Silver Loo. Chappell would never forget the elegant silver-haired Comte Bournaud snatching burning raisins out of the flame as they played at the wildly popular game of Snapdragon. Chappell smiled, the misted glass in front of him like a magic lantern screen where the pictures of his youth flashed and danced.

As he grew from boyhood to manhood, Lady Bournaud, for all her crusty demeanor, had been his savior, ensuring that he attended a good school, introducing him to the appropriate people, making sure he gained a valuable position with the secretary of state. These boons were not to be taken lightly by the son of an estate manager, with no money and no connections to recommend him. He had made the most of her help, working hard and diligently furthering every social connection that could aid his rise in the government.

But then the dark days came; Comte Bournaud died, and then Chappell's father fell sick with a wasting illness. Lady Bournaud was there even in her own deep mourning, comforting, sturdy, paying endless amounts of money for physicians who, though they could do little for the aging Mr. Chappell, at least made him comfortable. It had been a horrible, sorrowful time for Chappell, with Melanie's death, and his infant son ill at first. At least with Lady Bournaud at his father's side, David had known the man was comfortable and well cared for. David had broken away from his demanding London position and was in Yorkshire at his father's side at the end, comforting for both of them.

Eventually the darkness had receded as Alex grew, and some modicum of joy had reentered Chappell's life. The past few years had been entirely taken up with travel and work, friends, and then the honor and surprise of his knighthood in the wake of the end of the war. He had not been back to Yorkshire for four years, if memory served him right.

And now Lady Bournaud sent him a letter, calling on his indulgence, asking for the favor of his company at Christmas, when no work would be done in London anyway. He was ashamed even to have hesitated for a moment. He owed her more than mere "indulgence," and found that he looked forward to seeing the grand lady again.

"Drucker," he called over his shoulder.

His valet entered and waited.

"We will be going to Yorkshire for the Christmas season. Have my secretary attend me, for I have much to do if I am to take off the entire month of December. And I will want him to take down my letter of acceptance in response to this invitation."

* * *

"I . . . Oh, Lady Bournaud, I do not feel well at all."

It was late November. Lady Bournaud gazed at her companion shrewdly, noting the burning cheeks and pale forehead. So Beatrice was ill. And yet, she had been well just that morning. "What is wrong with you?"

"I have a sore throat and a heaviness in my chest," Beatrice said. "I very much fear putrefaction, my lady. Perhaps I should retreat to my bed. I would not want to infect you."

"Nonsense. I have outlived disease. I begin to fear I shall live forever," Lady Bournaud said. The crimson saloon was warm, overheated even, from the blazing fire necessary to keep old bones limber. And Beatrice was warmly wrapped in a woolen gown with a heavy shawl over it. That could account for the burning cheeks. "Come, kneel by me, child."

Obediently, Beatrice knelt on the carpet at Lady Bournaud's feet and gazed up at her. The comtesse felt her cheeks and forehead, then gazed steadily into her eyes. "Open your mouth."

"I . . . I beg your pardon?"

"I said, open your mouth. Are your wits wandering?"

Beatrice opened her mouth and the older lady stared down her throat. "Looks fine to me, but I will have Roth come see you," she said of her elderly physician, whose practice was twenty miles south in the great city of Richmond. Just then a wind whipped up and a shower of ashes billowed from the fireplace. A sleety rain began, tapping impatient fingers at the saloon window.

Beatrice looked down at the carpet for a moment, and then said, slowly, "No, my lady, I would not have you summon Mr. Roth all the way here for me, and in this awful weather."

"But I will not have you sicken," the comtesse said, her eyes shrewdly assessing her companion. She watched the flickering alarm cross Beatrice's face, and the quick calculation in the younger woman's eyes. Beatrice was not really ill; of that she was certain. But what had led to this charade was still a mystery.

But Lady Bournaud won, as always.

"I am sure I will be much improved by morning, my lady."
Her voice was meek, but rebellion blazed in Beatrice's deep
blue eyes.

"I am sure you will be," the older woman said, her face
crinkling into a smile. "I am somehow *certain* that you will
be. Now run off to bed and get a good night's sleep. I have
much for you to do if the first of our guests are not to find us
at sixes and sevens."

And that was the last Lady Bournaud heard of any illness
on Beatrice's part, though the woman's lovely sapphire eyes
did not lose the haunted expression, nor did her nervous tension break. Something was afoot, but for once in her life Lady
Bournaud was stymied. She could conjecture, but Beatrice's
heart was a closed book to her. Lady Bournaud did not like
closed books.

Three

December had arrived with every promise of chill winds and isolating snowstorms. It was not that the snow had really set in yet, though the high moors were white-topped, but that the hard wind wailed and battered the square manse. The locals would say about it that it "blew a bit thin," but for Beatrice, who had grown up in the south, it was a bitter season indeed. She had to remind herself often of her philosophy, that no weather was bad weather when you had a home and a fire to warm you, a soft bed at night, and good food. There had been a time when she doubted she would ever have any one of those things again.

She glanced around her room. It was not the largest nor the most ornate on the family floor—in fact it was a former dressing room converted into a bedroom so she could be close to Lady Bournaud—but she had come to love it over the last ten years. She had a simple modern bed, a four-poster with carved finials in the shape of pineapples. A washstand, cheval mirror, chest of drawers, and a table with two chairs by the window made up the entirety of her furniture, but she had made it homey with the addition of books and pictures, and a colorful Turkey throw rug rescued from the attic. It was home.

Much better than what she would have had without Lady Bournaud.

Lady Bournaud. The companion position with her had been gained through the unexpected advocacy of some ancient relative almost forgotten. And the comtesse had made life good again. Beatrice would never forget the old lady's kindness when, at twenty-eight, beaten and cowed by life's travails, she had arrived at Chateau Bournaud to the welcome of her new employer, a stranger to her and fearsome in her gruffness, but eventually respected, and then loved.

They had rubbed along quite well for over ten years, growing to know each other's crotchets, understand each other's moods. Their relationship was not seamless, but misunderstandings and quarrels were rare.

So Beatrice would not hide away in her own room during this season, a victim to an imaginary illness. It was not only that the old woman was too shrewd to be cozened a second time, but it was time to face whatever fate had in store for her. She must trust that the regard Lady Bournaud seemed to hold her in would withstand the inevitable battering it was about to take, once the guests . . . or rather guest, had arrived.

And so, with her determination to enjoy whatever unexpected pleasure life offered firmly cloaking her, she admitted that as winter arrived, the sharp frost had as its compensation the beauty of frost fairies on the window, their lovely arcing designs a wonder of nature. And the first drifting snowflakes needed no consolation to bear. They were lovely and fragile, and there was nothing more delightful than walking among their fluttering delicacy, watching their starry beauty melt on coat and muffler, unless it was coming back inside to a roaring fire and hot, spiced cider.

But still . . . it was all very well to determine that she must take things as they came; in truth it would not be so simple. Beatrice paced away from her bedroom window and sat on the edge of her bed, trying to compose her thoughts, trying to quell the ever-threatening panic.

He would be there soon. *He* would look upon her, disdain her at first sight, and denounce her to Lady Bournaud. She would cry; inevitably she would cry. And the comtesse, in her most gruff voice, would demand an explanation. But what could she say? Apologies were twenty years too late. Sorrow, as bitter as willow tea, was useless.

But again, there was only so much one could control in one's destiny. There was no changing fate. December had arrived, and soon the house would be full of guests.

A commotion outside the house! Beatrice ran to the window of her chamber and threw back the curtain. A carriage and team, with a trunk lashed to the roof! And an elegant, albeit foreshortened, view of a gentleman in greatcoat and gloves, muffler and hat.

It could only be him. He had sent word that he would arrive the first week of December, and it was now the end of that period. He was there. He would now be stepping into the house. Now handing Tidwell his hat and cane. Soon he would look upon her with scornful eyes the color of aquamarine and demand to know why Lady Bournaud had employed such a creature. The last words he had ever spoken to her had burned into her memory, every scornful syllable, the condemnatory tone echoing even now in her head.

Beatrice paced the floor of her chamber, waiting for the summons that was sure to come. The comtesse had made it abundantly clear that Sir David was being invited because she thought he would make Beatrice a pleasing companion. Oh, worst of appalling possibilities! She had some shadowy fear that a hideous scene would ensue.

Then she braced herself. She would face the scene awaiting her. Pretend nothing was about to happen. Act as if he were just another visitor, another welcome stranger in the home of her employer.

She descended the stairs. There were voices in the hall. A frosty breeze whirled around the marble floor and ascended even the curved oaken staircase. Beatrice could feel it on her feet as she turned the corner on the landing, then made her way down the rest of the steps, to hear Tidwell's gracious voice.

"Her ladyship is in her chamber, sir. She asked that the first of the guests to arrive be escorted up to her chamber, for she is, in her own words, sir, an old lady and must be coddled."

A rich, low laugh answered that statement.

Beatrice swallowed hard, turned the corner at the bottom of the staircase, and said pleasantly, "I will take our visitor up to her ladyship, Tidwell." She raised her gaze directly into the eyes of . . . a complete stranger, with brown eyes and a mop of dark hair that drooped over his forehead, the thick walnut-colored thatch matted down by dampness and his hat, now removed and in the butler's hands.

"Mark Rowland," he said, putting out one hand.

"Ah, Mr. Rowland! You are the vicar, am I right?" She swallowed, calming her thudding heart and breathing a sigh of relief. Reprieve. A few luxurious hours to rest, maybe, or perhaps just minutes. Who knew?

"That is correct. And you are . . . ?"

"Oh, pardon me! I am Beatrice Copland, Lady Bournaud's companion. I would be glad to escort you up to her, Reverend."

"Just Rowland, please. Yes, she has written of you often in her letters. I am anxious to see her; I have been remiss in my duty of late. If I had known about this quarrel—" He broke off and glanced at her as they made their way back to the staircase.

"I know about it, sir. Lady Bournaud told me about her reason for inviting you." Beatrice suppressed a sigh of exasperation. She did not like to think of this handsome, likable young man dragged up to Yorkshire at this time of year on a fool's errand. She could not understand what had possessed her ladyship to indulge in this mad bout of matchmaking when she had never shown the slightest interest in such a pursuit before. It frankly worried her.

"Good. I dislike concealment of any kind. I abhor slyness and artifice, in all its guises. I much prefer openness."

Beatrice smothered another sigh. Wasn't this going to be an interesting season?

* * *

The second visitor to arrive was one not on the original list. Lady Silvia Hampton was a child, it seemed to Beatrice later that day when the young woman arrived. She was all soft curves and pale loveliness, a girl of nineteen with brown eyes like a fawn and brown hair that was soft, like a catkin.

Beatrice, in her unofficial capacity as Lady Bournaud's ambassadress, greeted the young woman and guided her to her room, the one next to her own. Her first impression of brainless loveliness was ameliorated by some shrewd questions on Lady Silvia's part, and a brief conversation.

All Beatrice knew was that the girl, the youngest daughter of the Earl of Crofton and his countess, had been sent to Yorkshire as punishment. From Lady Silvia's own mouth came the further information that it was because of her parents' intransigence, not her own.

"They wanted me to marry Lord Boxton," she said, glancing at Beatrice to see if there was recognition in the other woman's eyes. "He is very well thought of in some society circles. But I do not like him and will not marry him."

Amused at the prim but firm tone, Beatrice said, "Why?"

Her brown eyes thoughtful, Lady Silvia said, "He beats his dog."

Beatrice was called away at that moment, but she thought there must be more to it than that.

In other circumstances this notion of Lady Bournaud's, to have a houseful of guests for the Christmas season, might have been enjoyable for Beatrice, who seldom saw a new face, but there was still too much to be agitated about. She could not guarantee that she would even be able to stay for the holiday. Her employer had spoken much, over the last two months, about Sir David Chappell—his wisdom, his rectitude, his goodness—and she feared that even her years of service to the comtesse would not override the knight's opinion of his elderly friend's companion. She did not think she would be ejected from the household, but she could not calculate what would happen.

It was late afternoon and the night had already enfolded the household in its wintry embrace. Beatrice whispered a prayer of thanks. One more day she was safe. He would not come now, this late in the day; darkness closed in so early in December. She directed the footman to fill the wood bucket by the grate in the crimson saloon before her ladyship descended for her first evening with houseguests. Mr. Rowland and Lady Silvia had been offered and accepted an evening meal in their rooms, allowing them a chance to recover from the inevitable traveler's fatigue. But they would all be gathering for an hour or two in front of the fire in Lady Bournaud's favorite room.

Beatrice was just arranging a dried bouquet on the glossy oak table by the crimson-draped windows when she heard the doors open behind her.

"I am so glad you could make it all the way up here," Lady Bournaud's stentorian voice intoned. "It has been far too long."

Surprised that she was downstairs already, and without ringing for her companion's help, Beatrice turned from her task and opened her mouth to ask her ladyship if she needed aid. And then she saw who was pushing the old woman's Bath chair.

It was Sir David Chappell.

She shrank back into the shadows, but her movement drew both pairs of eyes, the elderly gray and the piercing aqua.

"Beatrice, come out, child. Don't hide away as if you are a mouse. Come!"

There was no denying the summons. Swallowing past a dry lump, like clay, in her throat, Beatrice moved forward, her eyes downcast. She waited in silence.

"What is wrong with you?" Lady Bournaud's tone was impatient, and not to be ignored.

Beatrice looked up and stepped forward. It was a physical shock to see again those eyes, those much-admired crystalline blue eyes. And her gaze raced over him, taking in the still-graceful form, lithe, slim. There were lines around the firm mouth and silver in the light brown hair, but other than that he looked much the same as he had twenty years before.

But . . .

Hope welled into her heart. She had expected condemnation, denouncement, the pointed finger, the tone of rigid anger. Instead there was mild interest and complete . . . Oh, yes, she was not mistaken. This was an unexpected boon.

In Sir David Chappell's beautiful aqua eyes there was complete nonrecognition.

Four

Chappell sat back in the deep chair by the fire and watched the companion, Beatrice Copland, as she assiduously attended Lady Bournaud, pulling the old woman's frothy shawl around her shoulders. There was reliance between them, he could see. Lady Bournaud trusted completely Beatrice Copland, and the younger woman held the elder in affection, not just duty.

He was glad of that. The gruff old woman put many people off with her frosty manners and sharp wit, but for those who could see beyond the aloof demeanor she was a steadfast friend.

"Stop fussing, Beatrice," Lady Bournaud said.

"If I do not fuss over you, then what is my *raison d'être*?" she replied mildly. She straightened then and began to exit.

"Do not go. Sit with us."

"But you have not seen Sir David for some time," she said, her hands clasped together and working with nervous energy, the slender fingers weaving in and out of each other.

"I may doze off," the comtesse said, "and then poor Davey would be left with no one to talk to."

"Are . . . are the others not coming down?"

"I suppose," the old woman said vaguely. "Sometime. Sit!"

Chappell frowned. He hoped his old friend had not become a martinet at this age. "Please join us, Miss Copland," he added, to soften her order. "I would enjoy the company."

She flushed, but drew a low stool close to her employer.

His head in the shadows, he watched the younger woman's eyes, feeling that there was something familiar about her, something he could not quite name. And yet he felt sure if he had ever met such a lovely woman he would remember her. She was very much to his taste—slim, quick, intelligent. Her voice was husky and beautifully toned. She stirred some deeply buried instinct in him, some desire to shelter and protect. And yet that was ridiculous. She was clearly not in need of protection. But she seemed like an injured fawn, ready to flee at the first wrong move.

She was self-conscious under his observation. He could see it in her stiff movements and fidgety activity. He turned his gaze and stared into the fire, wondering if it was just his long celibacy that was making him abnormally sensitive to a lovely woman's presence. His last lover had been his mistress, the older, well-connected, politically astute Lady Corleigh, but she had died three years before. Since then he had felt little urge to take another. Their connection had been as much a meeting of the minds as of the bodies. She had been able to aid his career, though by the time they came together, eleven years before, he had been well on his way to his present elevated stature, and that through his own hard work.

Lady Bournaud and Beatrice were talking quietly and so he gazed at the younger woman. Still that recognition teased at his brain. "Tell me, Miss Copland," he asked. "Have you ever resided in London?"

"I . . . once, a long time ago, I had a London Season."

"And in what year would that have been?"

She seemed loath to answer. Lady Bournaud was watching her carefully too, the expression on her wrinkled face and in her pale eyes unreadable. Chappell waited out the silence, spending it, with pleasure, noting how the golden glow of firelight flickered and danced in the reddish highlights of the companion's hair.

"It was in the year ninety-six," she said finally, her voice low toned.

He had not thought her of that age. She must be forty, then, or something close. He tried to ignore the long-suppressed pain in his heart at the memory of that year. It was the year Melanie died, a terrible time, and one he would rather forget. He had spent weeks in a fog of anger and pain, recrimination, drunkenness. He let the subject lapse, not willing to canvass the remembrances of that year. It was likely that he had some dim memory of her from a ballroom or musicale, and that was why she seemed so vaguely familiar.

At that moment a young man entered the room and advanced to the fire. "Ah, this is where the party is gathered," he said cheerily. He bent over and kissed Lady Bournaud's withered cheek and pulled a chair over to sit near her. He held her hand in his own.

She squeezed the hand and said, "Davey . . . Lord, I keep forgetting not to address you thusly," she said to Chappell. "Mark Rowland, this is Sir David Chappell."

Chappell leaned over and clasped the younger man's hand, as Lady Bournaud explained the connection between them all.

"What her ladyship has not said," Chappell explained, as she finished, "is that I have her to thank directly for the honor of my knighthood. It was she who was my first and most important benefactor." He bit back a smile at the flush that rose in her pale, soft cheeks. She was never very good at being thanked, but he had never found a way to repay her yet, and likely never would. And so she would accept the full measure of his gratitude. He caught the gleam in Miss Copland's eyes and his attention was riveted by her once more.

She turned her face away.

"Miss Copland," he said quietly. "Miss Copland," he repeated, when she did not respond.

She wiped her eyes and then turned her gaze his way.

"Do I . . . Do we know each other?"

She hesitated, but then shook her head. "No, Sir David. I can honestly say that we do not know each other at all."

* * *

"Pardon me," Lady Silvia Hampton said to a maid burdened with a tray full of freshly polished silver, "but I seem to have lost my way. I am looking for the crimson saloon, and was told it was in this direction."

The maid dropped an awkward curtsy, almost tipping her tray. "'Tis this way, milady, down this corridor, an' turn right, an' then . . ."

Lady Silvia shook her head. "I shall never remember that. I am dreadful at directions," she said. Just then the butler, Tidwell, and two footmen heavily laden with trays bearing delicious-smelling pastries, came into the hall. "Ah, these gentlemen will help me I am sure. I have confidence that they are headed for the crimson saloon. Thank you," she said to the maid. "I shall follow them."

She caught up with them, her slippers making no noise on the gleaming wood floor, made the requisite turn, and said, chattily, "Mr. Tidwell, I have never been to Yorkshire, and I am looking forward to Christmas here. It is quite like a foreign country to me." She gazed up at the portly butler and noted his startled gaze at being directly addressed. Why was it always so? Butlers and footmen and maids were simply humans too, were they not? Why was one supposed to ignore them? It made not a jot of sense to her, and she had thought long and hard on the subject.

Just then one of the footmen pushed open a door and stood back to allow her to advance before them.

"Why thank you. . . . What is your name?"

"Charles, milady."

"Charles. What a nice name." She entered the room, but paused and studied the tableau as the butler and footmen carried their trays to a table by the window. Her father had told her tales of Lady Bournaud, what a frosty old woman she was, and how ill-tempered. That was the white-haired woman in the Bath chair, she supposed. Silvia had questioned the maid who had brought her up her dinner as to the other guests, not all of whom had arrived so far. Sir David Chappell; yes, that must be the older gentleman with the streaks of silver in his hair. She had seen him once at a London gathering, and had been impressed by his demeanor.

And she had already met the woman at Lady Bournaud's knee, her companion, Miss Copland. She had been very kind and comfortable. Perhaps she would be a new friend.

But who was the good-looking gentleman with the thick brown hair? She approached the group and stood, waiting to be noticed. The first to look up was the youngest gentleman, and she felt a shock of recognition when she looked into his dark brown eyes. There was something there, some . . . Oh, why could she not put a name to it?

She curtsied.

"Ah, there is the child," Lady Bournaud said. "This is Lady Silvia Hampton," she said, her voice raised. "She is the daughter of friends of my late husband's, Lord and Lady Crofton. My dear, Miss Copland you have already met," the old lady said, indicating the woman at her knee. The companion nodded. "And that is Sir David Chappell, and that young gentleman is Mr. Mark Rowland. Come here. Come in front of me and let me look at you."

Obediently, Lady Silvia joined the companion at Lady Bournaud's knee and knelt at her feet. She looked up into the aging gray eyes, examining even as she was being examined. Something passed between them, an acknowledgment that they were two very firm characters.

"I have been told you are a naughty and disobedient daughter, young miss."

"As the life I live is my own, and the only one I have been given, I think it behooves me to be careful with it, ma'am, and not fritter it away on worthless objects," she answered. "My parents wished me to wed an inferior. I would not do it." It was simply put, but it was the truth. The carpet, while thick, was not a comfortable place to be, and so she stood. She risked glancing sideways toward the good-looking gentleman, Mr. Rowland, and was pleased when he flushed slightly, and stood.

"My lady, please take my chair." He bowed and indicated

with a sweeping gesture the red-upholstered chair he had just vacated.

"But where will you sit, sir?"

"It does not signify. Please, take my chair."

Their eyes met again, and in that instant she felt the truth deep within her. Mr. Mark Rowland, vicar, was a man unlike any she had met before.

Rowland had felt his world shift in that moment, when Lady Silvia's pansy-brown eyes had met his. She was the loveliest woman he had ever seen, soft brown hair, plump figure, small of stature and with well-shaped hands that moved restlessly as she spoke, like independent butterflies. Her face was round and she had a dimple in her chin, and he was utterly enchanted. But her words, that her parents had tried to match her with an inferior, that stopped him. Was she an elitist? If so, he would know it soon.

As the others returned to conversation, while the footmen set up the table for late tea, he stayed at her side. "My lady, surely you would rather have remained home for the Christmas season?"

Her eyes placid, she said, "No, you see, Lady Bournaud has hit upon it. This is my punishment, you see, for not falling in with my parents' wishes. They think to bend my will by sending me someplace they find distasteful. But they do not consider that as we think the same on almost nothing, I may have a very different view of Christmas in Yorkshire."

"And what have you thought so far?" He studied her face, the rosy cheeks, the wide, innocent eyes. She was a child in many ways, he thought. Too young, and too highly placed, the daughter of an earl. He must remember that and quell his instant attraction to such a pretty young lady.

"Of Yorkshire? Oh, but you see I have seen so little yet. Perhaps some kind gentleman will take me on a walk and then I can judge."

"I would be honored," he said, hearing himself before he

even had a chance for second thoughts. He swallowed hard. "I would be honored to walk with you anywhere you might wish, my lady."

"Thank you, Mr. Rowland."

She smiled, and two dimples at the corners of her mouth winked. *I am merely enchanted by her looks*, Rowland reminded himself, trying to ignore the stirring of his body and the thumping of his heart. *That is all. And the physical is so small a part of who we are. I must not forget it.*

But then, of course, he proceeded to forget it, and lost himself in a delightfully frivolous conversation with young Lady Silvia.

Tea had been served and consumed, and Lady Bournaud drifted into a doze near the warmth of the fire. But it was only a moment and then she was wide-awake again, though the rest likely thought her dozing still. This gathering had been a good thought of hers. She had been too long without company.

And yet something was wrong. Beatrice had been forced into conversation with Davey, but she was not happy about it. What objection could the woman have to her handsome godson? Beatrice didn't know him; she had said so. Was it, then, that instant antipathy that she had occasionally observed between two people, the dislike that had no foundation in reason, but was more like the hackles rising on the back of a dog's neck at the smell of a particular person or another animal? If so, it was only on Beatrice's side, for Davey seemed properly taken with her.

She stowed away that thought for later, when she was alone. The heat of the fire felt good on her face, but the ache in her bones would not go away no matter how warm or comfortable she was. She would ignore it and soldier on, because she always had.

Now, there was something else. . . . Ah, yes, it was the look in young Rowland's eyes when he first observed Lady Silvia.

He was smitten, and he was not a young man of whims, nor of frivolous thoughts. This did not bode well, and she regretted again that she had been forced by the Croftons' old connection with François to accede to their request.

But Verity Allen would arrive on the morrow, with any luck, and then there would be an end to this unsuitable flirtation, if flirtation it was. Verity was the girl for Mark, raised to work hard and not expect riches.

Eyes closed, Lady Bournaud listened, separating voices in the low hum of conversation. Mark was speaking to Lady Silvia about his parish work as the curate to an aging vicar. Good. He was a poor man and Lady Silvia was a sensible girl, for all her flighty appearance. She would see immediately that Rowland was of a class that she could not stoop to, for all of his good character and pleasing looks. She must trust that, and to Mark's own good sense. He would not give his heart away where it could not be retrieved.

All would sort itself out, she hoped, and if not, she would make it work out properly. The next day would see the beginning of her campaign.

Five

It was early morning yet, but the day was frosty, with a few flakes of snow tapping tentatively against the windows of Beatrice's chamber. She stood, arms wrapped around herself, staring down at the frost that made the landscape look like an ice sculpture, everything coated in crystalline white, even down to the dead flower heads and the grass spears.

Humbling though it was, she had to admit that Sir David Chappell did not remember her. And she had lied to him, even when he seemed to see some familiarity in her eyes. But if he had forgotten, why dredge up the past? Or was that the coward in her running again, as she had twenty years before, running from responsibility, from accountability?

But, a sly inner voice whispered, *to bring up the past would only upset him, especially now, at this time of year. Why bring sorrow to him if he has healed?*

Had he healed? Or was he only good at concealing his deep pain? After all, he had never married again. That spoke of grievous injury unhealed, an open and festering wound still. A man in his position, elevated to the rank of knight through his own service to the crown, surely he would have found through all those years a woman who appealed to him?

Not, though, if he was still grieving for his dead wife. She didn't want to think about that, and was about to turn away from the window when a movement caught her eye in the stable yard, which her room overlooked. A rider approached. A young man? Beatrice frowned down at the scene; it was certainly hard to tell from this distance, but it looked like no one who belonged at the estate. She hustled out of her room. It could be a messenger, or a rider from another estate. One of the guests, Verity Allen, the young lady who was a relative of Lady Bournaud's, had not yet arrived, though she had been expected two days before. Was this news of her?

Wrapping her shawl around her as she went, Beatrice swiftly moved through the house to the garden door, which more directly led to the stable yard. The sharp morning air hit her lungs like a physical jolt. She coughed, pulled the shawl closer, and hurried still toward the stable, across the hard-beaten, frozen earth.

"Bobby," she called out to the stable lad who was in the doorway sweeping the entrance. "Was that a rider I just saw?"

He touched his cap and nodded, but before he could speak, Beatrice was startled into a surprised, "Oh!"

From the stable yard strode . . . yes, a young woman. But surely the rider had been astride? And surely . . .

She moved forward as the girl looked up, and stopped.

"Is this Lady Bournaud's pile?" the girl said in a cheerful voice. "I could not get a sensible answer, for all I tried in there," she said, hitching her thumb over her shoulder. The stableboy was gawking, mouth open.

Her voice was oddly accented, but her manner was open and lively. Beatrice, speechless at first, soon found her tongue. "Yes, this is the home of Lady Bournaud. I am Miss Beatrice Copland, the comtesse's companion. And you are . . . ?"

"Verity Allen. Pleased to meet you," the young woman said, striding forward and shaking vigorously Beatrice's outstretched hand. She then looked up at the house and said, "This is it? Criminy, but it is a god-awful-looking pile of rubble, isn't it?" When Beatrice didn't answer, the girl shot her a swift look. "Not supposed to say that, right? I opened my mouth again. It always gets me in trouble. Say, do you prefer 'Betty' or 'Beatrice'?"

"Please come up to the house, Miss Allen," Beatrice said, bemused by the girl's forthright, bold manner. "Why did you ride instead of taking a carriage, if I may ask?" she said, turning and assuming the young woman would follow her. She wanted very much to broach the subject of the girl's apparent arrival astride her mount, but did not quite know how to raise it.

"Because I am sick of riding in a carriage. London was awful, so hemmed in and so many rules. I wanted to ride there, but my uncle wouldn't let me. Said I was a disgrace and could not be trusted. But I always rode at home and saw no reason why I should not, now that I am in the country, ride here, too."

The girl, with her long, loping stride, threatened to out-distance Beatrice quickly, but by then they were at the garden door and they entered. Beatrice led the way down dark corridors, past the working part of the house to the family rooms.

Beatrice frowned at her as they approached the stairs. "You have no baggage, Miss Allen?" She stopped and looked at the girl's ugly stuff gown and heavy wool coat.

Catching her gaze, Verity looked down at her outfit. "Oh! You're looking at this awful thing. Yes, well, I save this for riding. The skirt is full enough that I can ride astride. At home I ride wearing breeches, but I have not been able to filch a pair here. My luggage is still in the village down yonder," she said, pointing out the window to the valley. "When the mail coach let me off, I borrowed a horse from the smithy and told them to send my bags up later. They can retrieve the horse at the same time."

"Oh," Beatrice said faintly. This was the girl Lady Bournaud was intent on matching with Mr. Rowland? She was attractive enough, though she did her best to conceal it with ugly clothes and her hair scraped back into an untidy bun. But she had glossy, auburn hair and her features were perfect: an aquiline nose, a pointed chin, and an eager look in her blue-green eyes. She was tall for a young woman, but it was hard to tell her figure in that awful dress and hideous coat. Beatrice hoped that the rest of her clothing was more suitable and would come quickly, because she could not appear in that dress at dinner. It smelled of the stable, and that was the least of its sins.

"I imagine you will wish to tidy up, though with no clothes . . ." Beatrice did not quite know what to do. She was saved by the other woman's cheerful good sense.

"I could borrow something from you for a few hours," she said, sizing Beatrice up. "We look to be somewhat the same size, though I am taller. That is, if you don't mind. I do want to make a good impression on Lady Bournaud, though you might not think it to look at me."

Won by the girl's infectious good humor, Beatrice relaxed. It was impossible to dislike her, though she was not sure what her employer would think. "Certainly. I think that is a wonderful idea. Let me show you to your room and find some clothing for you to don."

Dinner was a cheerful, almost rowdy affair. Lady Bournaud did not descend for the meal, sending word that she was feeling under the weather, but would join them later in the crimson saloon, as was usual. So Beatrice presided and found she was becoming inured to Sir David's presence. As long as he did not look nor speak to her, that is. She had carefully ensured that he was down the table several places from her, between Squire Fellows and his good wife, Mary; the squire and his lady were visiting as they often did, Lady Bournaud having asked them especially for their cheerful conversation.

She listened to the chatter as she ate her turtle soup.

"I *thought* I saw you in London," Lady Silvia was saying to Miss Allen, "and you looked so jolly, but my father is . . . well, a rather stiff gentleman, and I am allowed only so much latitude, you know. But I am so glad to meet you at last."

"Time and more we finished wi' that there Poor Law," the squire was saying to Sir David. "I be thinkin' the poor are not the one's benefittin', but the arseholes that willna pay their puir lads a decent wage."

"Now with all my children gone, I have no notion what to

do with my time, so I have taken in some of the girls of the parish, you know," Mistress Mary, the squire's wife, was saying to Mr. Rowland. "Especially the ones with no father or mother, poor wee lasses. I am giving them training in sewing and cookery. They'll make good wives or fine housekeepers by the time I am done, and then I hope to . . ."

The voices drifted and eddied with little need for direction from her, and Beatrice was at her leisure to observe and listen as the turtle soup was replaced by baked haddock. But the voice that drew her attention most was Sir David's. It had deepened with time, and mellowed, but still . . .

"Now with the war over, we can concentrate, I hope, on our domestic problems, like the Poor Law. I would like to see it repealed and some better form of relief invented." He was speaking to the squire.

"Yers," the squire said. "I see we be in agreement, sir. But Speenhamland," he continued, naming the system of topping up laborers wages from the parish coffers, "is a crime, sir, a crime, I say! Only benefits the cheap barstards what won't pay fer good help."

"But we cannot abandon the system without something in its place, you see," Sir David said earnestly. "We thought we were doing the right thing, back in ninety-five, by giving laborers something more to feed their families with. But the road to hell, as they say, is paved with good intentions. Just before I left London we had that dreadful Spa Fields riot, and I had second thoughts about coming. I should, perhaps, have stayed in London."

"Spa Fields," Beatrice said, unconsciously joining the conversation. "We heard about that up here. How did that come about? We heard that one poor soul lost his life and others were badly hurt."

The statesman shook his head, his lightly lined face drawn in an expression of weary sadness. "Hunt, I am afraid, is in it for his own glory. If it were not so, he would not lead men to risk their lives in the manner he does."

"You speak of the man known as Orator Hunt, I believe. He

is famous even up here. But the people need a champion, do they not?"

His eyes met with Beatrice's. "If you consider a vainglorious popinjay of a man a champion, then Hunt is that."

"You must see, sir, that here in the north, with little but what we hear second- and thirdhand, we have no personal knowledge. I am merely speculating." She said it mildly, though her heart was thudding at the quick anger in his voice, a tone she knew only too well.

"I know that is true," he said, and there was contrition in his voice. "I apologize, Miss Copland, if my spleen was vented at your cost. But he is a mere agitator, with no idea of how government works nor any real solutions to offer, and I hear too often people sing his praises. It is very goading when I feel sure he wants only to foment insurrection."

Squire Fellows frowned and chewed thoughtfully on a mouthful of boiled beef, the remove after the haddock. "Much in whut you say, sir."

His lady elbowed him in the ribs, and he glanced at her puzzled, until she made a swift motion that indicated his full mouth. He swallowed hard, and continued. "Much in whut you say, but still, we carn't continue, sir, carn't continue!"

"But armed bands of men training in your northern pastures is not the answer, Mr. Fellows."

"I see you are aware, in the south, of our intrepid militiamen?" Beatrice smiled tentatively.

"They are powerless, Sir David," Mr. Rowland said, joining the discussion. "And when men feel powerless, they are vulnerable to any talk that seems to promise a future. However ill considered you think their actions, they are desperate, and desperate men *will* do something."

"They must hold to the rule of law, though, and not go about alarming the populace. As a reverend, Mr. Rowland, surely you can see that a peaceful—"

"They are not alarming the populace. Oftentimes the populace is in support of these men, who only want, after all, to feed their families."

"Rubbish. They want more than to feed families. They want nothing less than to topple our government. And that is the sure way to the same kind of destruction we have seen in France over the last thirty years!"

Beatrice was about to open her mouth, alarmed at how the table conversation had become so surly, when Lady Silvia said, "I don't know how it has come about, but I seem to have lost my fork. Mr. Rowland, could you find it for me?"

"Your fork? Certainly, my lady, but how . . . "

Verity Allen, mischief lighting her odd, blue-green eyes, said, "I think it left with the last remove, Lady Silvia."

The subject was turned with the hunt for the fork, and Beatrice sighed in gratitude. They finished the meal in peace, until Verity looked up and her eyes widened. "Criminy! Look at the snow!"

"Snow?" Mrs. Fellows cried out in alarm. She pushed away from the table and waddled to the window, where, indeed, white flakes pelted the glass against the gloom of twilight. "Oh, we must go. We must. Mr. Fellows, gather yourself; we must leave at once!"

Beatrice concealed a smile and moved away from the table herself, knowing the guests would be leaving. The squire's wife was from the south, and even though she had been married for almost forty years and living in Yorkshire for all that time, she could not be sanguine about a northern snowstorm. By the time the squire had called for his carriage and the servants had retrieved all of their layers of clothing, the snow had thickened, and as Beatrice saw them to the door, it was gathering and swirling into drifts.

Dinner was finished and the company gathered in the crimson saloon, where Lady Bournaud was already bundled warmly by the blazing hearth, seated in her Bath chair in the choice spot. Sir David went to her immediately and asked after her health.

"I am as well as any old woman can hope to be. I ache, I forget things, I cannot move freely on my own, and I find dependence intolerable. That is how I am. Now, are you not sorry you asked?" She fixed on him her basilisk glare.

"Not yet," he said mildly. "I think I would need to be told to go to the devil before I would be sorry I asked."

She chuckled and reached out one knobby hand to pat his cheek, as if he were still the ten-year-old boy she remembered so well. Beatrice's eyes misted, thinking she had not seen her employer so joyful for a year or more. For that reason alone she had to be happy that Sir David had accepted the invitation, even though it was causing her some personal discomfort.

The room was warm, and Rowland, with the help of the footmen, directed the arc of chairs so all of the ladies could be comfortable, including herself. He really was a charming gentleman when he lost the seriousness he tended toward. And yet that solemnity of character was not grim in any way, it was just a habitual studiousness that was not unpleasing.

Though from Verity Allen's perspective, as vigorous and energetic as she was, it might look rather dour and staid. Beatrice sat back in the comfortable chair Rowland had pulled forward for her on the other side of her employer and watched the company. Sir David stayed by Lady Bournaud's left side, holding her hand in his. Mr. Rowland, seated between Lady Silvia and Miss Allen, was clearly hard-pressed to keep his gaze from wandering to Lady Silvia's radiant visage. He seemed entranced, and yet Beatrice caught him a time or two searching the young lady's expression with an earnest eye. In Beatrice's estimation, Lady Silvia was as lively as Verity Allen, but seemed almost prim by comparison, for the girl from the Colonies was very free speaking.

The window rattled, and everyone jumped except Lady Bournaud, who chuckled. "A good blow tonight," she said. "'Tis early in the season for this, I suppose, but we do get these storms rattling down into the valley. By morning you will not even be able to see the village from here, everything will be buried so deep."

"How exciting," Verity said, clasping her hands together

and trapping them between her knees. "I am glad my baggage came, for we might be snowed under until spring!"

Rowland snorted. "Highly unlikely, Miss Allen. There is always a thaw. There is no place in the world where one would be trapped for an entire season."

"That's how little you know," she retorted. "Where I live, if we get an early snow we can be submerged for months! One year, when I was eleven, we did not see the ground again until April, and by then we were surviving on dried venison and wormy flour."

Lady Silvia shivered, her eyes wide with wonder. "How could you bear it? What did you do all winter?"

"It was marvelous," Verity said, leaning forward, her eyes sparkling. "We would go tobogganing down the long hill behind the cabin, right across the river and halfway up the other side!"

"Tobogganing?" Lady Silvia said, enunciating each syllable carefully. "What is that?"

"It's a sled, only it doesn't have runners; it is just made out of barrel staves lashed together, you see, or nailed together with a cross board. And you slide down the hill on it, going so fast, and with the branches whipping through your hair and tearing at your bonnet . . . It is smashing!"

"Quite literally, if you did not avoid the trees, I should think," Lady Bournaud said dryly, examining the young woman who spoke. "How did you avoid instant death?"

"You steer, using a rope to guide it. But I will say if you were not careful, you could end up in the most awful pickle. One boy I knew went down recklessly and got a branch stuck in his eye."

Lady Silvia cried out and covered her face. "How horrible," she said, a sob in her voice. "Oh, how very awful."

"Oh, he recovered," Verity said nonchalantly. "He was blinded, but he recovered."

"Miss Allen, think of the company before you blurt out the first thing that comes to your head!" Rowland cast a quick glance at Lady Silvia who still shivered in revulsion.

Beatrice, watching the look of horror and repulsion on Rowland's face as he gazed at Miss Allen while he patted Lady Silvia's shoulder, wondered how Lady Bournaud possibly thought there could be a match between Rowland and the young woman from the Colonies. Their bickering so far had seemed more on the footing of brother and sister than lovers. "How long did you live in Upper Canada?" she asked Miss Allen, to divert the subject away from the gruesome.

"Oh, I still live in Canada." Seeing the company's blank stares, Verity added, "I mean, I shall be going back there as soon as Mama realizes I will have no better luck catching a husband here than I did at home."

Sir David laughed out loud at that ingenuous confession, and the girl stared at him in surprise.

"Did I say something funny, Sir David?"

"No, my dear child, you said something refreshingly honest." The knight wiped tears of laughter from his eyes.

Beatrice was spellbound, not having ever seen Chappell laugh before, and thinking what a rich, handsome sound it was.

"I fail to see what is refreshing about a girl admitting she cannot wed." Lady Bournaud's expression was set in a disapproving frown.

"Come now," Sir David said, recapturing the old lady's hand. "I think in Miss Allen's case it is not so much a case of being unable to wed, but perhaps unwilling?" He cast a smiling glance at the young lady in question, and then continued. "And if memory serves, I believe you told me a tale or two about your own adventures, and how you managed to remain unwed to the advanced age you were when you met the elegant and handsome Comte Bournaud and tumbled into love at first sight."

She swatted at him, but it was not an ill-natured cuff. "Do not think you are too old for discipline," she said, but chuckled.

Rowland was smiling, not even noticing Lady Silvia's rapt gaze, for once. "To return to the former conversation, I was just remembering that my sisters and I spent many a winter day sliding down the hill behind our home."

"Really?" Verity Allen said, in such a tone of disbelief that it started the whole company laughing.

Just then, from the doorway, Tidwell cleared his throat.

Lady Bournaud looked up toward her aged retainer. "Yes? What is it, Tidwell? You are sounding particularly phlegmy."

He bowed, and said, "My lady, there is a gentleman here."

"What on earth do you mean?"

"There is a gentleman. I have let him in. Should I show him to the fire, my lady?"

"A gentleman?"

"A gentleman." His tone was firm, and a look passed between him and his employer.

Voices, all at once, chorused, in quick succession, "Do show him in." "Yes, let him in!" "He must be frozen; bid him enter."

Lady Bournaud's voice carried over all. "Yes, Tidwell, show the poor chappie in."

Then, from behind Tidwell, came a dripping snowman.

Six

He moved forward stiffly, clumps of snow sliding off his shoulders with each movement. He was, it appeared, a youngish man, Beatrice thought, though it was hard to tell, for he was swathed in a greatcoat and muffler, and those were liberally coated with snow.

She was the first to react, and moved quickly toward him. "Sir, please come to the fire. You must be frozen!" She took his arm and led him toward the blazing hearth.

With her words the spell was broken, and everyone moved to help. Chappell was among the first, helping him off with his greatcoat and handing it to a waiting footman.

"Gracious, Tidwell," Lady Bournaud said, twisting in her seat to glare at her butler. "Why did you not do all of this before?"

The butler, standing behind the comtesse, cleared his throat and said, "He would not allow it, my lady, until he had personally asked the lady of the house her indulgence, since he will, perforce, be required to spend the night."

"What kind of looby are you, then?" Lady Bournaud said to the young man as he became unwrapped before the company's eyes.

"The frozen kind," he said, his words stiffly uttered.

"What's your name?" she demanded.

He bowed with difficulty, his breeches dripping ice and water as the fire warmed him. "I am Jacob Vaughan . . . Baron

Vaughan, if that matters. Where am I, by the way?" He shivered and sniffed.

Beatrice said, "This is the home of Comtesse Bournaud. I am her companion, Miss Copland." She examined the newcomer; he appeared to be in his early thirties, a well-set-up young man, with light brown hair and vivid blue eyes. He was not too tall, not, for instance, as tall as Mr. Rowland, and not broad of shoulder, but he carried with him an indefinable air of vigor, even in his pitiable frozen state. She gestured to the rest of the gathered company, who examined him with interested eyes. "This is Lady Silvia Hampton, Sir David Chappell, Mr. Mark Rowland—the Reverend Mr. Rowland—and Miss Verity Allen, from Upper Canada."

He nodded to the company, and turned his attention to Lady Bournaud. "My lady, I must beg your indulgence, it appears, for a night's lodging. I am on my way home—home being Wiltshire—from Scotland, and clearly cannot continue to the village as I intended." He sneezed.

Beatrice motioned to the footman. "Charles, bring Lord Vaughan a tisane. . . . Cook will know which one I mean. And a blanket."

Chappell watched the companion fussing over the younger man, and felt stir within him a warmth. He had seen her solicitude over Lady Bournaud, but now saw that it was a habitual attention to the needs of others. It was ingrained in her, it seemed, a sweetness of disposition and a concern for others that sprang from deep inside of her. "I think what the chap needs," he said quietly, "is a change of clothes."

"It is true, but has he any with him?"

Chappell turned to the other man. "Do you have your luggage, Lord Vaughan?"

"No. M'traps are ahead." He sniffed. "I hate carriages. Prefer riding, you know, and so I took a side trip to see a particular stream someone pointed out to me as a good fishing spot, and then got caught in this hideous storm."

"Do you mean you slogged through this . . . this blizzard on horseback?" Miss Allen said, waving her hand at the window that still showed, through the half-open curtains, the snow rattling against it. She half rose from her chair, a look of alarm on her pretty face.

Vaughan looked at his interrogator and frowned. "Yes. Why not? Wasn't like this when I started out."

"But your poor horse! Is it safe? Is it comfortable? Has it been bedded down properly? You know, warm mash will help the poor thing recover nicely, and if I were you I would brush it down immediately and cover it in a dry, warm blanket, and then . . ."

"Thank you very much," Lord Vaughan croaked. "So nice to know young ladies are still so caring. I sit here frozen, and you are only worried over Bolt's welfare!"

She glared at him. "You have all these people fussing over you. *And* a roaring fire, and blankets, and . . . and all this." She waved her hand. "But your horse may not. In Canada the horse would be taken care of first, for people can be more easily replaced."

Chappell, stifling a chuckle, said, "Children, enough. Miss Allen, there are no better stable hands than those in Lady Bournaud's employ. I think you can rest assured that his mount will be well cared for." He glanced around at the company, and then at Lady Bournaud. "What I was just saying to Miss Copland is that Lord Vaughan must change out of his wet things. If he does not have clothing, I think I can manage to lend him some, as we appear to be about the same size."

"I would be forever in your debt, sir," Vaughan said.

"Do that then, Davey," Lady Bournaud said.

Vaughan stood and bowed to the company, but his glance caught and stopped on Lady Silvia, who had been silent in all the to-do. His gaze was riveted. She did not meet his bold look, but rather stared, blushing, into the fire. It was clear to all that she knew of his close scrutiny. The reverend caught the direction of the baron's gaze and followed it to the young lady at his side.

Chappell noticed the brief interchange. He had noted earlier the way Rowland seemed protective of Lady Silvia, and had thought there was a romance in the air, but the sudden tension did not bode well, he thought. And once again, he was thankful to no longer be so young. "Come, Lord Vaughan, let's get you into something dry," he said, taking the other man's arm and guiding him away from the company.

Upstairs, Chappell summoned his valet, Drucker, and told him what he wanted. While Vaughan dressed, they talked. Or rather Lord Vaughan talked.

"Who is that lovely young lady?"

"Which one?" Chappell asked. "Miss Allen or Lady Silvia?"

"Is Lady Silvia the one with the enchanting brown eyes?" Vaughan allowed Drucker to straighten his jacket and tie his cravat. The valet had been drying and polishing Vaughan's boots in the meantime, and they stood ready for the gentleman.

"Yes. She is the daughter of the Earl of Crofton." Chappell, seated in a chair by the window, watched the calculation in the younger man's eyes.

"Not married, I take it. Nor betrothed?"

"No, from what I understand. However I cannot attest to whether her heart is engaged or not." The last was said with a wry tone, but the baron was oblivious.

"That doesn't matter. Women's hearts are soon turned." Vaughan glanced at himself in the mirror. "Can't thank you enough for the loan, Chappell, though these are not my sort of clothes." He hummed a snatch of tune and turned away from the cheval glass. "Shall we go back downstairs? Rejoin the company?" He rubbed his hands together.

How quickly the young recovered, Chappell thought. "Certainly. So, you are on your way home from Scotland."

"Yes." Vaughan grimaced. "I've got to get married, and a friend told me to come up and have a look at his sister. Gruesome."

Chappell, rising, stopped and stared at the other man. "What do you mean?"

"Well, 'twasn't so much that she was a quiz, though she was—not a patch on that lovely little dove downstairs, I can tell you—but she was a managing, shrewish wench, for all she tried to pretend to pretty manners. Too coy, too cloying." He gave a mock shudder. "Gruesome."

"I meant to say, you have to get married? What do you mean by that?"

He shrugged. "Don't *have* to. Mean to say, no one can compel me. Free man and all that, you know. But I've been a bit of a wastrel until now, y'know, and m'father says it's either marriage, or he'll ship me off to the Colonies." Shamefaced, he added, "We have interests in Canada, y'see, and he says I either marry and settle down to the business of gettin' an heir, or I go to Canada. Can't see m'self in Canada."

The two men exited the room and started down the long, winding staircase, lit dimly by the candles flickering in polished brass sconces.

"So I mean to find myself a cuddlesome bundle and get married. Shouldn't be so bad. At least a man can get married and still have his sport on the side."

Chappell put his hand on the other man's arm and was about to say something, but stopped. It was none of his business. He might find the young man's philosophy repugnant, but it was nothing but what he had been taught from the cradle. It was not his place to challenge or try to change the young man's ideas.

Vaughan paused and looked questioningly into Chappell's eyes, but then continued rambling on as they descended. "Just want a sweet-faced wigeon to keep the home fires burning, y'know. Children should be entertaining. And it's time I did it, stepped into tandem yoke. Assumed the harness. Got nabbed by the parson's mousetrap. Hey," he said, suddenly struck by an idea. Chappell looked back up at him. "Parson's mousetrap!" Vaughan said, eyes widened. "Fellow there, he was introduced as a reverend. If Lady Silvia were willing and Lady Bournaud let me stay awhile, she and I could be married during Christmas. Wouldn't that be a lark! Go to my parents' already wed!"

Chappell just could not hold his tongue in the face of such

nonsense. His own matrimonial experience had shown him the error of hasty choosing. "Lord Vaughan," he blurted out, "I think you should . . ." He paused, hammered his fist on the twisted oak railing, but then started again, his voice calmer. "From experience, my lord, if I were you, I would take more time in your choice of a life partner." Chappell looked down toward the saloon, where he could hear the voices of the company through the open double doors. "Marriage will affect your life far more than you think, and you should make your choice wisely."

"It's all chance anyway," Vaughan said cynically, stepping down to the same step as his companion. "Love don't tell you a thing. Had friends who married their heart's desire only to be bickering like fishwives inside of a year."

Disturbed, Chappell said, as they descended the last steps together, "Nonetheless, I would go slowly if I were you. It is the choice of a lifetime you are speaking of. At least take as much time choosing a wife as you would a good horse." The last was said with irony, but Vaughan's answer left him in great doubt as to whether the other man had gotten the message.

"But it *is* like a horse, you see, choosing a wife," Vaughan said. "As long as her wind is good and her legs sturdy, good teeth, decent disposition, nothing vicious about her, then she'll do."

In the face of such absurdity, Chappell was silent. If the young man got his way and was invited to stay, it boded ill for the peace of this Christmas season. He trailed after the baron into the saloon.

Beatrice noticed immediately that Chappell's expression held more than a hint of worry as he reentered behind the baron. The younger man went immediately to Lady Bournaud and bowed over her hand, though he spared a glance for Lady Silvia first. A smug expression crossed his too-handsome face.

"My lady, I thank you deeply for your splendid hospitality. I cannot thank you enough. I have been elevated from hell directly into heaven." He swept a hand around, indicating the warm room, blazing hearth, and assembled company.

Graciously, Lady Bournaud nodded. "Sit here, young man," she said, directing him to the chair that Chappell had sat in. The knight, having lost his seat to the younger man, moved around to the other side of Beatrice and pulled a low chair over to sit beside her. Beatrice felt the heat of his body near hers and agitation budded at his closeness, but she set herself the challenge of ignoring her perturbation.

"I have been trying to think," the comtesse continued, "where I have heard your name before, and it seems to me . . . Are you the son of Viscount Norcross?"

"I am. Do you know him?"

"I rather think we are related. Or at least your mother and I are."

Beatrice watched the comtesse's eyes. There was some scheme afoot, but she had no idea what her employer had in mind.

"Related? Is that so?" Vaughan sat back, very much a gentleman at his ease now that he was warm and dry and sitting with good company. A footman brought in the tray of decanters and offered the gentlemen port, which Chappell and Vaughan both quickly accepted. Rowland waved it off.

"Yes." Lady Bournaud looked over the company, frowning when she saw Rowland solicitously offering Lady Silvia a dainty glass of sherry. She turned her attention back to the young baron and said, "In fact, I believe my father was your mother's great-uncle on her maternal side."

"If you say it is so, my lady, I must concur." He grinned, his blue eyes twinkling. "I think I would agree to anything your ladyship might suggest, so smitten am I with your charm and graciousness."

"Pish tush, you scoundrel. But in light of that relationship, I have a suggestion to make."

Beatrice, an idea dawning in her mind, watched as the two bent their heads together and murmured, but was distracted by Sir David's voice near her ear.

"There will be trouble brewing in paradise," he said, "if this young man gets his way."

Trying to ignore the warmth of his port-scented breath, and the trill of pleasure that trickled down her back like warm bathwater, she turned her face slightly toward him, but then moved back when she found their mouths so close together. "W-what do you mean, sir?" she said, her voice unaccustomedly breathy.

"Lord Vaughan has spied Lady Silvia, and being in the market for an acceptable wife to keep him from the dread fate of the Colonies, has decided on a spot of instant wooing."

"Oh, dear," Beatrice said, glancing over at Lady Silvia, whose attention was wholly taken up by the reverend. Verity, she noticed, was restlessly prowling the room, exploring the nooks and crannies, upsetting knickknacks, and examining a porcelain horse she found on a side table.

"Yes," Chappell said. "That will fit in well with Lady Bournaud's plans, though, will it not?"

"You . . . you know of her plans?"

"I know her well enough to see when a spot of matchmaking is in the works. And look at those two," he said, indicating Lord Vaughan and his hostess. They still murmured together, and Lady Bournaud cast occasional glances over at the reverend and Lady Silvia. "They are conspiring."

"I do not know what has gotten into the comtesse," Beatrice fretted. "She has never done anything like this before."

Chappell sat back. "Perhaps that is the answer. Is it just boredom, or the doldrums that brought this on?"

"No," Beatrice said, worrying at her lower lip with her teeth.

"Is the other matchmaking, then, perhaps just a concealment for her real aim?"

"What do you mean?"

He smiled, but remained silent.

Had he guessed? Beatrice, her agitation growing, swallowed as he bent closer to her and put his hand on her arm. His face was close to hers, and she knew her cheeks were flushing an unbecoming cherry red, but there was no stopping physical reactions.

And she remembered all those years ago, how his mere presence in the same room had done exactly the same. How many evenings had she spent longing for and yet fearing his notice? How many times had she watched him when he did not even know she was there? She knew the angle of his jaw and the curvature of his ear, the crisp curl of his hair at the temple and slight hook of his nose. Those were still the same, even now, all these years later, as he leaned forward close to her, trying to hear what Lady Bournaud and Lord Vaughan were saying. But now there were crinkles at the corners of his crystalline blue eyes, and the curls were lightened with a liberal sprinkling of glittering silver.

He smelled so good, spicy and warm, like wool and cinnamon. And his hand on her arm flexed occasionally; to her addled thinking it felt like a caress. She sighed and tried to rein in her wild imaginings and wayward thoughts. This train of thought was not good, not at all. She must be sensible. And yet, how could she be, when his well-shaped lips were so close . . . ? He glanced up at her and caught her gaze. His own countenance, just by a tiny movement of his head, indicated that he knew she had been staring at him and wondered at it. If she could have blushed any deeper, without doubt she would have, but as it was, all she could do was look away into the fire, examining again the soot-darkened bricks and tracing the baroque intricacy of the carved hearth and mantelpiece.

"We have come to an agreement," Lady Bournaud said suddenly.

The entire company paid attention, for her ladyship's voice was a clarion call. Even Verity Allen strayed closer, standing behind Lady Silvia's chair as that young lady and the reverend directed their gazes to the comtesse.

Lady Bournaud cleared her throat and said, "I set out to re-create for myself the Christmases of old, with family and friends gathered around me. I am well satisfied with my decision so far, and in the spirit of the season and in light of his relationship to me, I have invited Lord Vaughan to stay here in Yorkshire for the Christmas season, and he has graciously agreed."

Seven

"Mr. Rowland has asked if he may visit you, my lady," Beatrice said, taking away the tray of breakfast dishes from Lady Bournaud's lap and placing it near the door for the maid to collect.

"I would like to see him," the old woman said, straightening her lace cap and pinning it more securely to her white hair. When she finished, she said, "My arms ache so. I wish it did not hurt to lift them like that."

"That is why you have me," Beatrice said, gently, affixing the cap more securely and primping her employer's hair.

Lady Bournaud caught her hand and patted it. "And for all my barking, I do appreciate you, my dear."

The compliment caught her so by surprise, that Beatrice was speechless.

The older woman chuckled. "Flustered you, eh?" She settled back against her pillows and watched as her companion straightened her side table, pouring a fresh glass of water and arranging the books, handkerchiefs, and oddments that were a part of Lady Bournaud's comfort. "So what think you of my scheme to liven up our Christmas season?"

"I think you have indeed found a way to liven things up, but that chance has played into your hands, too."

A secretive smile lifted the corners of the comtesse's mouth. "Indeed. I think the Almighty approves of my plans."

"I think we should not be assuming the Almighty approves or disapproves any of our infinitely insignificant doings." Beatrice sat on the edge of the bed and gazed down at the older woman. "My lady," she started, but then hesitated. She looked away, but then looked back, down at the elderly woman, who seemed to be shrinking as each month passed. "May I speak my mind?"

"Do I pay you to speak your mind?"

With a sigh, Beatrice rose. "No, my lady. You pay me to agree with you." She turned to leave.

"Wait!" Lady Bournaud had an irritable expression on her seamed face. The blue veins underlying her skin gave a cool tint to her face that heightened the arctic frost of her gray eyes. "Come back here." She slapped the bed, and Beatrice obediently resumed her position, seated on the edge of it. "I take it you do not agree with my plans for these young people?"

"I cannot help but think," Beatrice started, realizing that she had been given permission to speak more freely, "that you should let nature have some hand in all of this. You have done what you can to set things in motion, and it is all well and good to introduce young people to each other, but now you should let them find their own happiness." She stopped and stared down at the carpet. "And the older people, too," she finished.

"Ah." There was silence for a minute. "Is there something you wish to tell me, my dear? Something about your long-ago Season in London?"

"Why would you ask such a thing?" Beatrice knew that she had already said too much. If she was not willing to divulge the truth, then she must stay clear of the subject entirely.

A maid came into the room at that moment to retrieve the tray, and Lady Bournaud called out, "Nellie, ask Tidwell to fetch Mr. Rowland." The girl curtsied and exited. Turning back to her companion, Lady Bournaud said, "I would ask such a thing because there seems to be something . . ." The comtesse trailed off and studied Beatrice's face. Almost to herself she muttered, "All right, my girl. If you wanted to tell me, you would have by now. Go show Mr. Rowland in."

Beatrice moved toward the door, but stopped just short of it and turned. "My lady, you have ever been kind to me and you know how deeply I appreciate it, but . . ."

"But I did not purchase your soul, and your secrets are your own," the old lady finished irritably. "Go! I know that. Go tell Mark to come in."

Pulling the door closed behind her, Beatrice stood for a moment, staring down at the carpet. What she would not give to be divested of the weight she carried, the taint she harbored. But it was not to be. If she could just get through the next three weeks . . .

Mark Rowland approached from the top of the stairs, and Beatrice found a smile for the young man. She did like him. He was serious but not grim, though she had the feeling many would mistake his studious nature for austerity. She had seen something else in his eyes and on his face as he chatted to Lady Silvia the previous evening, but Beatrice was sorely afraid he was headed for heartbreak if that was how his preference was turning.

"Mr. Rowland, Lady Bournaud says you may go right in."

"How is she this morning?" Rowland asked, gazing at the door.

"As well as ever."

"I mean, her mood. She seemed . . . most inspirited last night."

"She is having the best time she has had for years," Beatrice said, her tone dry. "Do you know her well, Mr. Rowland? I do not think you have been here for some time."

"No, not since before I went to Oxford. But I spent a summer here when I was . . . oh, sixteen, I believe. Yes, I would have been sixteen that summer." He leaned against the paneled wall and stared down the hall into the gloom of the windowless expanse. "My aunt and Lady Bournaud are good friends, you see, and that year my parents died. I . . . I suffered a breakdown of sorts, a wandering of spirit. It was a time of great darkness and pain for me, and I was headed down a very unfortunate road. Aunt Selwyn sent me here. Lady Bournaud was there when I needed her, and yet she allowed me such freedom. I wandered the grounds, the moors, spent time, sometimes days, away from the house. And I found my calling. If it were not for her, I might have been lost in bitterness."

Moved by his openness and gratitude, Beatrice reached out and touched his arm. He gave her a quick smile. "I feel sure, Mr. Rowland, that you would have found your way, regardless, but I am glad Lady Bournaud was a part of your healing."

"Yes," he said eagerly. "She was, you see, and that is why I feel I can help her to heal this rift with my aunt Cordelia Selwyn. It is too bad, such a tiff between friends."

Beatrice remained silent.

Rowland's brow wrinkled under his sweep of dark hair. He pushed back the stray locks and said, "Perhaps I should have said nothing."

Beatrice, fuming internally, said, "No, it is all right, Mr. Rowland. I feel quite sure you will solve this . . . this rift between Lady Bournaud and her friend with very little difficulty at all."

Rowland brightened. "Do you think so?"

"I am sure of it. I guarantee you will mend whatever quarrel existed."

As the young man entered, Beatrice muttered, under her breath, "I am as sure of that as I am of her ladyship's duplicity."

Rowland slipped into the room. Miss Copland had assured him that Lady Bournaud was awake, and so though her eyes were closed, he moved toward the bed. She was vastly changed since that summer so many years before. Since then he had been taken up with his studies and then with the necessary work involved in maintaining a curacy. Any time he had free, he spent with his aunt Cordelia Selwyn, who was aging rapidly, though her mind and spirit were still copper-bright.

The comtesse, laying with her eyes closed, pale against the

white coverlet of her bed, seemed smaller than the stern and yet somehow welcoming woman he remembered from his youth. Since that time they had corresponded only by mail, but he had seen the steady decline of her penmanship, the letters becoming wavery and harder to read with the years.

"My lady," he said softly, watching the pale eyes flutter open and the knobby hand reach up and touch her white lace cap, settled firmly on her white hair. "May I speak with you?"

"Certainly, Mark. Draw up a chair. You see me in my morning attire; I have taken up the elegant affectation of staying abed until luncheon."

Mark dragged a chair close to the bed and captured one of her hands in his own, feeling how stiff the joints were and how crooked with age. "You are entitled to your ease, my lady."

She moved restlessly under the covers. "And yet I wish I could still walk. Losing the power of movement is an affliction I am ill prepared to bear. You've become a man, Mark, in the years since I last saw you." She rolled to her side and reached out her free hand, pushing the heavy hair off his brow. "You were so slim and dark and intense as a boy. You've filled out, and your spirit, it is . . ."

"Calm?" He smiled and squeezed her hand. "Yes, it is. I have you to thank for that. By the time I left here that summer the broken part of me had knit, and I had found my future."

"So you really are happy in your chosen life?"

"I am. I have not had a chance to tell you my good news yet. I have a preferment; Loughton, in Hampshire. It is a good living and due, again, to you. My patron is an old beau of yours, if I am not mistaken." He named the gentleman.

Lady Bournaud smiled. "Ah, yes. We were good friends an age ago, in London. I am so happy for you."

"But now, my lady," Mark said, gazing at the blue-veined hand he held in his own, "I was distressed to hear about your rift with my aunt Cordelia. You have been friends all your life.

What has come between you?" He examined the pale eyes and saw a shift, like a change of light, within them.

"Well, you know, I forgot to write to you. Cordelia and I have settled our little difference. Just a silly misunderstanding."

Rowland released her hand and settled back in his chair. He was silent for a moment, and the only sound was a clock ticking on the mantel and the fire in the hearth that popped and hissed as a coal dropped beneath the grate. He had seen the evasion in her eyes, but could not guess at the meaning of it. There had been a rift; that he knew, since his aunt had spoken of it during his last visit. He was about to speak, but Lady Bournaud put up her hand.

"I wanted to see you again. Likely the last time before I die."

"So you made up some absurd story?"

"Not exactly. Delia and I did have a tiff. Idiotic thing over who wrote last. But we made it up."

Rowland sensed evasion again, and yet he did not have the heart to pin the old girl down too closely. "You didn't need such a scheme to get me here, you know. If you asked me, I would have come."

The comtesse peered at him earnestly. "I suppose you would have. I'm glad you're here. You will stay, won't you?"

Rowland glanced out the window. "It seems we are all bound here, whether we like it or not," he said, getting up and wandering over, gazing down at the drifts that had piled up overnight against the hedges and trees. The snow glittered in the brilliant sun, an almost blinding reflection, but as his eyes adjusted he saw two figures walk the path that the gardener had shoveled from the front door around to the expanse of the west lawn. He frowned down, his attention riveted. One of the figures was slight and clearly female, dressed in a pale pink spencer and bonnet adorned with feathers that drooped and bobbed. The other was a man in a dark greatcoat and a curl-rimmed beaver.

It took only a moment to determine that it was Lady Silvia and Lord Vaughan. Rowland unwillingly acknowledged a pang in his heart and a surge of unwelcome jealousy. He fought it. It was unworthy. He had no reason to dislike Vaughan. It was un-Christian and unmanly to dislike the baron simply because he was handsome, wealthy, titled, and charming—in short, everything Mark Rowland, vicar, was not.

But that dislike was there, in his heart. And it was there, he knew, because of the budding affection he was experiencing for Lady Silvia Hampton, a lady who was as far above him as the North Star was above the earth. He had looked into her pansy-brown eyes, as soft as velvet, as beckoning as sunlight, and he had felt himself cut adrift from every other person in the room.

"Mark!" Her ladyship's voice was sharp.

Rowland turned from the window, certain that she had called him at least once before he heard, and perhaps more. He returned to the bedside and tried to settle back down in the chair. But all of the gentle peace of the morning was gone for him. He took a deep breath and let it out slowly.

Lady Bournaud examined his face, her gaze piercing. "What were you looking at just now?"

"Just the snow."

"Liar."

He was taken aback by her abruptness, but remained silent. In the past her commanding ways would have flustered him, but he had learned an inner calmness in the face of autocratic ways, and it stood him in good stead at that moment. In his years at Oxford, poor and often subjected to hazing and relentless belittling, he had come to inner peace. And, he hoped, strength. His thoughts were his own, and no man—nor woman—had the right to them.

Lady Bournaud chuckled. "You have indeed become a man, Mark. So, what think you of the company I have gathered?"

"It seems to be good company," he said truthfully. Lord

Vaughan was not one of her chosen guests, and so he could, in good conscience, omit him from his statement.

"And what think you of Miss Verity Allen?"

Mark shrugged. "A pleasant young lady."

"Is she not pretty?"

"I suppose."

"And vivacious?"

"Certainly that," he said, his tone dry.

"And she is of good family, too, but used to working around the house, according to her mother, my cousin Fanny. The girl has a good working knowledge of the kitchen, laundry, the care of infants. . . ."

Her voice droned on, and Mark stood restlessly and paced to the window again, interjecting just the right words to show her ladyship he was still listening. Enthusiastically, he agreed to some statement of her ladyship's, and then searched the scene below him. There they were, but there was a third person with them. Ah, yes, Miss Allen. That stood to reason. That girl was as restless as a three-year-old at a sermon.

Lady Silvia and Lord Vaughan were talking. Lady Silvia started to drift away, but Vaughan followed her, and then *pop*! Vaughan's hat was knocked off his head by a flush hit from a snowball. Rowland laughed out loud at the perfect hit from Miss Allen's deadly aim.

"Mark. *Mark*!"

"Pardon, my lady?"

Lady Bournaud sighed. "Go for a walk, Mark. I am going to rise now." When he hesitated, she pointed one crooked finger to the door. "Go!"

Lady Silvia sighed in frustration. Lord Vaughan just would not leave her alone, but insisted on accompanying her everywhere! And even Miss Allen's hit with a snowball had not deflected him. It should have, but he had just given her a cold look and gone back to earnestly boring his captive audience with some story of a boxing match in London.

She had met his type many times before in the ballrooms and salons of London during her two Seasons. Though in his case there seemed to be no viciousness at the core of his personality, neither were there any interesting traits, nothing that was not self-serving, nothing noble or fine. Not like . . .

"Fine day for a walk," said a voice behind them.

Silvia turned to see the object of her reflections. "Mr. Rowland! Do come and join us! Please!"

"As long as I am not intruding?"

His mellow, deep voice gave her a thrill of happiness, and she opened her mouth to answer, but Vaughan was already speaking.

"Matter of fact, old man, you are come at a most inopportune time."

"I think," Rowland said evenly, "that that is up to the lady to decide."

"You are most welcome to walk with us." Silvia gave Lord Vaughan a vexed look, then gazed back at Mr. Rowland. With a happy thought, she blurted, "And you did promise, as you have been here before, to show me the estate sometime."

"I would be most delighted to be your guide."

Just at that moment another well-aimed snowball hit Vaughan, knocking his hat askew and filling his ear with wet snow.

"That is it!" Vaughan growled, jamming his hat back on his head as high laughter drifted toward them over a snowy hedge. "Where is the troublesome vixen?"

"I think she is hiding by the cedar hedge," Lady Silvia answered. "Perhaps you should return fire?"

"I will indeed," Vaughan said. Without another word he raced off, bounding through the snow, scooping up a handful as he went.

Lady Silvia turned and gazed up at Mr. Rowland. Her heart raced. But contrary to her hopes, the young vicar did not take her arm, nor even move closer to her.

"I truly hope I was not interrupting anything just now," Rowland said.

"Not at all. Lord Vaughan was just telling me about some . . . Oh, I don't remember. I think it was a boxing match or some such nonsense." She couldn't seem to think, couldn't concentrate.

They turned as of one mind and walked. The day was brilliant but icy, the wind causing cheeks to pink and toes to curl up in boots. From somewhere they heard Verity Allen's high, giddy laughter float on the breeze. There was a scream, and then more laughter.

"I think Lord Vaughan found his target," Lady Silvia said.

Rowland grinned suddenly.

"What are you smiling about, sir?" she asked.

His smile became guilty. "I was up speaking to Lady Bournaud and I was looking out her window down here. I happened to see Miss Allen's first hit, that one that knocked Vaughan's hat off." He laughed, throwing his head back in a rare carefree gesture.

Silvia caught her breath and stopped, turning to face her companion. "You were looking down here?"

"Yes."

She couldn't ask. It was not ladylike. But oh, how she wanted to know if it was the knowledge that she was out there, walking with Lord Vaughan, that had encouraged him to come looking for them. This was such new ground for her. She was well versed in the gentle art of discouraging unwanted attentions. But how did one encourage a gentleman one liked, especially when he was reticent, as Mr. Rowland seemed to be?

"And you decided to come out for a walk?"

"Yes. I felt a sudden urge for activity."

It was enough, for the moment. They walked on for a while, and fell into an easy conversation of his expectations and hopes. Silvia listened to his enthusiasm for his new parish, Loughton. It was large, he said, and had its share of wealthy parishioners, but there were so many more people he hoped to be able to help, so many who needed the support of the parish just to exist.

And not just those of the Church of England, he said. His head down, staring at his boots, he told her about his hopes of bringing together Methodists and even Catholics. He was hoping, during his stay in Yorkshire, to ask Sir David's opinion about Catholic emancipation. He did not think that there could be any healing in England until that was a reality.

"Lord!" he exclaimed finally. His expression was chagrined, and he kicked at a snowdrift. "Here I have been boring you to tears, no doubt. The tale of the boxing match shall seem high conversational art to you by now. Shall I find Lord Vaughan and Miss Allen? Would you be better entertained?'

"No!" Lady Silvia's eyes widened. "Pardon me," she said breathlessly. "Mr. Rowland, if I have been silent for this half hour, it is because . . ." She twisted her hands together. How could she say what she wanted? Why was a young lady not free to say the things in her heart? And yet she couldn't. She couldn't say, *I have been silent because I have never heard a man say such fine things. I have been silent because love is a quiet thing, not noisy or pretentious, but soft-spoken and low-toned. It whispers, the better to be heard.* She wanted to say it, felt it deeply, but he was looking at her with those fine dark eyes, and it muddled her thinking. She could get lost in those eyes, in the amber fire that blazed deep within.

"What is it, Lady Silvia?"

He had reached out to her and put his gloved hands on her shoulders, holding her as if he would draw her close to his heart. She longed to move into his embrace and lay her cheek against the dark wool of his coat. She wanted to feel his arms around her for the first time, and know that the thudding of his heart was for her and her alone. She could almost feel the warmth of his breath, chasing away the frosty air as he laid a gentle kiss on her upturned face, then on her lips.

But there were no words for that kind of need, no ladylike way to show him her earnest desire. "I . . . I think you will make a fine vicar, Mr. Rowland," was what she finally said, and bitter was her self-condemnation when she saw the amber flames die within his eyes, replaced by cool obsidian flecks.

He dropped his hands from her shoulders. "Thank you, my lady. It is the passion of my life to find in service to others, a meaning to life."

They walked on, each lost in doubt and anxiety, both sure the object of their budding affection would never understand the secrets of their hearts.

Eight

"So, you see my fellow has taken no lasting harm from the soaking we both got." Lord Vaughan, teased and pestered into visiting the stables with Miss Allen, held the bridle of his steed, William Wallace.

Verity sighed and patted the chestnut stallion's smooth coat. "He is a handsome boy," she said. "What a bully name, too! I have a brother William, only this fellow is certainly more handsome than my brother. Shorter nose."

Vaughan laughed out loud, the sound echoing in the warm, humid, horsy depths of the elegantly appointed stable. "He is named after the legendary hero of Scotland. I got him from my Scottish friend, who is not very diplomatic about his politics," he said, returning his attention to the girl beside him. Young woman, really, for he judged her to be in her twenties, pretty much past the marriageable age, thank God. "I call him Bolt, most often, though. He is very fast."

"Well, I think he is a beauty." The horse tossed its head, and Verity kissed its nose.

Vaughan gazed at her quizzically. "What an odd girl you are! Do you always kiss horses?"

"More than gentlemen!" Verity retorted.

Clenching his jaw, Vaughan restrained a very real, very strange urge to kiss her and show her why men were preferable to horses. In the warmth of the stable the snow that coated her was melting and she was soaked, her hair lank and undone from its inelegant bun and her woolen coat dark with water. For all that, there was a natural attraction about her odd blue-green eyes and sharply pointed chin. *Kissable wench,* he thought, randomly. He was about to move toward her to put the thought into action, when she suddenly moved away and started walking around the large, dim stable.

Arms flung wide, she said, "What a magnificent stable!" She touched the polished wood supports and ran her hands over brass fittings. "I have never seen one like it. At home we have a barn constructed of logs . . . a dank, dark place. And cold! Wind rips right through the chinks between the logs. It serves as our byre and stable and chicken coop."

"Primitive country," Vaughan said moodily, watching her whirl around as if she were an opera dancer. Earlier, when he caught up with her, he had pinned her down and rubbed snow in her face for having the temerity to hit him with a succession of snowballs. It was then that he felt the first stirrings of attraction, the first physical warning that the lithe female body trapped under his, struggling and squirming though it was, was very womanly and desirable. That was exactly the meaning behind his words to Sir David about male freedom within wedlock. How glad he was that marriage did not prevent a man from sampling other feminine charms, because, though he still intended to woo the delectable and sweet-faced Lady Silvia—she was ideal marriage material, a prize his father would approve—Miss Verity Allen was a seducible bundle if ever he saw one. It would be a delight to tame the spitfire and feel her squirming with passion, and *not* get away.

The thoughts struck him as peculiar even as he watched her do an oddly graceful dance about the straw-covered floor, to the delight of a stableboy who had been dozing in the corner. She was nothing he had ever met before, and nothing he would normally think he could be attracted to, but there it was. He wanted to tumble her, and thought it was possible, given her passionate nature and chaperon-less existence, that he would achieve that objective. He had, after all, three weeks in which to accomplish it, and he had in the past performed seductions in much less time. A momentary qualm struck him, concerning the agreement between himself and Lady Bournaud. But they hadn't said a word about Miss Allen, and what the old besom didn't know couldn't hurt her.

"And what else can you tell me about your primitive country?" He stalked toward her, arresting her in midmovement and turning with her into a dark enclosure.

She gazed up at him in the dim light of the stall into which they had twirled. He pinned her against the wall of the stall with his weight, and she frowned, her elegantly arched brows furrowed; then with one quick movement was out and under his arm, and striding across the stable floor into the brilliant December sunshine. With a muffled curse Vaughan followed her into the sunlight. The icy coating over the snow heaps banked up around the walls glittered like diamonds against white tulle. Miss Allen, in her ugly brown coat, stood out against the pristine landscape like a dark blotch.

Impossible wench, Vaughan thought, and strode after her. If that was how she treated him then he would be damned if he would give her the honor of rejecting him again. His desire for her would be easily stifled, for he had never been a slave to his bodily needs. He was gratified to see that she was headed for the reverend and Lady Silvia, who strolled a pathway on the terrace. His time would be better spent on wooing the perfectly pleasing little lady rather than trying to seduce the unwilling Colonial wench.

"Ah, there you two are," he called out. He strode toward them and took Lady Silvia's other arm, leaving Miss Allen to walk alone along the long path up toward the house.

"Trouble among the youngsters?" Sir David said, coming up behind Beatrice.

Beatrice started, but then smiled over her shoulder. "Oh, I don't know. I hope not."

They stood at the window in the library, a mellow room

of oak and brass and muted colors of tobacco and old gold. The carpet was Turkish, plush and thick, with an intricate oriental design of some complexity woven in deep greens and bloodred. Bookshelves lined two of the stone walls of the ancient house, which were thick, giving each window a deep ledge. Sir David hitched up his trouser leg and sat on the ledge of one, gazing up at Beatrice, who stared out the window at the snowy scene that included the four young people.

"And yet I could not help but notice that you looked troubled just now," he commented, watching her eyes as he leaned back and crossed his arms over his chest. He had observed his old friend's companion often, while she was aware and also when she was unaware of his scrutiny. He had come to the conclusion that it was he who made her uncomfortable, though he was at a loss to explain that phenomena.

She shrugged, hugging herself, her arms wrapped around her slim waist, her fingers pleating the navy merino of her gown. "Lady Bournaud has a plan in mind, but I am only too aware of what happens when mere humans interfere in the workings of fate. Or providence, or destiny . . . whatever one should call it."

The knight indicated with a movement of his silvered head the couples outside as they meandered down a pathway. "You are worried about them, and Lady Bournaud's pairings?"

"Mmm, yes. I am, actually."

"Why do you care?"

She gave him a sharp look, and he was pierced by the intelligence of those eyes. She was nettled by his casual, unfeeling remark.

"I care because their whole lives are ahead of them. One misstep now and their lives could be ruined!"

Ah, now he was getting somewhere. "Is that what happened to you?"

Her eyes widened and glistened in the sunlight that slanted into the room. She shook her head, her lips moving but no words coming out. He put out one hand to touch her arm, alarmed at what his impertinent remark had done to her composure, but she moved back, stumbling on the thick carpet. She turned, then, and fled without a word.

He was left alone, gazing with unseeing eyes at the foursome in the snow outside.

Beatrice called herself a coward as she bustled up to Lady Bournaud's sitting room on the sunny south side of the house. She thought herself cool and collected, but it seemed that she was a bundle of nerves every time Sir David entered the room or spoke to her. Why could he not just leave? Then she castigated herself for her unkind thoughts. His visit was giving her employer so much joy, and she would not begrudge the old lady her happiness, not even at the cost of her own peace of mind. She should be grateful. He had not, after all, recognized her, not even when they were in constant close quarters, and she must be appreciative of that.

She stopped by Lady Bournaud's door, unwilling to go in to her employer when her cheeks were still flaming and her heart still pounding. The worst part was that she could find nothing in him to condemn. He was even more handsome than when she had known him twenty years before. And in that time he had added a gentleness to his charisma, a quiet inner strength that she found immensely appealing. Then she had found him attractive; now she found him intolerably enticing. His voice, his presence, everything about him.

If only he had become in some way or another coarse or vulgar, but instead he had grown in grace and dignity. And he had unerringly put his finger on the calamity of her existence, that one season that if she could, she would take back in every sense but one; she would still know him, if she was given that opportunity.

She paced the hallway. Nellie tiptoed by, carrying a stack of linens to the guests' rooms, but Beatrice merely gave her an abstracted smile. She rubbed her hands together. The hallway was drafty and cold with the sharp drop in temperature outside. Finally, she knew she was calm enough, and she quietly entered Lady Bournaud's sitting room, the adjoining chamber to her bedchamber and where she spent the afternoon most winter days.

The Bath chair was drawn up to the tall, deeply carved desk in the corner, and the comtesse was writing a letter. In the ten years Beatrice had worked for her, the lady had slowly moved from upright mobility, to a cane, and finally to a bath chair after a fall the previous winter. It had been a severe blow to the independence that was a hallmark of the widowed aristocrat, and she bore it ill, but was becoming reconciled to it gradually. Her one unfailing vanity was to allow no one to see that a footman—a young, handsome, and strong one—was invariably needed to move her ladyship from the first floor down to the ground level, where the crimson saloon, her favorite gathering place was situated. A big woman in her youth, she had shrunk over the last few years so she was not such a burden to Charles, the powerful young footman usually chosen for the task.

And so afternoons were spent here, in the sitting room, a cheerful salon of butter-yellow walls and rose tapestry furnishings. Sunlight seemed to expand in the room because of the yellow walls, and it added color to her ladyship's pale complexion.

Beatrice watched the old woman for a minute, acknowledging in her heart the love she had come to feel for her benefactress and employer. Though she would never say such a sentimental thing to the comtesse, who eschewed mawkish sentimentality in favor of a brusque kindness that seemed to belie any softer feelings.

"I am aware that you are standing there staring at me, Beatrice. I have not lost my hearing, though I may choose to use it selectively at times," the comtesse said, looking up from the letter she was writing.

"I just came to inquire as to whether you will be joining us for dinner tonight," Beatrice said, moving swiftly and silently to stand beside the desk.

"I think I shall," Lady Bournaud said, sliding a piece of blotting paper over the scrawl of the letter. "I would like to go to the window, Beatrice."

Beatrice obediently moved to the back of the chair and pushed her over to gaze down at the glazed landscape. In the distant valley the spire of the church was still visible, and the dark ribbon of the river wound through, glistening icily among trees and drab stone buildings. Distance was deceptive though, and the village was many miles away over treacherous roads in this weather. Lord Vaughan could have died in the short time it would take to traverse that distance.

"Ah, I see my pet projects are taking wing," she said, craning forward in her chair and looking down at the grounds below.

Beatrice looked down to see to what she was referring. The four young people had re-paired now, with Lord Vaughan and Lady Silvia in the fore, and Mr. Rowland and Miss Allen moving at a sedate pace behind them. "I wish you would not concern yourself so closely with the inner workings of that small quadrilateral," Beatrice said.

"Quadrilateral? I did not know you were a mathematician, my girl," the comtesse said, with an acerbic tone. "But I will be concerned with whatever and whomever I please. As always."

"As always," Beatrice echoed, her tone hollow.

The older lady turned her face up and studied her companion's expression. "Can you not be happy that I have found an occupation to my liking?" she asked.

"But it is meddling in people's lives, my lady." Beatrice sat down on the ledge, which was padded with mounds of soft yellow cushions. She stared into the glacial gray of Lady Bournaud's eyes. "Meddling in something you have only a dim conception of . . . perforce," she added hastily, seeing the anger drawing down the comtesse's thin lips.

"Each one of us can only have the vaguest notion of the internal workings of each person, what they think, feel, need. It is not given to us to have a closer knowledge, and that is how it was intended from the dawn of time. To interfere between men and women is to upset the fine balance that—" She stopped and threw her hands up in the air. "Oh, I don't know how to explain what I mean."

"Perhaps that is because everything you are saying is errant nonsense, my girl. You do not know what you are talking about. Some people don't know what is good for them until it is forced on them."

"But what if . . ." Beatrice shook her head and looked down at the two couples. "What if it happened that Mr. Rowland and Lady Silvia were the couple that were meant to be, and not he and Miss Allen? I can assure you, after watching them all, I must say the former is a much more likely match."

"Impossible!" The word exploded from the comtesse.

"But . . ."

"No. Utterly impossible. You do not know what you are saying." Lady Beatrice signaled that she would like to go back to the desk, and Beatrice leaped to her feet. "Mark is a decent lad, but his chosen profession is the church. And even if it were not so, even if he had gone to sea or taken a commission in the army, where there is hope of advancement and prize money, it would not matter, for the war is over and wealth unlikely at this juncture. He is virtually penniless. Lady Silvia's father is the most stiff-rumped gentleman there ever was. He was François's friend, or I would not have stood him. He would never countenance a match between Rowland and his daughter."

"But . . ."

"No. If Rowland has set his sights on rising socially by marrying Lady Silvia he will be doomed to disappointment, and it will be kinder for all involved if that idea is destroyed soon and for good. The girl's best hope of a decent marriage is to bring Vaughan to heel. He and I have had a serious talk and he is a pleasing pup. Good-natured, not a vicious bone in his body. Besides, the girl is too young to know what she wants. Vaughan is older, will take good care of her."

Remaining silent, Beatrice tidied the desk for the comtesse, pushing the bell she used to call her maid closer to her hand. She felt that her employer was dismissing the girl too readily. There were unrevealed depths to the child, of that she was sure. She just hoped that the poor girl did not acquiesce and marry to please her parents. She wandered back over to the window and gazed down again at the odd foreshortened view of the drama being played out in the wintry landscape.

She was just in time to see the figure of Lady Silvia, clearly visible in her pink attire, adroitly handing off Lord Vaughan to Miss Allen while she found room on the path for only Mr. Rowland. Beatrice smiled. Maybe there was hope after all that love would find a true path.

Nine

"Did you have a favorite place here during your summer?"

Rowland gazed down at Lady Silvia's upturned face. He was confused by her, and yet it was not an unpleasant state. He had given in as Vaughan had cut him out, completely expecting that Lady Silvia would naturally turn to the more sophisticated, more worldly Lord Vaughan as her companion, but she had very neatly handed him off to Miss Allen—Rowland still wasn't sure how that exchange had taken place—and now those two were off romping in the snow like a couple of puppies, while he and Lady Silvia were walking sedately down the path. She was so young, and yet in some ways she made him feel the junior, for her social skills were impeccable. Frighteningly so, really.

"Yes, I did have a favorite retreat. But it is not the sort of place you would enjoy."

"Nonsense," she said, slipping her arm through his. "Show me."

Her appeal was undeniable, the brown eyes gazing up at him so seriously, full of warmth and interest. He took a deep breath, and then glanced around. "This way," he said, guiding her over a drift and through the deep snow that managed to find ways to slither into boot tops. When they rounded the back of the estate and his objective came in sight, he smiled. "There it is."

Lady Silvia smiled and glanced up at him. "I should have guessed."

They slogged through the snow, climbing drifts, Rowland jumping to the other side and holding out his hand, helping her over the particularly deep ones.

Finally, they stood before it, and both were silent. It was an ancient Norman chapel with a square tower and long low nave that hugged the hillside toward the village. Simply constructed of mellow old gray stone and darkened with time, ivy clung to it, the last few wizened leaves stubbornly mired in the twisted gray reaches. It was utterly simple, devoid of ornamentation and certainly many centuries older than the house to which it nominally belonged. Rowland gazed up at it and sighed, remembering that summer years before and the first time he had entered the cool inner sanctum; peace had overwhelmed him with an intensity usually reserved for more passionate emotions.

"This is where I found my calling."

Her eyes shining, Lady Silvia said, clinging to his arm, "May we go in?"

"If you like." They approached, and Rowland put his shoulder to the enormous oak door, which opened with a rusty creak. A puff of air from inside touched their faces, the odor damp and dank. He hesitated. "It is musty. Do you mind?"

She shook her head, and they entered the dark interior. They passed from the tower into the nave, their boot heels echoing on the stone floor into the upper reaches of the darkened heights. Somewhere a bird fluttered, and a piece of straw fell to their feet, dimly seen in the pale light that filtered through the high Gothic arched windows.

Lady Silvia shivered. "It is so . . . peaceful."

"Why are you whispering?" Rowland asked, chuckling softly when he realized he was whispering, too.

"It just seems right to not be loud or . . . or boisterous," she said softly, moving closer to him.

"Are you cold, my lady?" He felt rather than saw her nod, and without conscious thought or planning he put his arms around her. She turned her face up. Her cheeks glowed like pearls and he felt a treacherous urge to kiss her face, to touch her rose lips with his own.

But it was wrong. There could never be anything between them, and he defiled the sacred interior of the chapel with the animal instincts that surged through his veins. It would be taking advantage of her trust, too, when the bestowal of that trust was like a gift she gave him. And so he let go of the urge, sent it up to the high vaulted ceiling like a prayer. Contentment filled him as they stood, his arms around her and her soft sigh echoing up into the tower.

He became aware gradually, as they stood in companionable silence, that her body was vibrating with shivers. "You are so cold," he said, his words coming out in frosty puffs. He pulled one glove off and chafed her hand.

She flattened her hand to his, his long blunt fingers stretching an inch beyond her slender ones. "Did not someone once say 'Palm to palm is holy palmer's kiss'? Or . . . or something like that?"

Steadily he gazed down at her, and then at their hands, palm to palm, the heat of his transferring finally to her. "He also wrote, 'Have not saints lips, and holy palmers too?'"

Her brown eyes widened. "Are you asking, with Mr. Shakespeare's help, to kiss me?"

He glanced around the dim interior, down the long nave, and at the high windows, grimed with a century's dust. "No, my lady," he said, giving her back her glove. "We should rejoin the others."

It was a misstep, Silvia thought, to speak flirtatiously here to a gentleman who took the sanctity of the church so very seriously. And yet, were not kisses exchanged in church? Certainly at the end of the marriage rite there was kissing. Mr. Rowland guided her outside and pushed the protesting door closed. The sun was sinking into the west, and the sky was blazing golden with dark streaks of coal and indigo where clouds gathered on the horizon.

"We have been outside far too long, my lady. I think you

should be by the fireside to warm up, or you will be chilled to the bone."

She was already so cold she could not feel her toes in her boots, nor the tips of her fingers, nor the end of her nose, but she was not willing to just meekly let the situation go. As awkward as it felt, she was determined to make him admit what was between them, even if he would never do so with words. He had taken her arm to guide her back over the snowdrifts but she stopped and would not be hurried.

He paused. "Is there anything wrong, my lady?"

He kept doing that, she thought, irritated, calling her "my lady," as if he was reminding himself over and over of the gap between their stations in life. She gazed up at him, noting the dark shadow along his square jaw and the silky curls of his hair, dark as walnut stain. She didn't know where she found the courage, nor the impertinence, but she said, "Will you kiss me now, Mr. Rowland, now that we are out of the chapel?"

His heavy brown eyebrows descended over his eyes. "I cannot. It would be sinful, for we are not betrothed. . . ."

"Are you so priggish, then, as to think a gentleman and a lady cannot indulge in a chaste kiss without being condemned?" Ah, yes, that had worked; he did not like being thought priggish. He lowered his head, his warm breath touching her mouth.

She closed her eyes, and when his lips touched hers she felt a rush of warmth, a swirl of giddy happiness that welled into her heart. It was true. He was the one. This was it, and this warmth, this wellspring of emotion was just the start, the beginning of their future.

Rowland pulled back and gazed down at her closed eyes, the fan of dark lashes that touched her cheek. This was madness, idiocy! This heady rush of emotion and mingled desire, this tangle of feeling and need and yearning, it would not end well. His hands gripped her shoulders too tightly. He loosened his hold, taking a deep breath and stepping back.

He stared wretchedly at her, watching as her eyes fluttered

open, the warm brown like the soft center of a chocolate bon-bon. Madness. He had steered clear of ladies over the years, knowing that for him, it would be years before he could wed, and that when he did, it must be to a wife who understood her lot as the wife of a vicar. It would be a life of labor with only spiritual rewards, never monetary. No jewels, no furs, no carriages, no London Season. She was a child of plenty, and he could offer nothing.

Not a thing.

And yet with such inviting lips . . . He stepped back toward her, dipped his head again, and was lost.

Sir David Chappell, delegated to find the young folks to round them up for dinner, sent Lord Vaughan and his playmate Miss Allen back up to the house and then set out to find the other two. He rounded the corner of the house and, shading his eyes against the setting sun, peered toward the chapel that he knew well from his childhood. Ah, yes, there were two figures near the dark gray of the building.

He cupped his hand around his mouth and was about to shout, when he saw the taller dip his head to the smaller in what could only be a kiss. Lady Silvia and Mr. Rowland, kissing! He stayed silent, but then, as the kiss lingered, he turned with a heavy heart and started back to the house.

Years in society had changed his old romanticism into realism. There would be no successful resolution to a love between a penniless vicar and a society belle, the daughter of an earl. And from his own experience he knew that marriage was difficult enough. If the two young people were foolish enough to persist, their love would never survive the hardships and difficulties that would be placed in their path by society.

He kicked viciously at the snow as he trudged up the slope toward the house. No, marriage was not easy even when all was made smooth for the two. He knew that by bitter experience. He had not thought of Melanie for years, or at least not in any conscious manner, but now all the sadness of that long-ago Christmas season flooded back to him.

His wife . . . how he had adored her! She was like Lady Silvia, petite and pretty, only blond and fair, vivacious, funny, adorable. Chappell entered the house through the door that opened out to the garden and kicked his snowy boots against the doorstep. As he divested himself of his greatcoat and made his way to the red saloon, he was lost in the past.

Life had seemed, for a time, complete. He had work that he thrived on, important work with the government, and he was good at it. Men whom he respected said that he had a future, and he had been honestly proud of their esteem, knowing it was hard-won.

And at home he and his beautiful wife had just been safely delivered of a boy, Alexander, and they both adored him. Melanie, though, had seemed sad after the birth, almost inconsolable, and he had been at a loss to understand her emotions. They had everything: each other, a child, a home, enough money to live on. It had seemed to him that life could not get any better, and yet he had come to her room many times and found her weeping. It had been confusing; he knew now with the wisdom of years that he had been cold and unsympathetic, merely pointing out, when she could not explain her tears, that she was being ungrateful. He had turned away from her in his impatience, angry that she was destroying what should have been a golden time for them with her moodiness. How differently he would do things now, if he had the opportunity!

But then the tears had stopped. He only remembered being thankful that she was back to her normal behavior. Yet, it had not been normal. She had been brittle, like ice, fragile and yet cold and untouchable. But at least she had smiled and laughed again, and he had thought that the coldness would pass as the crying had.

Had he known even then? Chappell sat down on a bench in the great hall and buried his face in his hands, overwhelmed by that long-ago misery, feelings he thought he had tucked away, never to be experienced again. It was this time of year, though, with the cold, the snow, the Christmas season creeping up on them. It was almost exactly twenty years ago that he had first suspected that his wife had taken a lover.

Ten

Dinner had come and gone. Chappell had watched with interest the interplay, the loaded phrases and significant glances, the hurt expressions and raised eyebrows. Vaughan was a masterful rake, Chappell knew, for the young man's exploits were well documented in London society, but he was clearly puzzled by Lady Silvia's continual snubbing of his advances. And Miss Allen, a likable if overly exuberant young woman, was, at times, hurt by Vaughan's brotherly treatment of her. And yet what could she expect when she insisted on buffeting his shoulder just as he was drinking wine, or making surreptitious slurping noises as he sipped his soup?

But now the young people had retired to the gold saloon to play a game of Forfeits, and Lady Bournaud, exhausted from the ordeal of being pleasant through dinner, had returned to her own chamber. Lady Bournaud had urged her companion to join Sir David in the red saloon for wine by the fire, and the woman, unable to politely decline, was now sewing by the pale wintry light thrown by the drifted snow outside and by the warmer glow of the fire and candlelight reflected off the crimson-papered walls.

It was peaceful. Sheaf of papers in hand, Chappell watched her covertly. The atmosphere was cozily domestic, with only the crackle of the fire and faint sputter of the guttering candle to break the hush. The last time he had experienced anything comparable was before his mistress had died, three years before.

Lydia had been older than he. When he was thirty-four, her age of forty-two had seemed to make little difference, but she had aged quickly, probably because she was ill, though she had never told him that. Passion between them died early; what was left was their political alliance and deep friendship. But then, he had never truly loved her. He had been flattered when she made advances to him, for she was the widow of a very powerful man, and it was whispered that she took under her wing—and into her bed—only those whom she felt would become politically important. She was an intelligent, and more important, an astute woman.

But still, he had never loved her. He hadn't wanted love, for love meant betrayal, and he had sworn after Melanie's death that he was done with the softer feelings of the heart. Never again would he trust a woman with his emotions. Lydia had known that—he had told her his story early on—and had never asked for more than he could give. And yet he knew his aloofness had hurt her. Toward the end he had realized that though he had never been in love with her, he had still come to love her, as contradictory as that sounded.

Her last words to him had been a plea to let go of the hurt once and for all. And he thought he had until the emotions had swept back over him that evening. It was different though. Now he knew that he had to forgive himself for what he had been then, the twenty-seven-year-old David Chappell, unsure of himself, hurt by the wife he adored's infidelity. And in turn, it helped him forgive Melanie. Adored, spoiled, and petted her whole life, she had been, he knew now, suffering from his preoccupation with his work and his obsession with Alexander.

And that brought him back to the present, sitting in a pool of golden light watching Miss Beatrice Copland, who seemed to him to be everything that Melanie had not been. As a young man he had chosen a wife with a young man's needs. Melanie was pretty, flirtatious, vivacious, a diamond her first year, and even as a young matron, the center of a circle of devoted admirers. He had been proud when she chose him to marry, and thrilled when she presented him with a child in their first year.

But with the wisdom of the years he could look back and see that their marriage would have devolved to the bickering, quarreling misery he had seen some of his friends suffer, or it would have grown cold and aloof, with each partner having a separate life, separate friends, and separate lovers. With age came insight, and now at forty-seven, he would choose someone like . . . Miss Copland. Quiet, intelligent, modest, giving, she was everything a discerning man could want and more.

But how to approach her? How to touch a cool heart? She seemed, at times, almost repelled by him. He knew there were women who preferred other women, but in his experience it did not mean that they disliked men, and often they were the easiest friends for a fellow to have, undemanding and with no fear of entanglements or untidy emotions. But Miss Copland withdrew when he approached though she did not do so with the other gentlemen, so it was *him*. Was it just that she was aware of her employer's clumsy attempt to matchmake? For that was what was in Lady Bournaud's mind; he was now sure of it. Perhaps Miss Copland had been hurt by a man and did not wish to repeat the experience. Or perhaps . . . he went back to the remark he had made to her just that afternoon and how it had stung her, the remark about her Season.

It was a puzzle, and he dearly liked unknotting the intricate weave of an enigma. It was what made him good at his job, which involved a good deal of diplomatic language, the greatest tangle ever devised by man. And yet this mystery was none of his business. He must be mindful of that.

He glanced down at the papers in his lap. It was an opening, and he wished to start a conversation with her while he had her as a captive audience.

"Listen to this, Miss Copland," he said. He knew he had a good reading voice, and he used it as he read. "In that pleasant district of merry England which is watered by the river Don, there extended in ancient times a large forest, covering the greater part of the beautiful hill and valleys which lie between Sheffield and the pleasant town of Doncaster . . ."

She looked up and smiled. "Is it a travelogue, sir?"

"No," he said, pleased that he had engaged her interest.

"A history then? For that is Yorkshire, south of us in West Riding."

"No," he said. "It is not a history. It is the opening of a work my friend Walter Scott proposes, his first book set in England. It has to do with the tensions between the Normans and the Saxons shortly after the conquest, and is set, as you pointed out, in this very county. He is tentatively entitling it after the hero, Ivanhoe."

"Walter Scott," she said, clipping a thread.

"He has written mostly poetry, until now, though he has published a couple of novels. His poetry is very good: 'The Lay of the Last Minstrel,' and 'The Lady of the Lake'?"

"Of course I know of whom you speak." She tilted her head to one side and observed him. "I did not know you were interested in poetry."

"I think it is safe to say, Miss Copland, that there is much you do not know of me."

Her ivory cheeks stained with rose, and he was caught by the youthful glow it gave her. Why a blush? He had not said anything outrageous. Who was she? And why did she fascinate him so? He could not imagine, and yet there was something between them. It almost felt like unfinished business, though that, of course, was ridiculous. They had only just met.

"I have no doubt," she murmured, and got up, gathering her sewing together as if she was going to leave.

"Don't go," he said. "Stay. Do you like poetry, then?"

"I do."

He watched her face for a moment. "Do you perhaps write poetry, Miss Copland?" He knew he had hit on something by the deepening blush in her cheeks. "You do. You do write poetry."

"Very bad poetry, sir," she said with spirit, looking him directly in the eyes. "I write very bad poetry, and only for myself."

"Let me read some. Let *me* be the judge."

"No. It truly is only for my own perusal, sir. Good evening, Mr. Chappell. I hope your stay so far is enjoyable."

And she was gone. No amount of persuasion would entice her to stay.

With all of the miracles of the modern age, Lady Bournaud thought, why could someone not create glasses that would not slide down to the tip of one's nose and pinch off one's breathing? She pushed them up once again and tried to follow the inanity of a novel that chronicled the adventures of a young girl who seemed to be perpetually idiotic and unlucky, in that every house she entered was haunted, and yet still she ventured abroad after dark with only a guttering candle and no weapon.

A tap at her door did not make her jump or scream, as it would have the imbecilic heroine of the novel. She merely called out, "Enter."

When Chappell entered, closing the door behind him, she smiled and indicated the edge of the bed. "Come, Davey. Do you, by the way, mind that I insist on calling you by your childhood name, even though you are a mature man and a statesman of some repute?"

"No," he said. "It takes me back to when I was a towheaded child following around the great lady of the house and getting underfoot."

"I'm glad. It would not have changed anything if you *had* minded, but I am still glad," she said, as the bed creaked under his weight. She examined him closely. They wrote often, but there was nothing like having him in the house again, right there for her to examine. He was a handsome man, though the beginnings of age were showing. His mouth was bracketed by faint lines, and the skin under his chin was getting softer. Nothing like her own great wattle of skin, of course, she thought. When she looked in the mirror now she almost did not recognize herself, for all of her former healthy fat had melted away, leaving too much skin. She had always been a big woman, handsome rather than beautiful, they had called her. When she was twenty it had mattered to her, but when she was forty, and meeting François Bournaud for the first time, it had not because he thought her beautiful, and by then that was all that mattered.

She watched her protégé's eyes, and saw in them worry over something.

"What is it, Davey? Why have you bearded the lion in its den?"

"Why does Miss Copland seem so frightened of me?" he asked without preamble.

"Frightened?" Lady Bournaud removed her glasses and laid her book down on the snowy coverlet. "Is that true? Beatrice is not a coward. Have you said something to her?"

"Nothing! Nothing but the most bland banalities. Or . . . well, she made some reference to ruining one's life with a misstep, and I did ask her if that was what had happened to her. But it was just a passing reference and she had been avoiding me before that. I make her uncomfortable."

"Well, whatever it is, Beatrice Copland is not a coward. Though she has never told me so, I think that she has suffered great hardships in her life, and not been bowed by them."

"What do you mean?"

Lady Bournaud pursed her lips and fingered her chin. What should she say? How much? But she did so want this to work. Beatrice deserved it, and yet there seemed to be obstacles of the woman's own making. So anything she could do to encourage the interest Davey was clearly feeling . . .

"I shall tell you a story. I don't know if I have ever told you this." She settled back in her pillows and sighed. "Your father gave me a list of all of your kinfolk to write to after his passing."

Chappell nodded.

"He did not want to leave all the work to you, because he knew you had your own concerns."

There was a moment of silence. The senior Mr. Chappell's death had come a bare month and a half after Melanie's. Lady Bournaud rarely referred to that time, for it was horrible and dark, both of them grieving, she for her recently deceased husband, and then her protégé's sadness, and then the death of her dear friend, Arthur Chappell. It had seemed for a while as if God had deserted them both, and she had spent her share of time weeping disconsolately in the dim reaches of the chapel, though she would have denied it had anyone confronted her with that weakness.

"And so," she continued, "I struck up a correspondence with a distant relative of your father's, a very old woman . . . or so I thought her then, for she was my age now."

Chappell shifted restlessly, and Lady Bournaud put out her hand. "Patience, my dear boy. You must learn to humor the elderly. Surely you have learned that in your profession, dealing with all the lords in the House. Anyway, your ancient relation told me, about eleven years ago, of a girl, the niece of a friend of hers, who needed a position badly. She was of a good family, but due to the profligate ways of her father and the self-absorbed selfishness of her mother, she was left penniless after their death. He died of pneumonia in a sponging house and the mother died shortly after of shame, for all I can tell. This young woman, a Miss Beatrice Copland, had obtained a position of governess, but had been let go. Your kinswoman did not say, but I think the scion of the family expressed a dangerous preference for Miss Copland and the female head of the family dismissed the girl rather than have her son make a fool of himself. When I first heard the tale I thought that perhaps Miss Copland was an adventuress, but upon meeting her, I dismissed that idea. By that time she had been alone for almost two years with no family, no position, and nowhere to go."

Chappell was still now, perhaps sensing that she was coming to the meat of the story.

"She was a bundle of bones. She was thin and threadbare, and looked like she had not had a decent meal in weeks." Lady Bournaud turned her face away, for she felt the water come to her eyes and she hated the sentimentality that occasionally overcame her great pragmatism. "I think she had been eking out an existence on whatever savings she had managed to put by, but when she arrived here she could not have had enough to even hire a carriage, for she walked up from the village with her meager belongings. If I had not taken her on, I do not know where she would have gone."

"Why are you telling me this?"

Lady Bournaud turned her face to look into his eyes, her snowy eyebrows knit. "So you will understand her better, I suppose. She could have used her suffering to gain sympathy. She could have told me the story to convince me to hire her, but she did not. She conducted herself in the interview as if she had a choice, too, and was evaluating me. It was foolhardy, I suppose, but I respected her then, though I was not sure how much use she would be as a companion. So self-contained! So withdrawn. I had a chatterbox before her and so she was a welcome relief, but she could not have known that."

Chappell shook his head. "None of this explains why she shies away from me. Am I repulsive?"

"Davey, do not be absurd. You are not a coxcomb, but you must know you are a pleasing young man. I am sure Mistress Lydia thought so," she added, a wicked glint in her eyes.

"You are not supposed to know of my amorous adventures," he scolded.

"Precious few adventures, seems to me," she retorted. Becoming serious again, Lady Bournaud said, "She has never reflected back on that time, except to occasionally speak feelingly of how valuable a warm bed and good food are."

"We spoke for a while," he said, plucking absently at the coverlet. Lady Bournaud smacked his hand and he grinned, stopping his unconsciously destructive behavior. "She told me she writes poetry, but she will not let me read it, she says. It is too bad, according to her. I would prefer to judge for myself."

After a brief internal struggle, Lady Bournaud said, "It so happens that I have at least one sample. If I let you read this, Davey, you must promise not to tell her about it."

"I promise," he said, with only a moment's hesitation. "Where is it?"

She directed him to her writing desk in her sitting room, and guided him, with her stentorian voice, to the secret compartment.

"One would think these were the secret papers of the immortal bard, so well is it hidden,"Chappell said, bringing it back into the bedroom.

She shrugged. "Read it."

He did so out loud

> *"Autumn creeps o'er the moor on chilly feet,*
> *Soon to be tucked under the snowy white mantle*
> *Of winter's bright night, to sleep,*
> *And dream of spring's warming, so gentle.*
>
> *But I . . . I dream of a fire in winter,*
> *Warming, melting, thawing a heart*
> *Froze by a disconsolate longing so bitter,*
> *Buried in arctic tears glazed by old hurt."*

"It is so . . . sad. So very sad." He laid the paper on his lap, after tracing the fine slanted writing. He looked up and smiled. "But she is right. It is rather bad poetry."

"We judge differently, my dear boy. I judge it good because it gives me the faintest glimpse into her soul, and that is a rare, rare sight, seldom offered. As I said, I was happy she was so closemouthed when first we met, as my previous companion was a chatterbox and I cannot abide senseless nattering on. But Beatrice has been with me for over ten years, and yet sometimes I think I know no more about her now than I did that first day. There is a melancholy deep within her. It is not so much a morose disposition, or a gloomy or tragical outlook, but more a . . . a sadness from the heart, as if there is a wound that has never healed."

"Never healed," Chappell repeated. He slipped off the bed. "I would ask to keep this, but I think it is not wise, so I will tuck it back in its hiding spot."

"I think that is best," Lady Bournaud said drowsily, "since she does not even know I have it."

"I thought that this was given to you," Chappell said, holding the paper by one corner and gazing at it. He was horrified by the invasion of privacy he had just committed unknowingly.

"No, idiot. Did you think she would freely give me something so revealing of her inner self when we were just speaking of how self-contained she is? I was still able to get about a few years ago, and I came across the poem slipped under a blotter in the desk in the library. She must have been interrupted as she wrote. She used to do the household accounts in that room—probably still does—and I think she must have been sitting there writing and hid it when a maid came in or some other interruption occurred. She never said anything about it, so she either forgot it was there or assumed some maid found it and used it to light the fire with." There was a long pause. "I would give much to know what it means."

"I don't know." He bent over his elderly patron and kissed her cheek, hearing her breathing slow and the soft snuffling that meant she was dozing off. "Thank you, my lady, for the insight into the fascinating Miss Copland's character. You are a disgraceful old meddler, but I love you anyway."

She chuckled sleepily, and he left the room humming a tune, a piece of music that was on everyone's lips the year of Melanie's death. At one time he could not abide it for that reason, but for some reason it was stuck in his brain. The words, if he remembered correctly, were about a village maiden deserted by her cavalier.

At one time the tune had reminded him of a particularly vicious argument he and Melanie had had while she badly played the tune on their piano. He thought perhaps it was the first time he had accused her of having a lover. In hindsight he could see that she used the piano as an excuse not to look into his eyes.

But now he hummed the tune as he closed the door to the comtesse's suite. Strangely, it brought back the few pleasant memories of that time, now: holding his son for the first time, his pride in his family, the brilliant future plans he was working so hard toward. He was long past the depression, even though the memories were still painful. And he had forgiven Melanie, and himself, too. Or at least he hoped he had.

He was ready to move on with his life after a long period of holding on to pain and recrimination. But was he ready to seek love again? Or was he too old for that tender emotion?

Eleven

Lord Jacob Vaughan trudged grimly through the snow, not quite listening to Miss Verity Allen's chatter as she commented on everything from the weather to his horse. Somehow, though he had intended to get Lady Silvia alone for a half hour's walk, it had turned into an expedition involving all four of them to gather mistletoe and evergreen boughs for the rapidly approaching Christmas day festivities. How had it happened?

He had, the previous night during a silly game with lettered squares, asked Lady Silvia to walk with him in the park the next day and she had agreed, but then at the breakfast table it appeared that she had mistaken his invitation for something entirely different and had invited Rowland and Miss Allen along as well. He had thought he was being perfectly clear about his intentions toward Lady Silvia, but that could not be.

Infuriating.

It would not have been so bad if Rowland would just keep Miss Allen busy, but somehow the old sobersides had managed to finagle things so that Lady Silvia was on his arm, and a fellow couldn't very well cut out another fellow, could he? Especially a man of the cloth.

The day was brilliant, with puffy white clouds drifting across a sky so blue it looked like thick cerulean paint spilled across the heavens. It was warming things up, and the snow was melting into itself, the drifts shrinking and becoming increasingly sodden with meltwater. Miss Allen was wearing again the ugly brown coat that irritated him for some reason. She looked like such a guy in it. Had the girl no fashion sense? He assessed her expertly in one quick sideways glance. She should be wearing hunter green and antique gold topped by a jaunty hat adorned with a quail feather, or perhaps a scarlet military-cut jacket and a shako. She would look dashing in that garb.

Moodily, he cast another glance toward her. She had so much energy! It was like walking a spaniel pup, for she bounced off the cleared trail constantly, fetching back interesting branches, dead weed heads that stuck up out of the drifted snow, or chased off when she saw or heard an unusual bird.

He craned his neck and looked over his shoulder. Behind them, Rowland had the neat, pretty, well-behaved Lady Silvia clinging to his arm just as a properly raised young lady ought. Vaughan knew very well that she could not prefer the sober and silent Rowland to himself, so he could only think that she felt sorry for the vicar. He honored the sweetness of character that she would tie herself to the brooding and repressed reverend for the afternoon, but such sacrifice was really not necessary. It went quite beyond the bounds of politeness.

"Vaughan, what is your home like?"

He snapped out of his unusual introspection to feel his arm grasped and Miss Allen, panting from her exertions, hanging on to him. Irritably he thought he should shake her off, but it would not do to look obstreperous in front of the gentle Lady Silvia. He shrugged. "Vaughan Hall is good enough, I guess. It is home, but I don't spend much time there anymore. Have rooms in London."

"I hate London," she said, giving a dramatic shudder.

"Why?" he asked, interested in spite of himself. He found that his spirits were lifting as he and Miss Allen bounced along in step. They were like his carriage team of grays, he thought, well matched and high-spirited. Though the girl at his side was much prettier than even his best horse.

"Pretentious, drunken louts," she said, her usually ebullient and cheery tone virulent with distaste. "And so many rules! I was the death of any peace my aunt had, for I was always

A MATCHMAKER'S CHRISTMAS 99

spilling ratafia and stepping on toes, and being overly familiar with the lads *she* said. . . ."

He lost the rest of her comments. "Overly familiar with the lads?" What did that mean? He looked her over with interest, from her glossy auburn hair and clear brown complexion to her generous mouth and sparkling blue-green eyes. Yes, there was that tug of interest again, of sexual attraction.

"Oh!" she said suddenly, pointing. "I think that is the wood that Tidwell said was the oak grove the mistletoe could be found in."

She let go of his arm and dashed off, galloping through the snow in a most unladylike way that made Vaughan want to laugh out loud. As much as he tried to resist, he was never bored in Miss Allen's invigorating company. He raced off behind her, leaping snowdrifts and pelting snowballs after her into the woods.

But her brown coat disappeared in a forest of brown and gray trunks. The snow had not drifted in as deeply into the wood, for there was a break of evergreens at the edge of the forest, and even in the dim reaches of the forest it was melting off, shrinking away from the trees and leaving patches of wet leaves visible. "Miss Allen," he called, "where are you?"

His own voice echoed, taunting him. "Impossible wench," he grunted, and followed her tracks as well as he could, where there was still snow. He tracked her down to find her staring up at an enormous tree with a trunk twice as thick as one of the pillars in front of the Bournaud home.

"I suppose you expect me to climb that monstrosity," he said, leaning back to stare up, his hands on his hips.

She gave him a disgusted look. "No! I will do it."

"No you shan't," he said, shocked that she would even consider such a thing. "How old are you?"

She frowned. "What has that got to do with anything?"

"How old?"

"I am twenty-four."

"And you have not yet left off climbing trees? Why can you not be more like Lady Silvia?"

A hurt look pulled down her mouth and furrowed her brow. "Sourpuss," she said. "You are too great a lummox to be able to climb this tree properly. I shall do it."

"Fine. I would like to see you try." He stood back and folded his arms over his chest, watching her intently.

She eyed the tree with expert assessment, stripped off her gloves, threw off her heavy greatcoat, and rucked her gown up between her legs. Then she grabbed a handhold on the rugged bark. Vaughan watched in amazement as she tackled the tree, competently placing hand and foot in secure spots and gaining the first branch without too much trouble. From there it was as if she were a monkey, scampering from branch to branch until she was twenty feet off the ground.

"I found it," she crowed.

He watched as she stripped the branch of the parasitic plant, throwing it down onto her coat where it lay spread out over some snow. She stared down from the tree.

"Is that enough, do you think?" she called out, one hand cupped around her mouth.

"How many kissing balls do you think you will need?"

"One for each saloon, and one for the servant's hall," she said, not catching his sarcasm.

"There's enough," he said, watching nervously as her foot skidded off the branch and she had to scramble for a foothold. "Come down out of there."

"Am I making you nervous?" she said impishly, letting go of the branch and teetering precariously. "Are you a Nervous Nellie, Vaughan?"

"Come down here now, you infuriating imp!"

"Certainly, Vaughan, but I just want to show you a trick I learned from my brothers," she called down.

She came down about ten feet, and he felt the tension ease out of him with each downward movement. Despite her words, it looked like she was going to behave herself. But then she stopped and sat down on the lowest limb.

"What are you doing?"

"I told you!" She turned around so her back was to him,

and then wiggled back on the limb, so that her knees were over it securely, then she let go and leaned back.

"Watch out!" he called, just as she started to fall, or so it looked.

But instead of falling, she swung upside down and she was staring him in the face, grinning, her hair tumbling out of its pins. "You look most odd, Vaughan, upside down."

"So do you, wench," he said. "Now come down."

She tried to grab for a handhold as she swung her legs over the branch, and for one agonizing moment Vaughan thought she was going to fall.

And then she did and was coming at him, skirts flying, hair flying, legs flailing. She landed on him and he felt all the wind knocked out of him as he hit the ground with a re-sounding thud. When he opened his eyes it was to see her blue-green ones, slightly dazed, staring down into his.

Everything stopped for those few seconds. She was not heavy, but he was very much aware of her coatless body pressed down upon his own as they lay together in the wet snow. He licked his lips and saw her eyes riveted on his mouth, and then before he knew what to make of her expres-sion, she had pressed her mouth over his in a haphazard kiss, her warm breath melting with his own as her generous mouth worked in an inexperienced melding.

And then she was off him, her knee hitting his groin as she stumbled to her feet. He doubled over in some pain as she staggered over to her coat, shook it out and gathered the mistletoe, stuffing it in the capacious pockets of the ugly brown garment.

"I shall find the others," she cried, her voice oddly breathy and her cheeks flaming red. She raced back the way they had come.

Rowland felt a contentment steal over him. He supposed they should be gathering boughs or some such nonsense, but a walk in the woods with Lady Silvia was much nicer without the added distraction of any kind of labor.

"Will you have a house in Loughton?" she asked, as they talked about the village where his curacy was to be.

"Yes. It is small, a cottage really, but of sturdy stone and with a patch of land. Mr. Leslie—he is the vicar I am replacing—he and his wife had a garden and kept goats and a couple of sheep."

"Sheep? Really? I adore lambs! They are so pretty and sweet," she said, sighing.

Rowland did not want to say that Mr. Leslie liked lambs, too, with mint jelly and new roasted potatoes. He glanced over at Lady Silvia. Her head was so close it was almost resting against his arm, but she wore an absurdly attractive bonnet with dyed pink feathers nodding at a rakish angle, and he could not see her face.

"It is a modest beginning, but it is all I could ever want or need. I am not an ambitious fellow."

"Are you not?" she asked. She turned her face up and searched his eyes. Hers were a lovely melting brown, like a melange of caramel and chocolate.

"No," he said carefully. He longed to boast, to puff himself up, to expand his consequence so she would think him as fine a fellow as Vaughan, and he felt ashamed of that urge. It was pride, or . . . He wasn't sure what. Why did he want to appear more than he was in this lovely lady's eyes? "No," he continued, sternly quelling his baser urges. "I have modest wants and my ambition has more to do with the people I will serve. I want to bring together those in the community who feel that the church has not served their needs. Too often I think my fellow churchmen think more about advancement and money than the spiritual needs of their flock. Not," he hastened to add, "that most are morally at fault. I did not mean to imply that."

"No, I think I understand," she said, holding his gaze. "But I wonder, would . . . would a wife not be able to help you in this? Women are connected in a different way with people than men, I think, and we often see a different side, a perhaps more honest side."

"Do you think that folks conceal their faults?"

"From their vicar? Yes. Who would not? Especially a gentleman so . . ." She paused and her cheeks flamed. "A gentleman so good as you. No one would want you to see their bad side. A wife would be more likely to see and hear about the true conflicts of the parish, I think."

Rowland's heart sunk, but he had to be honest. As much as he would like to pretend things were different, it was the moment for absolute truthfulness. "I wish I could afford to marry, but that is not likely to be for some years yet. When I do, I will look among a class of young ladies used to the rigors of a modest household. Being the wife of a parish vicar involves a certain amount of labor, for though I will naturally keep a housekeeper and perhaps a maid, there will be much, if I marry, that my wife would have to do for the family. Cooking, sewing, preserving . . . that sort of thing. A man in my position would be wise to choose a young woman from, perhaps, the merchant classes, or a squire's daughter. . . ."

"Someone used to poverty," she said sharply. So he would warn her off, would he? Had she been so very blatant? She glanced up at his handsome face, the dark tumbling locks over his broad forehead, the coal-dark eyes. Or was he just speaking generally?

"Well, not poverty, certainly, but a modest budget."

"Do you think that a young lady of a higher class could not learn those things?" she asked.

"I don't think she should have to," he said earnestly.

"So you think she should be allowed to remain in the slothful privilege in which she was raised?"

He quirked one eyebrow. "My lady, there is no answer for that that is not insulting in some way."

"I know." They walked on in silence for a while. Silvia was silent because she was doing some honest soul-searching. She had never had to do anything in her life but what was pleasurable. She had learned to play the piano, paint, sew, and sing. She could make conversation with a duke or a bishop or even the Prince Regent himself if she had to. She knew how to gently discourage an unsuitable suitor and how to deflect unwanted attentions. But what did she know of running a household on a limited budget? How did one know how much food to order, what to cook and how, or how to hire a maidservant? Since she had been staying at the Bournaud estate she had observed that Miss Copland took care of all of those things, including such housewifely duties as mixing the tea and ordering the provisions. Perhaps it was time to pay the companion a visit. Perhaps with some help she could learn those skills. With that knowledge she could learn if she was suited to be the wife of a vicar or not.

She was an advocate of not making assumptions. She had always, in her life, taken pains to learn anything she needed to know from a direct source, and deciding whether she was a fit wife for Mr. Mark Rowland would be no different. He made her heart beat faster, and she thought that he liked her, too—surely the kisses between them proved that—but there was more to marriage than that. If he was practical, well, she was, too. She would go about this in an orderly fashion. Her decision calmly made, she turned the discussion to other, more innocuous subjects.

"Where is that boy with the sledge?" Vaughan peered through the woods. "And where are the others? It is getting colder." He stamped his feet in the snow.

Verity peeled off her gloves, stuck two fingers in her mouth, and let out a sharp whistle. The whistle was returned, and a moment later the boy, a small but strong lad of about thirteen, arrived pulling the sledge. His cheeks were rosy and he was out of breath.

"Where did you hare off to, Bobby?"

"Found a hill, Miss Allen," the boy said, his eyes shining. "This here sledge ain't much on flat, but you should see 'er go down a slope!"

Verity laughed. "I can imagine." She was tempted to tell the boy to take her there. She would like nothing better at that moment than to careen down a snowy slope just like she and her brothers used to do when they were children. She had done nothing half so much fun since arriving in England, and her abundant energy had her insides humming like a top. How the ladies she had met in London could abide just standing around all the time looking bored or languidly reclining, she just did not know. It seemed a waste of time to her.

She glanced over at Lord Vaughan, who was loading a heavy log on the sledge. He made her feel all tingly inside, but she didn't think he felt the same way for her. He certainly did not seem to approve of her "hoydenish ways," as her aunt had called them. She sighed. She could not even bear to think of that kiss she had forced on him under the tree. He had said nothing about it when he caught up with her, and she wouldn't be the first to raise the topic. "I suppose we should look for some evergreen boughs, Bobby," she said, leading the way. "I saw some likely trees back on the main path."

As they followed the boy with the sledge, Vaughan looked her over with a frown. "So you have actually had a Season in London?"

"Hard to believe, isn't it?" Verity said ruefully. "I was a trial to my poor aunt, I can tell you. I cannot dance, and everything she tried to dress me in just looked terrible. I am too tall, my arms are too long and freckled, and I cannot walk correctly. Not like my cousins. They are lovely swans while I am a goose."

"Then you can be a Christmas goose," he joked. "Why did you come here in the first place? It sounds as though you loved your life in Canada."

"My mother was afraid that I was turning into a fellow, I think. And she was convinced I would only get worse, and would never find anyone to marry me." Sighing deeply, and relieved that Vaughan was still talking to her after that wretchedly awkward kiss she foisted upon him, Verity kicked at some sodden snow as Bobby and the sledge pulled ahead of them.

"I miss home," she continued wistfully. "Especially this time of year. But it is not so bad. Home is not the same anymore, not like it was when I was a child. My mother has talked my father into moving into town and letting my oldest brother have the homestead, and I could not live with Patrick—my oldest brother, you know—because he has a wife. They are having a fourth child and there is no room for me. Town there is almost as bad as here. Worse in some ways! You would think they would be different, but they try so desperately to ape the manners of "home." They still call England home as if any of them are ever moving back here! Well, I can tell you, Canada is *my* home!"

Vaughan put his arm over her shoulder and gave her a shake. "This is not so bad, is it? Staying here?"

Eyes shining, she looked up at him. "No, *this* is jolly! Lady Bournaud is marvelous. I'll bet when she was young she was like one of those old warrior queens, you know, like Boadicea. And all of this," she said, waving her arms around to indicate the forest, "it is rather like living back home, only with a much grander house than anywhere in the Colonies. All I miss is riding my old mare, Feather."

"I hear that is how you arrived," Vaughan said, leaving his arm over her shoulders. She was well matched in height for him, almost as tall as he.

Grinning, Verity said, "It is! I could not bear to wait in the village while they hitched a carriage and all that fuss and bother, so I borrowed a horse and rode up."

"Astride, I hear."

"And why should I not?" Her expression earnest, she said, "I think it is hideously ridiculous that women are forced to ride in that unnatural pose! Sidesaddle! I would like to challenge a man to do it without the most unnatural contortions. And they say it is for female health, but I would think that men are the ones . . . I mean for their bodies . . . I mean . . ." Her face flaming, she fell silent.

Vaughan was torn between the urge to guffaw wildly or draw back in horror. Was she saying what he thought she was? Was she really referring to a man's private parts in that way? "And what, Miss Allen, do you know about a gentleman's body?"

"I have seen my brothers swimming naked," she muttered. "That is all. It is truly not such a big mystery. Anyone who has seen a stallion knows what men have."

Vaughan released her and doubled over with laughter, roaring until he thought his sides would split. He staggered sideways and put out one hand against a tree trunk so he would not fall to the wet ground laughing so hard. Miss Allen stood staring at him in perplexity, but when he could speak, still gasping for air, he said, "A s-stallion. I . . . I hope you haven't used that comparison to too many young unmarried ladies, or they will be sorely disappointed at male dimensions on their wedding night!"

Catching the joke, Verity laughed, too. "I never thought of it that way! Lord, and that is what I told my cousins, one of whom is getting married in the spring. Do you suppose I should write her a letter to let her down easily?"

"Let her down? Rather free her from horror! I mean, imagine if you will . . . No," he said, putting up one hand, "perhaps I had better not pursue that train of thought even with *you*, outrageous female though you are. But no, I cannot imagine how you would broach that subject in a letter, and what would happen if it fell into the wrong hands? Better let well enough alone," Vaughan said, staring at the girl before him and shaking his head. "Miss Allen, you truly do amaze me. I have never met anyone like you."

They walked on and caught up with Bobby, and went about the business of gathering heavily scented evergreen boughs for the Bournaud house. Vaughan did not even think about the fact that he could not care less where Rowland and Lady Silvia had disappeared to, so caught up was he in their operation.

But there was a subconscious thread to his thoughts that he

was barely aware of as he laughed and talked with Miss Verity Allen, self-consciousness between them broken down irrevocably.

Marriage. He wanted to get married, oddly enough. He had been something of a rake for years now, though he had never hurt anyone, nor had he ever abandoned a woman, nor impregnated one. Very lucky he had been, but mostly because he had consorted with more knowledgeable women, ones who knew how to handle such matters. He was not a seducer of innocents, and so, though he could quite easily see Miss Allen as an enticing conquest, he now acknowledged that as unsophisticated and naive as some of her conversation had proved her to be, she was not a fit target for seduction.

But back to marriage; he now thought that he had entered a time of his life when a wife and children were something to be desired, not something to be avoided. He was thirty-three, and if he was to have children he wanted them soon, while he could enjoy them the way his father had. For the Viscount Norcross had been a good father, imbuing his son and heir with a love of the outdoors and outdoor pursuits. They had, together, fished, hunted, rode, and drank, and the elder had taught him much about moderation in all such pursuits.

His mother he had seen less often. She and his father lived separate lives in many ways, with different friends, different pursuits, different interests. It was how he saw his own future marriage: he and his wife as partners in bearing and raising children, but with necessarily much different lives beyond that.

He paused in the act of hacking a branch from a fir and watched Miss Allen throw a snowball at Bobby and receive in return a chilly face washing. What a woman! He could see her as a friend, a companion in many pursuits. Her life in Canada had been rough-and-tumble, partly because of the nature of the country, but partly because of her family life, being raised with brothers. She hunted, fished, rode splendidly . . . not the attributes he had ever thought attractive or desirable in a woman. She had canoed silver streams, hiked through primeval forests. . . .

What would it be like to go through life with a woman like that? Did she want to marry? What kind of mother would she make?

He pushed away those thoughts, horrified by them. As a wife, Verity Allen would be a failure. He could not see her deferring to her husband, nor would she stay home quietly while he was off enjoying himself. No, she would make a fellow an uncomfortable wife.

But perhaps she could tell him more about Canada, because, if he was honest with himself, it sounded like the kind of place he would like to see. As his father's heir he had been circumscribed by his duties from entering the army when he had wanted to. As a result, he longed for adventure, for something beyond the rake's routine of London Seasons and house parties and hunting frightened foxes. Miss Allen had met wolves, hunted for bear, ridden through the wilderness. She had learned the language of the natives of her country and had lived among them. She was not genteel, but she certainly was not boring, either.

He threw the branch on the pile on the sledge and said, "I think we have enough. If you two infants will stop gamboling, we can find the main path and go back to the house."

The two reluctantly gave up their snowball fight and called a truce for the time being. They trudged through the snow toward the main path, found it, and started out toward the edge of the woods, their coats and boots sopping wet from the melting snow.

"We shall probably find Rowland and Lady Silvia back at the house sipping tea." Oddly, he did not envy Rowland his company for the afternoon. He had thoroughly enjoyed the outing.

Twelve

"Yes, I think the evergreen boughs along the stair railing will do," Lady Silvia said, holding a twisted evergreen garland up to the oak. "What do you think, Miss Allen?"

The young woman shrugged. "I guess it is fine."

Once they had returned from their expedition, they had begun to decorate the manse with their findings. With some coaxing the gentlemen had agreed to help, but only in the actual physical labor. A table had been hauled into the great hall, and the evergreens and ribbons piled on top.

Lady Silvia stood, hands on hips, and said, "Am I the only one who is to decide where things go?" She glared at Miss Allen. She had expected that the only other young lady would be of some help.

But Verity was sitting at the table frowning down at the mess she held in her hands. "I cannot do this," she said.

"What are you trying to do, Miss Allen?" Rowland stood behind her and looked at the item in her hands.

"It is supposed to be a kissing ball," she said, blushing for some reason. "But it is lopsided."

Vaughan laughed out loud. "Yes, well, look who is making it."

"What do you mean by that?" Verity said.

"I mean, you are the most unartistic female I have ever seen. I would bet that you do not paint or sketch or net or even do needlepoint."

Stung, Verity threw down the mess of glossy greenery and

white berries that she had been trying to fashion into a circle. "There is precious little need for a painted screen or a netted purse where I live, Lord Vaughan."

She said his name like an insult, emphasizing the "Lord" appellation, and he frowned. "Then why are you even attempting this?" he said, grabbing and shaking her sad creation. "Suddenly fixated on kissing?"

She colored, and he felt for a moment as though he had hurt her with his casual and brutal reference to her odd behavior in the bush that afternoon. But that was ridiculous. It was quite clear to him that she had no normal feminine feelings.

"Not at all," she said, summoning all her dignity. She sat up straight, a strangely regal creature. "I am doing this because my mother told me so much about her childhood in England. I just wanted to experience it as she had." She looked down sadly at the monstrosity in her hands. "But you are right. I have no artistic ability. I have made an abominable mess of this." She held it up pathetically and sent a beseeching look toward Lady Silvia. "Can you help me?"

Vaughan felt an unwelcome tug at his heart at the pain he had caused her. Damn it, he did not feel anything at all for her but a reluctant sort of liking for her gallant nature and vigorous sense of fun. After fighting the urge for a moment, he finally gave in. "Oh, for God's sake, it is easy. Look," he said, sitting down beside her. "It can be fixed if we just add some more of the mistletoe here, and stick some kind of a red bow there in that bald spot."

Her brilliant eyes shining, she gazed up into his face with admiration. "I think you can do anything you set your hand to, Vaughan."

He shrugged off the compliment, but it left a warm spot in his heart, and he affectionately nudged her with his shoulder. "Come on. Let us make more of these. You said you wanted one for each saloon and one for the servant's hall, did you not? If that is so . . ."

* * *

"Have you always done this for Lady Bournaud?"

Beatrice, with a neat apron over her navy sarcenet dress, stood at a table in the pantry where the tea chest was kept. It was a large, elaborately carved monstrosity made of dark wood with numerous drawers, all of them locked. The keys were on her own key ring, and she was the only one with access to the valuable resource. She glanced over at Lady Silvia, who stood at her elbow watching and asking questions.

"No, not at first. When I first came here Lady Bournaud had a housekeeper, but she was getting on in years and became ill. Lady Bournaud pensioned her off and she went to live with a sister in the village. She died just two years ago." Beatrice took a scoop of the bohea and mixed in a little China, and then put it in the box the cook would retrieve it from in the kitchen. This was the servant's blend, and very generous Lady Bournaud was thought, too, to give the staff real tea—and with some China, too!—and not the second-hand leaves. "I took over her duties. It is a modest household and it is not an onerous task." She took another handful of China and put it in a porcelain bowl. She mixed in some hyson, then added some of the cheaper bohea, a smaller amount this time.

"What are you doing? Why do you put different kinds of tea leaves together?"

The pantry was dark and chilly and Beatrice frowned, wondering why Lady Silvia was suddenly so interested in a housekeeper's work. "The China tea, this lovely dark leaf, is very expensive," she said, holding up one leaf fragment. "It is fermented until it is ready, and is from a very good supplier. Lady Bournaud is generous with the household expenses and likes a good cup of tea, but still we mix with the less expensive blends."

"Can one tell the difference?"

Beatrice took a pinch of each type and said, "Hold out your hands." She dropped the leaves into the girl's cupped hands. "Now, smell each one."

The young woman complied, and a look of understanding

crossed her smooth face. "I see. This has a much . . . I don't know how to explain it, but it smells nicer," she said, holding up the hand with the China tea in it.

"So the trick is to keep all the lovely properties of the China, blending it with the less expensive varieties."

"Is this what a wife would be expected to do if her husband was of a modest income, say a tradesman perhaps, or . . . or maybe a vicar?"

Beatrice did her best to conceal a smile. So, that was the child's intention. She could not help but honor so sensible an approach to her future. If Lady Silvia truly was considering marriage to Mark Rowland, then learning how to take care of his home was important, though not many young women would think of it while in the early stages of love. She gazed over at the girl for a moment and then said, "Why don't you do some of this? We'll work together. And then I need to count the linens for the guest rooms and confer with Cook about dinner." It was early morning yet, and this was her daily work, a comforting routine of housekeeper's chores.

"Do you mean you will give me a few household lessons, Miss Copland? I would appreciate it. My education so far, I fear, has been sadly lacking. My mother wanted me to learn only those accomplishments that would make me popular with the gentlemen."

"Certainly," Beatrice said. "Now, in the porcelain bowl," she said, stirring with a wooden spoon the dark leaves and the lighter bohea, "will be the brew we serve at tea. For Lady Bournaud I mix a special batch for her late-night tea, with some chamomile to help her sleep."

They worked together for a few minutes, Beatrice talking occasionally about one aspect or another of tea ordering, how to tell if you were getting a bargain on leaves, and where to get the best. She took a spray of dried herbs that hung from a nail—dried chamomile she told the girl beside her—and stripped the leaves off, talking about collecting herbs from the garden for their properties brewed as tea, as well. Lady Silvia was attentive and asked intelligent questions, proving an apt student. But gradually conversation turned to more personal matters.

"I know it is impertinent," Lady Silvia said, taking over the task of stripping the dried leaves from the woody stalk, careful, as Beatrice had showed her, not to crush the leaves prematurely and lose the essential oils. "But I am so curious. Why did you never marry?"

"I never had the opportunity," Beatrice said. "My family lost its money and I had to go out to work; I am afraid that made me quite unmarriageable."

"But Sir David seems quite taken with you." The girl's mild brown eyes glittered with interest in the dim light from the wall sconce. "Have you considered marriage now?"

Beatrice swallowed and closed a drawer of the tea chest with a slam and locked it. "Tea is quite expensive, which is why it is kept locked. It is not that we do not trust our serving staff, but . . . well, it has always been done this way. I guess that is its explanation."

Lady Silvia gazed steadily at her without comment.

Beatrice turned and with a bright smile, said, "I have heard that your Christmas trip here is some form of punishment. Have you found it thus so far?"

Taking the hint, the girl allowed the subject to drop. "No, I really am much more fond of quiet living than of London, but I could never make my mother understand that. Finally, when they wanted me to marry Lord Boxton and I said no, she became angry, and my father, too. He said if I did not agree to an engagement, I would be sent away."

"Was Lord Boxton so horrible?" Beatrice carried some of the tea in a bowl out to the kitchen and nodded pleasantly at the scullery maid, who was peeling potatoes for the evening meal's ragout. The scent of rosemary and thyme filled the air from the *bouquet garni* the cook used to flavor the meat for the stew.

Lady Silvia followed, her pretty face pinched in a scowl. "I know some people would think he was perfect, and he always treated me well, but . . ." She sat down on a high stool pulled up to the floury pastry table. "I'll tell you why I will never marry Lord Boxton. I have told no one, but you are unlikely to be in London anytime soon, and besides, I know I can trust you." She said it simply, with a nod, as she brushed flour into a pile. "There is a fellow, his name is . . . well, people call him Daft Willie. He is sweet and kind, and we have become friends. He is not someone you would turn to for conversation, but Willie is good-natured and accepts people as they are. I like that, for it is a trait seldom discovered, especially in London during the Season. He is exceptionally well born, which is the only reason my mother lets me near him."

Her expression changed, the brown eyes becoming hard and glinting like dark marble. "Lord Boxton and his . . . his *friends* set up poor Willie so that he somehow ended up in a ballroom during the premiere occasion of the Season *n-naked* except for his boots. I am not supposed to know it was Boxton who tricked him into it, for Willie did not tell me. If anyone found out I knew, they would think he did and Boxton would make him suffer for it. I only know because I overheard Boxton and his despicable cronies laughing about it after, and making fun of Willie's . . . his anatomy." Her voice was shaking with anger and tears rose into her eyes. "Willie is pudgy, you see, and . . ."

Beatrice sat down beside her and laid one calming hand on the girl's shoulder.

Lady Silvia steadied her voice, looked up at Beatrice, and said, "How could I marry someone like that? He thought it was funny. And poor Willie does not even realize that it was meant as a torment. He thinks Boxton is his friend. I was *overjoyed* to leave London. It is a cruel place, and the young men there are a breed apart, who think it is entertainment to "box the watch," in other words to beat up old men who are only trying to do their jobs. I hate it. Boxton himself I have seen kick a dog, and I know he beats his horse if the steed does not instantly obey. He is beneath contempt."

And that explained her attraction to the gentle Mr. Rowland, and the possibility of a life as wife to a man like that.
Beatrice slipped off the stool, got some hot water from the
kettle on the fire, and made a pot of tea, adding extra leaves
to make it strong. "You did the right thing, my dear. Marriage
is so close a bond, a woman must suffer if her husband is
cruel, even if he never inflicts his cruelty on her. Now, let us
go through some of the household accomplishments a young
woman might need as wife to a man of modest means," she
said. They spent the next hour in such a lesson, and Beatrice
promised, at the end of it, to meet Lady Silvia the same time
the next day for more.

In one of the pleasant rituals that had become a part of
their day, the company met for tea in the late afternoon in
the gold saloon. Lady Bournaud sometimes took part and
sometimes not, but this day she sat in regal splendor, her
icy blue gown spread over her withered legs and her snowy
hair piled in an elegant new style, fixed with ivory hair
combs. The younger people trooped in, followed by the
footmen with laden trays.

Tidwell directed the operation, commanding a table be
brought to Lady Bournaud so she could pour tea for her
guests. Beatrice watched it all from her chair at her employer's side.

Chappell, the first to arrive, stood by the window looking
out over the familiar countryside. It had started raining some
time during the night and continued for the better part of the
morning, and all of the snow had disappeared, so the countryside was painted in a palette of drab browns, grays, and
greens once more. Afternoon had brought the sun out, and so
the pathways and road were drying.

He looked back over the company, the chattering, lively
young people, the quiet, smiling Miss Copland, and the
watchful Lady Bournaud. It was clear to him what his former
mentor had in mind. Matchmaking. Lady Silvia and Lord

Vaughan, Miss Allen and Mr. Rowland, and, yes, himself and Miss Copland. In some ways that was the most unlikely match of all, for he never got beyond her cool façade, her icy wall of composure, and he was too old to make a fool of himself as he might have if he were younger.

And yet she drew him like iron filings to a magnet. He had seen innumerable examples of kindness to not only her employer, but also the guests and even the serving staff. He was attracted by that, and by her soft voice, aura of gentleness, her intelligence, grace, loveliness of face and body, and yet . . . and yet . . . who *was* she? It nagged at him as he watched her pass the teacups that Lady Bournaud was filling.

It was likely just a general impression from having met her in her London Season so many years ago. That had to be it, and yet she had never owned meeting him. He shook his head at the self-centeredness that would have her remember him, when he was not particularly memorable then, just a minor bureaucrat in the government, too tired most of the time to join his wife in social evenings.

She shrank away from him, though, whenever he brushed her arm, any time he came too close, and every day, he noted, she seemed more haggard and worried. Every morning found her more reticent and silent in his presence, and for her sake, it was worrying him.

At a signal from Lady Bournaud, he joined the cheerful company.

"Davey, here is your tea. I remember that unlike many men who say they abominate tea, you admit to enjoying it."

He took his cup. "I remember many a time, my lady, when you allowed a young boy to partake with you, and what a great honor he knew it was even then."

"Pish tush." Lady Bournaud waved off the compliment, but looked pleased.

"I spent the morning with Miss Copland learning the art of blending tea leaves," Lady Silvia, elegant in a pale green cashmere half dress of deceptively simple lines, spoke up, her voice betraying a nervousness that Chappell could not figure a source for.

Miss Copland said, "And a very apt pupil she is, too."

"What the devil—oh, pardon," Lord Vaughan said, bowing hastily to the ladies. "Why would you want to be mucking about with a bunch of leaves?" He came to stand by Lady Silvia.

"It is a household accomplishment every wife should have familiarity with," Miss Copland said. "Even if it is not necessary for a lady to do it herself, she should know the mechanics, for one never knows when a housekeeper will quit, or fall ill. And every lady should know what constitutes good tea and what is bad."

"Seems a waste of time for someone of Lady Silvia's status. I mean to say, there will always be someone in the kitchen who can do that sort of thing, won't there?" Vaughan's brow furrowed, and he looked around the company.

"We often did not have tea when I was young," Miss Allen said from her post near the fire. She gave the largest log a poke with a fire iron. "We harvested dandelion leaves and made tea out of that."

"Dandelion leaves?" That was Vaughan again.

"Useful things, dandelions. We couldn't afford coffee, either, so Mama roasted the roots of the dandelion and then ground it. Didn't make a bad brew. And in summer, the leaves are good as a salad."

Vaughan snorted. "Sounds like you were a self-sufficient lot, living off weeds."

"We had to be self-sufficient," Verity said, her eyes serious for once. "And resourceful. The first winter we almost starved. I was only three the year we emigrated. Papa was a half-pay officer; he was wounded and couldn't go back to his commission, so we emigrated, but we timed it poorly, getting to our plot of land in August of that year. Papa barely had time to build us a shelter before the cold weather, and we didn't have enough time to grow a crop, nor any money to buy food. Our nearest neighbors were three miles away, and if it hadn't been for their kindness, we would have starved."

There was silence in the warm saloon, and every person there eyed the warm fire, the heavily laden tray of cakes and tiny sandwiches, the elegant gilt furnishing and thick rugs. Firelight glinted off the silver teapot, and a beam of light from the window shone on the crystal chandelier.

"It is only when you do not have enough—enough heat, enough food—that you truly learn to appreciate simple things like good bread, milk, a piece of chicken," Miss Copland said feelingly, breaking the silence. "A cup of good tea is a miracle," she said, holding her patterned china cup with reverence.

Chappell felt Lady Bournaud's significant glance. Yes, Miss Copland had suffered, and at that moment he determined, by fair means or foul, to find out her history.

"We are accustomed to so much. You would not believe what some people say when I must ask for money for food and shelter for the poor," Rowland said, staring into the hearth. "Some people have managed to vilify the poor in their own minds. Religion—our religion, anyway—has, for too long, taught that each person was put into their place on this earth for a reason, and that it is a sin to want to rise out of that position. Some use that to justify not helping the poor advance, and sometimes even to deny them basic comforts. They have come to the conclusion that the poor feel deprivation less. One woman of my acquaintance even concluded that her desire for a new hat and a poor person's desire for adequate food caused the same degree of pain to the sufferer."

"Women," Vaughan snorted. "Silly creatures." Realizing he was outnumbered by the breed he denigrated so freely, he looked around with alarm, but the only one to take him up on it immediately was Verity Allen.

"And are not the fops and dandies of London society silly creatures, more vain and superficial than even the silliest woman of your acquaintance?" she cried, giving a last vicious poke to the wood in the fire before hanging the fire iron back in its place by the hearth.

"Very true," Lady Silvia said. "And at least women do not do such idiotic things as . . . as bet on which raindrop will trickle down the window first, or which drunk will fall in his place at the gaming table first. Or other things."

"I surrender," Vaughan said, laughing. "Men can be just as silly, vain, and careless as women."

The general conversation broke up, then, with Verity taxing Lord Vaughan about his own activities in London, and Lady Silvia softly asking Mr. Rowland about his parish work. Lady Bournaud had dozed off for a few minutes, and so had not heard the spirited debate, but awake again, and seeing Chappell standing alone, she signaled him to come closer to her. He pulled a low stool to her knee and took her hand in his own, feeling the knotted joints with alarm. He had not realized her arthritis was so far advanced as to make her fingers so stiff. It made him understand the increasingly erratic writing in her monthly letter to him, and appreciate it that much more. What effort it must cost her!

He and Lady Bournaud and Miss Copland made a tight, cozy circle by the hearth as the sunlight faded from the room and the shadows lengthened. Tidwell removed the tea table and Lady Silvia sat down at the piano, providing the company with a light, tinkling tune as Mr. Rowland turned the pages for her, leaning over occasionally and whispering as she glowed, her eyes sparkling.

"Children," Lady Bournaud said, picking up Beatrice's hand, too, with her free one, "I want this Christmas to be one that François will smile down on from heaven. I want music and laughter and good food and wine. I want presents for everyone, even the servants, and boxes for the parish families. I want the village supplies of bonbons and fruit jellies decimated, and every child smiling queasily on Christmas morning. Can we manage it?"

Beatrice, her eyes shining, squeezed her employer's hand. "We can, my lady."

Chappell laughed out loud. "We can."

"But to that end, I need your help. Christmas is less than one week away. Davey, will you accompany Miss Copland into the village tomorrow morning? I have a rather long list, and it will take two of you to accomplish everything on it. And I don't trust those flibbertigibbets," she said, indicating the young folk, "to do anything serious."

"My lady," Miss Copland protested, her eyes wide with alarm, "I can do it all myself. We need not bother Sir David with such menial labor, surely."

"Miss Copland," Chappell said. "Please, think nothing of it. Lady Bournaud knows she can call on me to even haul coal if need be." The comtesse chuckled, and Chappell squeezed her hand at this private joke between them. "And I have business in the village myself. I would be delighted to accompany you, and may I ask you to partake of luncheon with me at the Dove and Partridge?"

"Done," Lady Bournaud crowed. "I will feel easier getting all of these tasks accomplished, for one never knows when the weather will close in again."

Beatrice, clearly nonplussed by being routed so effectively, could do nothing but agree or look terribly ungracious, and she could never do a thing in her life ungracious or mean, Chappell was convinced. She was the one lady in the world he would bet had nothing in her life to be ashamed of, nothing to look back upon with regret. He would stake his entire wealth on that.

"We will go early," he said, "Is ten o'clock all right, Miss Copland?"

She nodded. "I suppose it will have to be."

Thirteen

Beatrice sat in her bedchamber, staring unseeing at the mirror in front of her, the mirror that told her that though she was no longer the girl she once was, pretty and thoughtless, flirtatious and self-absorbed, the years had not been terribly unkind to her. She had stopped caring long ago, though, about looks and other surface attributes. Time and earnest reflection had made her value the internal accomplishments of a good heart much more.

If only she could believe that the penance she had done in all those years had made up for the havoc her thoughtlessness had wrought a lifetime ago. But it did not feel like it had. Would it ever? Or was she overcompensating for something that was understandable in a young and frivolous girl?

She sighed deeply. And now she was just stalling, keeping Sir David waiting down in the great hall. She rose, brushed a strand of thread from her neat gray spencer, and prepared to spend the day with a man she had wronged so deeply he had never recovered.

Chappell checked again the pocket watch in his vest. He looked up the stairs, convinced that Miss Copland would send down some excuse for not going, but no, there she was. He looked up the long staircase as her slight, gray-clad figure moved like a ghost along the gallery to the head of the stairs and then down, swiftly, silently, her gloved hand resting lightly on the carved oak balustrade, adorned now with evergreen garlands. The day stretched ahead of him, a day with Miss Copland, one day in which to sort out the reasons behind her reticence and aversion to him. They were two adults; surely they could come to some understanding between them.

"I apologize, Sir David, for keeping you waiting," she said breathlessly.

"Not at all," he replied, offering her his arm. "If we are ready now, the carriage awaits us."

Hesitantly, she laid her hand on his arm and he felt triumphant at such a small gesture.

The ride into the village was not a long one, but it was complicated on this day by slippery roads, wet still from the melted snow. Chateau Bournaud nestled halfway up the moorside above the village of Harnthwaite. Below them stretched the long gray-green stretch of Harn Moor, named for some ancient Viking settler who owned enough land to make him the premiere citizen and worthy of a valley named in his honor. Or so went local legend.

All of this history Chappell had absorbed as a motherless youngster, wandering the hills and then coming back to Chateau Bournaud with eager questions for the elegant French comte and his unlikely English wife. He began to speak of those days, and the traveling time sped by. To his pleasure, he found that Miss Copland enjoyed the stories of his life as a child and what Lady Bournaud was like at forty and forty-five, active and athletic, striding over the hills, walking staff in hand, with little Davey in tow.

He glanced over at her as she still chuckled over a story of Lady Bournaud's inflexible iron will and how it brought her into conflict with an equally stubborn Yorkshire farmer. Her oval face glowed and she eagerly watched out the window as the first sight of Harnthwaite came into view. As isolated as the chateau was, a visit to Harnthwaite was, he knew, infrequent enough that it counted as a rare treat. The carriage rattled over the low-sided stone bridge into the commercial section of town, which comprised one row of stone shops facing an expansive village green.

"Where shall we go first, Miss Copland?" he asked as the carriage slowed.

"I need a sizable order from the drapers first," she replied, "and I would like to give him some time to make it up. Lady Bournaud is ordering dress lengths for all the female servants—they are not to know about it until Christmas morn, you know—and matching ribbons. I need to obtain a miscellany of buttons and pins and needles and thread, too. . . . Oh, a whole list. I do not expect you to wait for me, you know. I will be just fine going about my business, if you have tasks of your own to accomplish. Everyone in Harthwaite is a friend."

"My business can wait," he said, opening the carriage door and jumping down. He gave her a hand down onto the cobbled street of the main road. "I know it is not necessary, but it will be my pleasure to escort you and carry your parcels."

Her cheeks burnished like apples, and she nodded, looking awkward but pleased. A good start, Chappell thought.

He tossed a couple of coins up to the driver. "This is for you and the lad," he said, indicating the groom, a young man of not more than teen years. "Take the team to the inn's livery and have a pint on me."

"Thankee sir," the driver said, touching his cap. He turned the team to go around to the livery stable.

"Now, you said the draper. Is it still Mr. Ford's for quality dry goods?" He took her arm as she nodded, and headed, by memory, toward the shop.

Beatrice found that a gentleman escort was a great help, for she did have parcels, even though she had not yet even begun her shopping in earnest. Lady Bournaud's list was long and detailed, for her intentions seemed to have blossomed from merely celebrating Christmas in a grand style within the walls of the manse, to a wish to ensure that every child and every family in the valley had an equally merry Yule, not excepting the most ancient of widowers, a gentleman known to all only as Old Merrick. Even he was to have a cord of firewood, delivered split, and a bottle of rum from the tavern. And all of this Beatrice must effect in one day.

Sir David's aid and advice was invaluable, but she found it was garnering her much more attention than she had ever had in Harnthwaite. The elderly "church ladies," as she thought of the parish mainstays, stopped her on the street, and she was forced to introduce Sir David Chappell, and then he would smile and bow and wish them the bounty of the season, all while holding her arm close to him and smiling over at her as she spoke until her cheeks were cherry red, she was sure. As they learned of his connection to the chateau, the ladies exchanged significant looks, and she knew they stood in a tight knot after she and her escort moved on. She could hear their hissed chatter and excited gabble, even many shops away.

It was embarrassing. And thrilling. For a while she could enjoy the illusion that with this gentleman at her side there could be something more in the future, some sweet dream of love, even though she knew it to be impossible. Sir David had changed over the years, she found, after all, but for the better. His temper had mellowed, his voice deepened. His eyes were kinder. But his touch was still just as thrilling as it was to the silly young girl she had been. Thank the Lord he did not remember.

"Shall we stop for luncheon now?" he said, indicating the tavern, the Dove and Partridge just a step or two away.

She was tired, she admitted to herself. "I would enjoy a cup of tea and some of Mrs. Gould's pigeon pie. It is truly remarkable, with a crust that melts in your mouth."

"Then pigeon pie it shall be."

In a trice they were seated at the window in Mrs. Gould's best parlor, reserved for those she considered gentry, or at the very least, genteel. Mrs. Gould herself insisted on waiting on them. She had known Beatrice since her very first day in the valley, when Lady Bournaud's future companion had been set down by the stage at the Dove and Partridge, and, shabbily clothed, had declined hiring a carriage but had walked the entire way to the chateau, even though Mrs. Gould had protested that it was at least five miles, and up moor, too.

Being staunch Yorkshire, Mrs. Gould had respected and applauded Miss Copland's unwillingness to take a boon for which she could not offer payment, and had been her most vocal admirer ever since. And so she questioned Sir David minutely, until she recognized his name and remembered him as a lad, and his father, the respected Mr. Arthur Chappell.

Her round face lit in a genuine smile of pleasure. Wiping her hands on the snowy cloth tied around her waist, she said, "Aye, nouw I do 'member ye! An' yer pa. Nobbut more honorable than yer pa, nouw, was there? 'E were the grandest gentleman, an' well I remember ye nouw as the sprig whut would foller Lady Bee 'round."

Lady Bournaud's name, being so "Frenchy" and awkward to pronounce, had been shortened for years in the village to just "Lady Bee."

"That's right, Mrs. Gould. Only, if I remember right, you were not Mrs. Gould then?" Sir David looked up at her from his seat by the window and smiled.

"Aye, you've a sharp mem'ry," she said. "I were just Gladys then, sir. I were a maid here afore Mr. Gould started wooin' me."

His antecedents gave him the right to be bearing her favorite, Miss Copland, company, and Mrs. Gould plied them with her best cookery, which was superior country food. Finally, he sat back, satisfied, as Beatrice finished her meal with a cup of tea. "I do not remember when I have eaten that much in one sitting," he said, as a young girl—from the plump looks of her, a Gould sprig—cleared their dishes.

Beatrice, content for the moment, watched out the window. The village green, opposite, was the site of considerable activity, since the scene of nativity was to be played out there in a makeshift byre being constructed by Mr. Gould's livery stableman, who happened to be handy with a hammer. School had let out early, there being no sense to be gotten from children with such important things on their minds as sugarplums and holidays and the whiff of snow in the air, and so there were an abundance of warmly dressed children dancing about the man, making his task impossible.

"Miss Copland, I feel that you are far away."

Beatrice, with a start, looked across the table at the man who sat there, a man she had never thought to share space with again. When he had visited four years before she had managed to be "ill" for the four days of his visit, but she was happy that she had not been able to impose the same deception on her employer this time. It had been a salutary lesson in her own unimportance to find that Sir David did not even remember her, and she had been worrying for nothing. He had assumed such a major part of her own thoughts and memories that she had completely lost sight of how little she must have mattered to him twenty years before. And yet their last confrontation had been so dramatic and so unpleasant. . . .

How time had changed things! He had been drunk and spewing vile accusations that held too much truth for her to be comfortable even now, looking back on them. But here and now he smiled over at her, waiting for her acknowledgment.

"I suppose my mind was just wandering." She indicated the scene out of the window. "I was remembering my own childhood in Dorset and how the villagers would celebrate this season."

He frowned. "Dorset. How strange. I feel like I knew you were from Dorset."

Her stomach clenched into a tight knot. Had she, with that simple slip, unveiled her past to him? But he merely shook his head, his brows furrowed.

Then his expression cleared, and he said, "Ah, well, likely just one of those strange things, like knowing what someone is going to say or do next. And so, how did the people of Dorsetshire celebrate?"

They talked generally for a while, but then the conversation turned to his own childhood in Yorkshire. "Those were marvelous days. Lady Bournaud made sure every day of the twelve brought a new wonder. I can never adequately thank her for all she has done for me in my life. She is a rare and wonderful woman."

"I think you have repaid her by becoming the man you are," Beatrice said softly, wiping a crumb off the table. "She talks about you often. She is very proud of you."

"And yet there was a time when I thought I was going to become something very different." The lines in his face, lines that had only been hinted at twenty years before, deepened. "This . . . this time of year did not always hold pleasant associations for me. The greatest tragedy of my life happened twenty years ago this week."

It was coming. The moment she had been dreading was coming. Beatrice could not answer, but neither would she flinch from hearing him tell the tale she knew only too well.

"But I will not dwell on tragedy," he said, with a sudden smile that lit his handsome face and his crystal-blue eyes. "It is in the past, and I do my best not to dredge it up to suffer again."

"Have you recovered from the . . . the tragedy?" Beatrice asked.

He was silent, staring absently out the window as he fingered the brim of his hat, which sat on the table. "I don't know if one ever fully recovers from tragedy." He looked back into her eyes. "Look at Lady Bournaud. She has never been the same since that awful winter when her husband died."

"I did not know her before that, so to me she is unchanged."

"Ah, but she was a smiling, happy woman, the Lady Bournaud of my youth. Still stern, still with that inexorable will, but cheerful and bright. Energetic."

"I would have liked to have known her."

Sir David stood and picked up his hat. "Miss Copland, if you will excuse me, I have a private errand or two to run while I am in the village. I would leave you in the excellent care of our hostess, Mrs. Gould, while I do my tasks. May I return to you here in a half hour?"

Beatrice said all of the necessary things, and then he was gone, striding away and out the door. She followed his progress down the street until he was out of sight.

It was just a few days to Christmas Eve. Twenty years ago this very day she had been a flighty young girl staying with an ancient relative in London, enjoying her first taste of freedom. At nineteen she had not a serious thought in her head but a desire for more gaudy finery, a yen for admiration, and a thoughtless belief that she somehow deserved better than the modest circumstances of her life.

Her family had never been wealthy, but had enough money to afford the doted-upon daughter of the house one Season, one chance to find a husband, to attract and capture a man of means. Had she taken her quest seriously? Had she acknowledged that her attractions were modest, and if she wanted to attract the notice of a man of quality who would overlook her modest dowry, she must refine her behavior, take from society the best it had to offer, make connections that would further her objective?

No. Flighty and headstrong, she had fluttered through the list of acquaintances her mother had sent with her, despising all of the elderly women who could have been invaluable help to a husband-hunting chit. Only one name had caught her notice, and that was Mrs. Melanie Chappell, a young matron, newly delivered of a son, who matched the girl Beatrice had been then for flightiness and thoughtless pleasure seeking.

Coming from a village where she had been among the premiere families had spoiled her. London was a shock for Beatrice, when she realized that she was on the bottom rung in London, where every girl was pretty and most were better dowered, better bred, more accomplished, and with prettier manners. As a result, she acted even worse, took more chances with her reputation, was sillier, more vain, more full of her own importance. She couldn't look back on the girl she was with anything less than shame at the chances she let slip away, the decent young men she snubbed just because Melanie told her they were beneath her. Melanie discouraged her from marriage to a man of modest means. "Don't get married," she had said, "because you will only get fat and ugly and your husband won't like you anymore and won't take you to gay parties, but will expect you to stay home with the baby. If you do get married, at least make it worth your while. Marry into money." And so, urged to aim higher, every vanity encouraged and every vice approved, Beatrice had stayed in London to become even more vain, flighty, and heedless. Melanie Chappell had been a boost to her self-esteem, a valuable ally who gave her nothing but compliments and expected nothing but approval.

Beatrice gazed out the window of the tavern, watching the stableman build his makeshift byre, but her vision was clouded with that long-ago time, as the Season dwindled into late autumn, and then winter. She should have gone home. Her modest allotment of money was gone, and her mother's letters were becoming increasingly frantic, but Beatrice had ample reason to stay, or so she thought.

She was in love with her best friend's husband.

Mr. David Chappell. Then he was a young man of about twenty-seven years, but to her eyes he had been mature, attractive, vital, vigorous, with an intensity that sparkled in his crystalline eyes and shot darts directly into her heart, silly chit that she was. She envied Melanie fiercely, envied the casual caresses the young woman clearly abhorred, was jealous of every endearment David gave his beautiful wife.

And yet she had, on occasion, seen another side to David Chappell than loving husband. He was, then, a hard-working aide in the employ of a government official. He was entirely caught up in his work, so much so that really, looking back on it, Beatrice remembered seeing him only very occasionally, though she spent much of her time with

Melanie, whole days sometimes, staying overnight on occasion in the modest Chappell town home. With the wisdom of years, she could see now that he was working so very hard, sometimes not arriving home until midnight, because he knew that to rise from his lowly position would require long hours and dedication. He was doing so for his family, for their future.

But Melanie was bitter, claiming that her husband preferred his work to his family, even though she, herself, seldom spent time with her new son, Alexander, preferring to let the nanny and his wet nurse care for him almost completely. One night when she was staying over, Beatrice had heard David Chappell come home, and almost immediately he and Melanie had launched into a ferocious argument. Beatrice had been shocked at the bitterness between them.

And so she was torn. It was clear to her then that there was a rift between David Chappell and his young and beautiful wife. As a friend, she heard much more intimate details than she should have, but Melanie was not shy about telling her new friend everything. And yet still, seeing the agony between them, and sympathizing with Melanie, she was certain that she was hopelessly in love with David Chappell.

What did that love amount to? Once he had given her a careless compliment, had told her that she was a pretty girl, or something mild to that affect, and she had felt sure that he was in love with her, too, though of course as an honorable married man he could not admit it. She had floated through several days not knowing even when people addressed her directly, so full of love and hope was she.

How Melanie could have remained unaware of her friend's infatuation Beatrice would never know, for she blushed every time the man entered the room—seldom, since she only saw him once in a very long while—and she even stole a stickpin that was his and kept it pinned inside the bodice of her dress, just to feel him close to her heart.

From the distance of twenty years she could see that it was girlish infatuation, a sign that she should have been safely married with a suitable object for her questing affections, but that was not to be. Everything changed that Christmas season.

The first step on the irrevocable road to ruin came when Melanie and she were at a Christmas ball given by a well-known hostess, who though of good *ton* had a certain reputation for entertaining very "loose fish," gentlemen no one else would acknowledge. They were soon beset with admirers, Melanie particularly because she was so very beautiful, with the added attraction of being safely married.

One in particular, Viscount Oliphant, made a great fuss over both of them, swearing to anyone who would listen that he could not decide which of the two friends was prettier. Beatrice thought him everything a gentleman should be. She was not alarmed at all when she saw the man whispering in Melanie's ear, because she was used to the attentions of Melanie's cavaliers. And she didn't think anything of it when she could not find Melanie for an hour during the night. Her friend had likely just retired to the lady's withdrawing room or to the card room, she thought.

And so Melanie's confession a few days later came as a complete surprise.

Beatrice was staying at the Chappells' town home for a couple of days in the middle of that December, and she and Melanie were having tea while they went through some invitations. But Melanie laid them aside and gazed at Beatrice earnestly.

"I have to tell you something, Betty," she said.

Beatrice, Betty as she was known then, had looked up, alarmed by the agitation in Melanie's voice. "What is it, Mel?"

"I am in love," Melanie said, her voice low and trembling.

Beatrice was silent. She didn't think she quite understood. Of course Melanie was in love; who should not love David Chappell if not his own wife?

"I am in love with Ollie . . . Lord Oliphant."

Beatrice was silent because she was stunned. The look on

her face must have told the story, for Melanie grabbed her hand and held it to her bosom, and there were tears in her eyes. "Oh, Betty, I do not know what I am going to do! Ollie says he will kill himself if I do not give him some sign that I love him, too, for he is so deeply in love with me that he is desperate!"

"Kill himself? Mel, you must tell him that you are married, that nothing can—"

"But he knows I am married." Melanie dropped Beatrice's hand and said, with a good deal of self-consciousness, "Married women have friends . . . lovers . . . all around us; you know they do, Betty. So why should I not enjoy Lord Oliphant's attentions?"

Beatrice had been appalled, but so enmeshed was she in Melanie's life, so sure that anything Melanie did or said was "bang up to the mark" in popular cant, that she was soon persuaded to think that there was nothing so wrong in Melanie's being a little in love with her Ollie.

But then had come the first request of what would become, over the weeks, an avalanche. Her eyes glowing, Melanie had leaned over and said, "Betty, he wants me to spend the night at his house in Cheapside! Can you imagine anything so deliciously wicked?"

"Spend the night? But you can't. How would you explain it to your hus—"

"Shhh!" Melanie had glanced toward the door of the parlor in which they sat and lowered her voice. "It could be easy. All I would have to say is that I was going to spend the night with you at your aunt's house."

"But, if David ever found out . . ."

Beatrice had protested, refused, but in the end her fear of losing Melanie's friendship, and thus all hope of seeing David Chappell occasionally, had weighed more heavily than her internal conviction, not admitted then but acknowledged since, that she was a shill in an evil game of deception. It was wrong and she had known it, and yet knowing it, had still participated.

If it had ended at a few nights of passion shared illicitly by Melanie and her viscount, then guilt would have been the only price. But there was much worse to come, and Beatrice could not see herself as anything but culpable in Melanie Chappell's tragic death on Boxing Day of 1796.

"Shall we go on with our mission, Miss Copland?"

The words, spoken so close, made her jump, startled back into the present by Sir David Chappell's more mature voice in her ear.

Fourteen

And so the day continued.

The greengrocer's store was filled with good things to eat, shiny red apples, fragrant Seville oranges, carrots, cabbages, and onions, with bunches of herbs, rosemary, and thyme hanging in drying bunches from the time-darkened ceiling beams. Beatrice had a long conversation with the owner about the wishes of Lady Bournaud, since initially the fellow evinced some skepticism of the generous, indeed, ample, provisions the comtesse wanted to make for the people of Harnthwaite over the coming winter. Eventually she prevailed, once Sir David came forcefully to Beatrice's assistance, demanding that he take the lady at her word once and for all.

They descended the step to the walkway outside of the shop.

"I didn't think he would ever admit that perhaps you might know what Lady Bournaud's wishes were!" Chappell shook his head in bemused frustration.

"You cannot blame him. Lady Bournaud has been so insular for most of the last twenty years, I gather, and folks have gotten used to not much notice from the great house." Beatrice, buffeted by the strengthening wind, tucked her hands in her muff and glanced up at the sky, which was beginning to darken with clouds. It looked like snow, she thought. Smelled like snow, too, in that inimitable north country fashion.

"Where to next, Miss Copland?" the knight asked, taking her arm.

Oh, if only she were who he thought, Beatrice mused, looking up at the man next to her as they walked down the stone path along the line of shops that huddled together like cats in a rainstorm. He seemed to enjoy her company, and she had found, to her surprise and dismay, that the infatuation she had for him those many years before had not abated as it should have, and was even now strengthening, turning into a more mature esteem and respect, with that old tremor of attraction.

But she would think of that another time, alone at night, when it would not show in her expression.

"We shall first stop at the post office, which has, I believe, some packages that Lady Bournaud ordered from London, and then on to see the vicar. Every child of the parish is to receive a gift from Father Christmas, and every family a goose."

"Lady Bournaud has at last gone mad," Chappell said with a laugh.

Beatrice chuckled, "I think so." Comfortably, like old friends, they walked and talked. "You must miss your son this time of year."

Sir David nodded, squinting off into the distance at the bare limbs of the trees that lined the village green and stretched up into the sky. "Very much. This will be the first year we are not together for Christmas. But he will barely miss me, I think. Life in Paris will be lively for a handsome young man like Alex."

"I think you underestimate his attachment to you, Sir David. I am sure he will have moments of sadness among the gaiety."

He gave her a grateful glance. "As selfish as it sounds, I hope he does miss me at least occasionally. But what about you, Miss Copland? Have you no family to miss you?"

"My parents are both long gone," she said. "Lady Bournaud has been more family to me these past years than anyone."

"Pardon me for my impertinence," he said. "But I wonder what you have planned for your life after Lady Bournaud's demise?"

She gave him a shocked look.

"I know it sounds heartless, Miss Copland, but it is not, please believe me. I have reason—more than you—to be grateful and to love the old woman, but perhaps I have more reason to notice, not having seen her for four years, that she has declined. She is eighty. I cannot be easy about how you will go on once the St. Eustace horde has descended upon Chateau Bournaud."

She was warmed by his concern. "I have put by enough of my wage to live, sir," she said, her chin going up in an unconscious display of reserve. "I will be all right. Retirement to the village will suit me."

He gave her a long look. "I feel you were meant for more than that, my dear. Were you never a young girl, and did you never dream of making your mark on society?"

"When I was a young girl, sir, I thought and spake as a young girl, but when I grew up, I put away girlish things, to paraphrase the Good Book."

In the inadequate protection of a bare-limbed tree, he stopped and turned her around, putting one gloved finger under her chin and turning her face up. "I wish you would not put away all girlish things, Miss Copland. Christmas is a time for becoming a child again. Dream, Miss Copland." His mellow voice held a low, urgent tone. "Let yourself dream. I feel strongly that your girlish dreams were stamped out far too early and in too vicious a fashion. Let your imagination drift and ask for what you would most like in the world."

Beatrice closed her eyes, unable to look directly into his sky blue ones for fear he would see the guilt in her soul. How could she dream? Dreams were for those who deserved them. She was not being a martyr, she was just honest with herself. She took a deep breath and opened her eyes again. "I have put aside dreams; they are for other people. Shall we go see the vicar, sir?" she said, turning away.

* * *

They were finally on their way home as the dark clouds gathered on the horizon and scudded uneasily across the sky. Chappell glanced sideways in the dusky gloom of the carriage interior at the woman next to him. How close had his earlier words come to the truth? A shudder had raced through her; he felt it under his fingers, and how her chin trembled. What had she suffered? Who had hurt her?

Why could she not dream?

Watching her as he had in the past weeks he had seen her kindness, the innate goodness that could not be feigned. She cared for Lady Bournaud, even when that crusty old dame was snappish, as she tended to be when in pain. And the staff turned to Beatrice with every complaint or worry, and she made all smooth. She even found time to teach Lady Sylvia the finer points of housewifery.

But what had he seen of time for herself? Even sitting quietly she was usually engaged in sewing for the household, or for Lady Bournaud. She had a thousand concerns, and was, inevitably, the last to retire at night and the first to appear in the morning. Even today, a rare day out for her, she had spent it in selfless activity, joyfully fulfilling her employer's detailed and extensive wishes.

She was tired. He could see it in the way her eyes drifted almost closed with the rocking rhythm of the carriage, and then they snapped open, and she shook herself, as if to try to awaken. How would she react if he offered her his shoulder to lean on? He would like to do that. His body stirred at the thought of her soft curves fitted under his arm and leaning against his body.

He smiled wryly in the dim interior. How she would draw back if she knew his thoughts that very moment! But he could not help the attraction he felt for her, the wish he had to hold her close and protect her. He felt protective of her, wishing to shelter her from life's difficulties and the sadness that must come to her eventually when Lady Bournaud passed on. Was

it just the story Lady Bournaud had told him about her difficult life? Or was it something in *her*?

Her chin was lowering again as she drifted toward slumber,
but with a sway of the carriage she snapped to attention and
put one hand up to smooth her hair, glancing toward him self-
consciously.

"Yes, Miss Copland, I know you were almost asleep."

She smiled and rolled her eyes. "I am so sorry. I did not realize I was so tired."

He hesitated, but then said, "It is understandable that you
are so sleepy; you have had a very full day. Why do you not
put your head here and close your eyes?" He put his arm over
the back of the seat and indicated his shoulder.

The shock on her face was immediate, but just as quickly
replaced by a wide-eyed guilty expression. "I couldn't. Th-
thank you though, for the kind thought."

The result was that she made a concerted effort to stay
awake, even lowering the window and letting cool air stream
in against her face. They chatted for a while, bumping along
the increasingly rough road toward Chateau Bournaud. It
was late afternoon, and with the cloudiness it was getting
dusky very quickly. The landscape outside of the carriage
was a palette of dull gold and green, taupe and rust. Beyond it all, looming like a silent giant in the distance, was
Harn Moor.

As they approached the chateau, above the noise of the
wheels they both heard a thudding and craned their necks,
looking out of the windows. Across the dull green lawn of the
house, speeding on a chestnut steed, a slight figure with flowing auburn hair bent over the horse's neck. Behind the rider
another horse followed, mounted by a heavier figure with
short-cropped hair. They were heading on a direct path for the
walled lane along which the carriage bumped and jolted, and
Chappell said, "That is Lord Vaughan behind, but who is the
front rider?"

With a smile in her voice, Beatrice said, "I do believe that is Miss Allen on the forward mount! Yes, I can see her skirts fluttering around her legs."

"But . . . but she is mounted astride."

"She disdains sidesaddle as unnatural."

Both were silent for a moment, but then Chappell, uneasiness growing in his stomach, said, "I do not think our driver has seen them yet; he has not slowed the team. What, is the fellow asleep?"

"Why does Miss Allen not turn away?" Beatrice clutched the window frame and stared with wide eyes.

The riders were on a collision course with the carriage, though Chappell could not believe the young people would be so foolhardy as to take the stone fence in the dusky late afternoon, and with wet earth and slippery gravel their only purchase on the other side. And yet, he thought, they were going to do it. He held his breath, certain that danger was imminent.

At that very moment, Miss Allen, standing in her stirrups, sailed over the stone fence with Vaughan close after her, clearing the fence and the lane just before the carriage horses, sensing the stable near and their long-awaited dinner, quickened their pace and trotted past the same spot. They reared, and the driver shouted at them, but they settled down almost immediately and continued without incident. Chappell heaved a sigh of relief and fell back in his seat. "Idiotic children! That could have been very bad indeed, if the timing had not been just as it was."

Beatrice smiled and shook her head. "But it was just so, wasn't it? Miss Allen is a bruising rider! I do not think one man in twenty, let alone one woman, could have done what she did."

"It was still a risk."

"And Lord Vaughan right behind her," she chuckled. "He is no child, you know. He is above thirty. How well those two are matched! But what kind of vicar's wife Miss Allen will make, that is another question entirely."

"Vicar's wife? Ah, yes, Lady Bournaud's matchmaking plans."

The carriage pulled up to the front door just then, preventing further conversation. Tidwell met them at the door and told them that Lady Bournaud was eagerly awaiting their return in the crimson saloon.

"Thank you, Tidwell," Beatrice said, handing her spencer and hat to a maid hovering near the door. "She so seldom goes into Harnthwaite herself, she is eager for news, no doubt."

"Oh, no doubt," Chappell said wryly, giving her a sideways glance. The day in Harnthwaite had been designed for far more than the errands commissioned.

They joined the old lady, who was reading a book and shaking her head over something in it. She looked up as they approached, her glasses sliding down to perch on the tip of her nose. "You are back, finally."

Chappell strode to her and kissed her cheek, then crossed behind her to the tray of decanters. Beatrice joined her at the fire.

"We got everything done, my lady, even down to the cord of wood and measure of rum for Old Merrick. Mr. Ford said he would take that commission on himself, as he always likes to visit the old gent and smoke a bowl of tobacco."

"Ah, yes, Ford is a good man. None of those absurd affectations of gentility some of the new shopkeepers have assumed, just good, honest north country ways." Lady Bournaud put out one knobby hand and touched her cheek. "You look tired, Beatrice. Too much for you?"

"I am not getting any younger, my lady."

"Pish tush. We have had this conversation before. When I was your age I was striding the moor early every morning with that lad in my wake." She pointed at Chappell, who was pulling a chair closer to the ladies.

"That she was," he added, his light eyes sparkling. "Comte

Bournaud was the one who liked to lay abed late, if I remember right."

"Very true. François would still be abed when I came home, and I would crawl back in with him." A smile of reminiscence quirked the old lady's lips.

Beatrice felt her cheeks burn, but pretended to busy herself with the tea tray.

"You are shocking Miss Copland, you old reprobate," Chappell said.

"Good, Davey. I am happy to still be capable of shocking folks occasionally."

"You will never imagine the sight that greeted us as we came up the lane," Beatrice said, sternly ignoring her employer's teasing tone. "Miss Allen was riding the mare Bellanoche as we came home. She took the stone fence along the lane without so much as a hesitation, and who was behind her, matching her folly for folly, but Lord Vaughan!"

Lady Bournaud shrugged. "So he treats her like a friend, a boon companion. Doesn't mean a thing."

"I think they are well matched in other ways, too," Beatrice said.

"I am aware of your matchmaking efforts, my lady," Chappell said, sipping his port and leaning back in his deep chair.

"Are you? How odd. I have admitted no matchmaking."

"Do not try to cozen me, you old fraud. I have rousted wilier opponents than you and cornered them."

She chuckled and shook her head. "I have done what I can, but now it is up to the young people."

"Only the young people?" Chappell asked, giving her a significant look.

A broad smile wreathed her wrinkled face. "Young, old, what do I care?"

Chappell dropped a slow wink, and she broke into open laughter, the sound like a rusty gate.

"But now you are going to let nature take its course, are you not, my lady?"

The comtesse gazed steadily into her protégé's eyes. "I think I have done all that is humanly possible, Davey. The rest is up to the gentlemen in question."

"And the ladies," Chappell added, and his gaze settled on Beatrice.

She would not let tears come to her eyes, Beatrice scolded herself. If only they would let her alone and stop taunting her with what could never be! Not that either of them knew what they were doing to her. Standing abruptly, she said, "I will see how dinner is progressing."

Dinner was a bright and noisy affair, with Lady Bournaud as full of noise and chatter as the rest of them. Mrs. Stoure, a genteel but poverty-stricken relation of Squire Fellows, was visiting for the evening, and later, in the red saloon, she played at cribbage with Lady Bournaud while the young people played a noisy game of Pope Joan, much teasing going on when one got "matrimony" and another "intrigue."

Then their card game broke up in a general agreement that a word game was preferable. Beatrice watched and worried. Mr. Rowland's dark eyes rarely left Lady Silvia, and it was clear to everyone—or should have been—that he was head over ears in love with her. And yet every chance he got he deferred to Vaughan, even giving him the seat next to his favorite, who looked near tears at the slight. Vaughan, oblivious to the undercurrent of emotion running between the reverend and Lady Silvia, monopolized her, engaging her in a conversation about mutual acquaintances, of which they had many, it seemed.

Verity, looking miserable and jealous, drifted behind the grouping, restlessly knocking over knickknacks and moving things around until Rowland irritably told her to sit in one place. They bickered like brother and sister for a few moments, and then Verity sat down in a chair and began kicking at a stool. She was dressed in an ugly confection of mint green and puce, unbecomingly cut and too short for her elegant height, and her hair was carelessly dressed.

Beatrice, watching in dismay, did not hear Chappell approach until he was directly behind her, where she stood by the tea table.

"So what do you think is going on here?" he asked.

"I don't know," Beatrice admitted, trying desperately to still the thumping of her heart and clamoring of her senses from the knight's closeness. "I know that Mr. Rowland is attracted to Lady Silvia, and if I am not mistaken, Miss Allen is in the depths of infatuation with Lord Vaughan."

"In other words, all of Lady Bournaud's careful work is falling in disarray."

"M-Hmm," Beatrice murmured. "But why Lord Vaughan is making such a dead set for Lady Silvia I do not understand. He seems to me to be the sort of young man who would not be interested in settling on a wife, and Lady Silvia is clearly not flirt material. And she has shown no interest in him at all!" In fact, Lady Silvia was eyeing the doorway, looking for an avenue of escape from the baron's interminable stories, it seemed.

"I can solve some of the mystery, I think," Chappell said. He took Beatrice's elbow and guided her to a chair in an alcove where there was a comfortable grouping. He crossed the room and came back with a glass of sherry for her and brandy for himself. "Now, do you wish me to gossip a little?"

Beatrice concealed a smile as best she could. Sir David had leaned forward and said "gossip" in just that tone of voice reserved for confidences of that nature. Against the backdrop of Lady Bournaud's triumphant neighing over a point won in cribbage, she said, "I would dearly love to hear your gossip, Sir David."

"Just—" He stopped, gazed at her earnestly, and said, "Just David, Miss Copland. I feel I know you so well, I would deem it a privilege if you would call me by my given name."

She shook her head before he was even finished. She couldn't do it, couldn't call him "David," as Melanie had. She looked away, concealing the tears that started in her eyes. She heard him sigh.

"All right, Miss Copland, I will not overstep the boundaries of our friendship. But one day, I think, you will tell me what I have done that you are so reserved toward me."

She couldn't look at him.

"The very first night Vaughan arrived here," Chappell said, leaving behind the sensitive subject, "he told me that he 'must' marry. His father is putting some pressure on him to settle down with a wife and start having a family. The alternative is that he go over to Canada and manage the family interests there."

"Oh," Beatrice said, risking a glance at Sir David. He was sitting back in the deep chair, sipping his brandy, and she felt some of the tension drain from her. "I suppose that explains his interest in Lady Silvia." She frowned and watched the young couples near the fire. Lady Silvia had tried to maneuver Mr. Rowland into the chair closest to her during a general displacement as the gentleman helped the ladies to a plate of sweets, but Rowland deferred once again to the baron.

"But why does Mr. Rowland, who is clearly in love with the little lady, give way for Vaughan?"

Chappell frowned and shook his head. "I can only guess, having spent some time talking to Mr. Rowland, that he knows how impossible is his preference for Lady Silvia, and is trying, honorably, to help his competitor for her hand, knowing the baron stands a much better chance. And Vaughan is not a bad fellow, just . . . energetic."

"But if Vaughan would only open his eyes, he would see that Miss Allen is infinitely better suited to him!" Beatrice gnawed her lip, frustrated for the young people. "They have so much in common."

"Is not the old saw that opposites attract?"

"Not true, I do not think. There must be some foundation, something in common, and Lady Silvia appears to abhor everything about Lord Vaughan."

"Why do some ladies take against a man who seems to have nothing against him?"

Beatrice glanced over at Chappell and found his gaze was on her. She could not trust her voice to answer. She turned her gaze back to the grouping of young people. "Even if Rowland knows he can never marry Lady Silvia, he cannot make the girl prefer Vaughan when she so clearly does not."

Rowland stood beside the fire, the glow of the flickering flames dancing across his brooding, handsome face. At that moment Lady Silvia stood, in an unpardonably rude display that was completely against her character, and joined Mr. Rowland at the fire. The reverend's face lit with a yearning so powerful it was painful to Beatrice. His hand went up, as if he would stroke the earnest young face turned up to his, but then it fell back to his side and clenched.

"Oh, it is so hard," Beatrice murmured.

"Impossible love?"

"Being young," Beatrice answered without looking toward her inquisitor. "Being young and confused and giving your heart where there can never be a return of affection."

"Are you speaking of them, now, Miss Copland, or yourself?"

"Of young people everywhere." Her tone was hollow, even to her own ears.

Vaughan, clearly miffed by Lady Silvia's blatant attempt to brush him off, stood casually, stretched, and moved over to the hearth. Verity Allen had finally settled down by the fire, sitting in an unladylike cross-legged pose as she roasted some chestnuts in a flat pan. It was oddly graceful though, her position, and she glowed with health and vitality. Vaughan joined her on the floor and teasingly pulled the pins from her untidy bun. Her auburn hair cascaded down her back in rich waves, and Vaughan threaded his fingers through it as Miss Allen gazed at him, her eyes full of longing.

Vaughan cast a glance over his shoulder, trying to catch Lady Silvia's eye, it seemed, but the younger girl was engrossed in conversation with the reverend. And so the baron began a flirtation, laughing with Miss Allen over something, touching her cheek, her hand, her arm.

"Oh, I hope they know what they are about," Beatrice said sadly, shaking her head.

"What do you mean?" Chappell said.

"Someone can so easily be hurt when games are played with hearts. Look at Miss Allen's eyes," Beatrice said. "They are glowing. She has never met anyone like Lord Vaughan before, and he is going to break her heart. I . . . I must do something . . . must stop this idiotic flirtation. . . ." She started to rise, but Sir David put one hand on her arm.

"She would not thank you," he said quietly. "It is *her* heart, and she is commander of it. You can alter the course of events, but you have no idea if this is the way they are meant to go or not. If you interfere, you may alter forever what was meant to happen, how these young people were meant to sort out their lives."

Beatrice searched his eyes. The light blue held pain, she thought, and it cut her to the core. She could have prevented that old pain, she thought, could have done something about it. How different his life would have been if she had acted differently, been stronger, wiser!

Chappell felt her tremble under his hand. It was as if his speech had some resonance with her beyond the tableau they were viewing. Had he meant more by it? Beyond a deep belief that people must work out their own destinies, he did not think so. He was comfortable that his life had progressed as it was meant to, and he had no regrets. Well, no, that was not entirely true. There were things he would have done differently in his past, but whether those changes would have altered the course of his life, he was not so sure.

"Do not worry about the young people, Miss Copland.

They have their lives ahead to work things out. They are all good people, and we must trust in their own wisdom." He moved his hand down to cover hers, and stroked it, feeling the soft skin under his thumb. "In two days it is Christmas Eve day," he said, changing the subject. "Promise me one waltz."

"There will not be dancing, Sir David," she said, rose blooming in her cheeks.

"I think there will be. I am sure there will be. Promise me." His voice was husky and he cleared his throat.

Her eyes wide, she said, "I will."

Fifteen

Listlessly, Lady Silvia listened as Beatrice consulted with the cook, listening to the woman's complaints about the footmen's rapacious appetites, and then planned the ritual stirring of the pudding for all the company. It was to be a real, old-fashioned Christmas, and the staff was fully in the spirit, even though it meant much more work for them than the usual quiet Christmas with only Beatrice and Lady Bournaud to attend to.

Beatrice joined the girl at the table. "It is, as you can see, up to Cook how she will do things, but close consultation with the staff is necessary so there are no surprises."

Lady Silvia murmured something in response, but continued to gaze absently out the high window, which, since the kitchen was in the basement, had a view only of bushes and dead grass.

"My lady," Beatrice said.

No response.

"My lady!"

"Hmm?" The girl looked up, her brown eyes wide.

Beatrice sat down on a stool beside her and took the girl's two small hands in hers. "Lady Silvia, do not take this amiss, but I cannot help but observe that you are distracted and . . . unhappy."

Tears welled in the pansy-brown depths, and the girl shook her head. "It is nothing, really, Miss Copland. You have been so kind, and I . . . and I know I haven't been attending, but . . . but . . ." She burst into tears.

Beatrice followed her instincts for once and pulled the girl into her arms, rocking her. "There, there," she said, patting her back. The weeping, instead of subsiding changed to heaving, gasping sobs. Beatrice gave the startled scullery maid a look that told the child to leave, and the kitchen, for the moment, was empty. "What is it, Silvia? What is wrong?" She pushed the girl away, pulling a handkerchief out of her sleeve and dabbing at the girl's eyes.

"I did not know love would hurt! I have always thought that it would be so simple. I would f-find the gentleman who most appealed to me, and he would like me and want to marry me."

"But that is not so?"

"N-no! Mr. Rowland keeps trying to hand me over to Lord Vaughan, as if I am some distasteful gift that he wishes to foist off on someone else. And Lord Vaughan is so horrible and talks of nothing but boxing and hunting and g-guns! And then he will try to talk about p-poetry and fashion and gossip, and I don't care for any of that, but he will not leave me alone and Mr. Rowland will not rescue me!" She said it all in one long stream with only sniffs and sobs punctuating her speech.

Beatrice patted her back and shook her head. What could she tell the girl? That her first experience with love would not be profitable, but that she must lift up her chin and go on? Hollow words when one was young and in love. "Be patient, Lady Silvia."

"You do not understand. . . ."

"But I do! I know that is the hardest thing to do, but you *must* be patient. You have . . . Let us be blunt. You have fallen in love with Mr. Rowland?"

She nodded and sniffed, dabbing at her nose with the wisp of cloth.

"He is a good man. Does he care for you?"

"I don't know. I thought he did. Sometimes when he looks at me . . . But . . . oh, I do not know!"

What could she say? It had been pointed out to Beatrice

that Mr. Rowland's prospects were not sufficient that the earl, Lady Silvia's father, would ever consent to a marriage between them. "Have you given your heart prematurely, my dear?" Beatrice asked, as gently as she could.

Her smooth brow furrowing, the girl stared down at her hands and pulled at the cloth. "I did not think I was. I thought I was in control and that I would be guided by his behavior, but then when I wasn't looking my heart floated away like a bubble, and now he h-holds it." Lady Silvia, cupping her hands to illustrate, stared down at them as one tear dripped off the tip of her nose. "And I had meant to be so sensible!"

It was a simple, heartrending wail of despair. "Love has a way of taking all of your good sense and tossing it out the window," Beatrice said sadly. "Courage, Lady Silvia. Courage. I cannot think that you have lost your heart to no end, but you must be prepared to be patient."

"Do you think there is a chance?"

"There is always a chance." Beatrice was torn at that moment, between destroying every shred of hope the girl had in what looked like a difficult situation, or shoring up her faint hope in the knowledge that life could and sometimes did work out for the best for those who were patient. "You must be calm and accept what destiny has in store for you. Be strong. After all, if you win the day and you and Mr. Rowland marry, you must be strong to be a wife to a reverend. They work long hours, you know, something like a doctor, for they are ever at the parish's disposal. So you must learn to be calm, and to believe that everything that happens has a purpose."

Good advice, Beatrice thought. Was she so unwise as to give advice she could not follow herself?

"Rowland, I would have words with you!" Lord Vaughan strode up the nave to the crossing in the old church, where Rowland knelt at the altar.

Rowland stood. He had been lost in contemplation, and Vaughan's loud voice echoed profanely in the sacred interior. "I would have *you* remember where you are, my lord," he said sternly. The baron was his superior in the outside world, but in this holy place all men were equal.

Vaughan, looking stricken, said, "I am sorry, Rowland. You are right, of course." His expression troubled still, the man nodded and turned, waiting at the door.

Rowland turned back to the altar, made obeisance, calmed himself, and then left the church with Vaughan, who looked chastened, he was happy to see. Outside, the early promise of the day before Christmas Eve had changed, and a sharp wind sliced up the moor from the valley, tossing the bare limbs of the tree and whistling around the ancient stone foundation of the chapel. For Rowland, who last remembered the chateau in summer, it seemed desolate, as dreary as his heart, which was the very subject he had been praying about. He had come north with peace in his soul, but now it was tormented with earthly desires and he needed to regain that serenity if he was to believe that he was fit to serve in the church. The tribulations of physical life should not disturb him the way they had, but there it was. He was full of agitation.

"Now, what is it that concerns you, Vaughan?"

They walked up the damp path from the chapel toward the house, but Vaughan's earlier impetuosity had abated. He frowned down at his feet and then looked at the man at his side. "We must talk. About Lady Silvia."

"I cannot think that we have anything to discuss about her ladyship."

"But we do," Vaughan said, stopping and forcing Rowland to stop as well.

Rowland turned and looked at the baron, examining him with a dispassionate eye. Vaughan was the very type of fellow who had tormented him and made his life a living hell in school. He was athletic and thoughtless and vigorous, but without any real viciousness at his core, unlike some of the boys whose torture Rowland had suffered. But he was not good enough for an angel like Lady Silvia. Not half good enough. And if they were social equals . . . But, he thought, calming the worldly urges of competition and envy that spurred his anger toward the other man, they never would be social equals. That knowledge was what made him, in his better moments, guide Lady Silvia toward the baron. The two should have a chance to see if there could be anything between them. Vaughan was, after all, at his core a good man, better by far than many Rowland had known. And it was not as if he himself had any hope of winning the lady's hand.

"No. We do not have anything to talk about concerning Lady Silvia. She is her own woman and will live her life for herself."

"Have done with that, Rowland," Vaughan said, planting his fists on his hips. "She is a girl, a marriageable, pretty little chit, but just a female. The business of her life is to marry, and marry well. She would make me an admirable wife, and I happen to be in the market right now for just such a commodity. Do not let her silly infatuation, this churchish, idiotic softness, make her pass up an eligible offer."

Rowland gritted his teeth together. "It seems I was wrong about you, Vaughan."

The baron nodded, with a quirked half grin. "Good."

"No, not good. I had been thinking that there was nothing too amiss about you, that you were, at the very least, good-hearted, but now I see that you are a doltish, superior, smug, churlish example of male idiocy, not worth Lady Silvia's tiniest finger!" He whirled on his heel and started toward the house.

As he strode toward the doorway, he heard Vaughan's words floating behind him. "Do not think this is over, Rowland, because it is not. If you will not discourage the chit, I will be forced to point out to her what life as your wife would be."

Rowland stopped and slowly turned. "Do not be so presumptuous, Lord Vaughan, or you will only embarrass her and humiliate yourself. I know my place, and I know my future. Lady Silvia, unfortunately, will not be part of either."

She had been coming to find him, to test her new resolution of strength and calm, as Miss Copland had advised. Frozen in her spot, within hearing range but out of sight, she had heard his ringing words, that she would never be a part of his life, nor his future. Tears would start, but she swallowed them back and stood, immobile, waiting for both men to go away. What had preceded Mr. Rowland's speech she could only guess, but it was as final a blow to her hopes and cherished wishes as any could ever be.

Lady Silvia had, at nineteen, just lost the first love of her life. Quivering, feeling sure that her actual, physical heart was shattering into pieces, she walked aimlessly, lost in contemplation.

What would she do now? She had thought falling in love was a happy thing, full of sweet and tender moments, whispered confidences, gentle kisses. Instead it had been a time of uncertainty, doubt, and soul-searching, punctuated by moments of delirious happiness when she and Mr. Rowland could walk and talk—and kiss. She would always have that to remember. It was the moment when she had first been sure.

And she was sure. She stopped in her perambulation. He *was* the one, and she would be good for him; she knew it! He was inclined to seriousness, if not melancholy, and he needed a wife who would keep him connected to the everyday, to people and life, for he was studious and deep, while she was far more practical than was consistent with her elevated station in life. No matter how hard she had tried, she had never been good at the giggling, the silly gossip and frivolity that the girls around her fed upon. And yet she was not intellectual; she was far too pragmatic for that. She was just what he needed, and she would not give up her dream without a fight. She nodded once. There had to be a way.

She looked up and realized that of all places, she had wandered to the stable. The big doors were open; she had heard that morning Lady Bournaud order a footman to go to Squire Fellows to gather Mrs. Stoure's things, as she would be spending Christmas Day with them, so that explained where the big, formal carriage was.

But she could hear a voice, and it was a feminine voice. Curious, she stepped carefully into the stable, but she need not have worried about her elegant half boots, for the stable floor was pristine, as clean as any ballroom. She moved forward and the crooning tone became understandable words as she came closer.

"Yes, you're a good lad, aren't you? Vaughan don't know how to treat you right, does he? Acts like you're just another beast, but you're much more than that. You're a clever lad, and a beauty. Doesn't have a brain in his head, your master, does he?"

Silvia peeked around the corner of the stable to find Verity, dressed in that ugly brown stuff gown of hers, brushing a big chestnut stallion. The animal quivered all over and nuzzled Verity affectionately, snuffling and snorting as she fed him a lump of sugar.

"If only the gentlemen were that easy to tame," Silvia said.

Verity, calm and unruffled in the presence of horses where she was not with humans, looked up and smiled. "Prefer horses, really. They smell better most of the time."

Silvia wrinkled her nose. She moved tentatively into the stable. "I . . . I have generally been nervous around horses. They are so big, and I am so small."

"Nothing to be nervous about. Important to calm yourself in their presence, you see, for they are very sensitive creatures; sense your nerves, makes 'em jumpy. Worse than any green girl at her first London ball, and Lord knows I have seen plenty of *them*. Come here."

Edging forward, Silvia watched Verity, noticing a side to

the girl that she had not seen in all the time they had spent in the same household. Here, in the stable, Verity was absolutely at home: calm, collected, in her element. She pulled off Silvia's glove and placed a lump of sugar in her palm, then took her wrist, pulling her closer to the stallion.

Silvia tugged at her hand, but Verity said, "No, hush. Calm, remember? Hold your hand out flat, now."

Doing as she was told, Silvia flattened her hand out, palm up, and the stallion snuffled, and then daintily took the sugar. It tickled, and she stifled a giggle. It was not so bad, really, she thought, as Verity released her from her iron grip. The girl was awfully strong.

And yet . . . Looking her over curiously, Silvia noted how beautiful Miss Allen was. She had a pointed chin, perfect skin, even, white teeth, and her eyes were an unusual, lustrous blue-green, like top-quality jade. It would have been impossible not to notice that she was completely and utterly fascinated by and infatuated with Lord Vaughan, but the man treated her like a boy, cuffing her familiarly. The night before he had used her callously, trying to get Silvia's attention by caressing Verity's hair and face. It was unthinkingly cruel, especially given the way Verity clearly felt about him. But the dolt didn't know it. He had likely not intended to be cruel.

And yet, she was perfect for him. Silvia, watching Verity finish her brushing, was taken with an idea. Vaughan was clearly on the hunt for a wife. Verity Allen was of impeccable family background, a relation to Lady Bournaud herself. But Vaughan would never see her as a potential wife while she smelled of the stable and acted like a twelve-year-old boy with a bad case of hero worship whenever she was near him.

"Miss Allen," she started.

"Oh, please don't call me that. I am so tired of it. Just call me Verity, will you?"

The beseeching look in the young woman's eyes was irresistible, and even though it was unthinkable on such a short acquaintance, Silvia, warmed by the pleading expression, said, "Verity. And you must call me Silvia."

"Done," Verity said, sticking out her hand. She looked at it, then wiped it on her dress and stuck it out again.

Silvia, stifling a smile, took it in her gloved left hand and shook. "Mi—Verity, will you come to my room? My abigail has been wanting to show me a hairstyle she wishes to try on me, but I have not been sure of it. If she could try it on your hair first, I could see what it looks like."

Such an utterly absurd fabrication deserved to be laughed at, but Verity, an open expression on her guileless face, said, "All right. Sure."

Seeing a solution ahead to at least one of her problems, Silvia sighed with satisfaction. "Good. Come up when you are done here."

Gazing at herself in the mirror, Verity shook her head. "Doesn't look like me." Of course, since there was no one to hear her, there was no answer. How she had allowed herself to be primped and prodded into this absurd imitation of a London belle, she did not know, but now she was committed to it, for Silvia had insisted she come down to dinner this way.

There was a rap on the door. "Are you ready?"

It was Silvia's girlish voice. With a deep sigh, Verity said, "I guess I am as ready as I ever will be."

Together, arm in arm, they descended as the dining room doors were opened for the company. Sir David Chappell was the first of the guests they met, and though his eyes widened, he was too much the gentleman to comment on Verity's changed attire and hairstyle. He bowed and greeted them formally.

Precedence was not observed, as the gathering was being conducted more along the lines of a family party, so Silvia and Verity were still arm in arm as Vaughan strode in from the library. He stopped. "What happened to you?" he said, gaping at Verity.

She stiffened, feeling dreadful embarrassment steal over her. This was what she had been afraid of, that he would think she was doing this for him.

"Does she not look beautiful, Lord Vaughan?" Silvia squeezed Verity's arm in silent encouragement.

And that was when Verity first understood that it was all meant for this moment, that the hairstyle story was just a ruse to gently cajole her into more ladylike attire and primping. She swallowed, praying the same idea would not occur to Vaughan. She could not stand it if he laughed at her. It would be more than she could bear. It had been like heaven the night before when he had sat down beside her just as if he wanted to, and had patted her hair and touched her face. But soon she had realized that the caresses were much as one would give to a puppy.

"She looks . . . different," he said, staring at her, his slow gaze traveling over her and taking in the change to her hair and her clothing.

The rush of other guests to the table finished the subject, and Verity sank into her chair between Sir David and Mrs. Stoure. She would have sat beside Silvia, but the girl had been claimed immediately by Vaughan, and she had somehow maneuvered Mr. Rowland on her right.

Dinner rushed by in a blur. Sir David was kind, helping her to choice bits of fish and game, noticing when she did not eat much. Normally her appetite was good, but tonight, for some reason, she felt queasy. Lady Silvia, in her kindness, had noticed her feelings toward Lord Vaughan and had been trying to force him to notice her. But nothing would make that happen. On some elemental level he was attracted to her; she had felt it when she was pressed to him in the stable, and when she fell on him from the tree. It had given her the courage for that ridiculous kiss.

But men would always be men. The genteel, delicate, pretty Lady Silvia would always be the one they preferred.

And who would not? Verity cast a glance across the table. She was perfect, even when flustered by the overeager attention of Lord Vaughan. Her cheeks were pink and her eyes wide, but her manners were . . . perfect.

Dinner progressed, and then they joined Lady Bournaud in the red saloon, as was the custom. It was the last night before Christmas Eve, and a table was set up in one corner, for the task before the young people was to make up the baskets for the staff. Normally Beatrice would do it all herself, but this year, with the added burden of company and her dual duties as de facto hostess and housekeeper, she was just too busy, and had asked the two younger ladies that afternoon if they would mind lending a hand.

The table, a large round mahogany table at one end of the saloon, was heaped high with good things and gifts. Silvia, in her pretty way, asked Lord Vaughan and Mr. Rowland to help, and both being gentleman, agreed.

"Though I do not know how much help I shall be," Mr. Rowland said, his expression bemused. "I have ever been clumsy with duties of this nature."

"Oh, but in your role as parish reverend you may be asked to help at the village fair or the harvest bazaar," Lady Silvia said, looking at him sideways from under her lashes.

Vaughan sat down with a grunt of disapproval. "I shall not be a damn bit of help," he said.

Lady Silvia turned to him, wide-eyed. "Oh, come now, Lord Vaughan. Do you not tie your own flies for fishing? Making bows for the baskets is simpler, truly."

Verity could not but admire her new friend's adroit handling of every objection. Her own upbringing had been devoid of the lessons she supposed would have taught her such finesse. Her mother, overwhelmed with the task of merely surviving the wilderness at first, had been wholly consumed with practical issues, cooking and laundry and gathering food, gardening. Those things Verity could do. She knew how to cook an entire meal over an open fire, and could gut and clean a deer. She knew how to tan hides, gather wild rice from the lake nearby, and . . .

Without thought she began to talk out loud as she picked up a length of ribbon to tie into a bow onto the handle of a basket. "At Christmas, at home, we would spend the week before making apple pies, bread, and ginger biscuits, and my father made gifts for us all out of wood and deerskin. An Indian woman from their village taught Mama how to make moccasins . . . that is, slippers from hide decorated with beads."

Vaughan said, "Is that the odd beaded footwear you had on the other night?"

"Yes." Verity looked up from the basket she was filling and smiled. "I brought some pairs with me when I came over—thought my English cousins would want to see what life in Canada was like—but no one was interested." Her smiled faded and she did not go on. It was the one thing that had bothered her most about this land she was born in. Not a soul was truly interested in any part of her past, and the life she loved so much and had been forced to leave behind, though some of the London gentlemen had pretended interest until they found out there was no Colonial fortune in her family.

"I would like to see them," Silvia said.

"I would as well, Miss Allen," Rowland said.

Verity frowned and squinted. Were they merely being kind to the Colonial clod or did they really want to see them? She found that she had become preternaturally sensitive about condescension and being humored, but her hypersensitivity did not sense any hypocrisy from Rowland or Silvia.

"All right. I brought some other things, too, if . . ."

Silvia smiled and touched her arm. "We would be fascinated," she said, gathering Rowland into her gaze and then turning it back to her new friend. "I have never been anywhere but London and Bath, and now Yorkshire. I would like to hear about your home. It will make me feel almost as if I have been there."

Verity blinked back the water that rose in her eyes. Never a weepy female, she was shocked at her own susceptibility, but she had missed being part of a family circle, as she was at home among her brothers, in the long months since she had landed in England. This felt almost like home.

She stole a glance at Vaughan. He looked frankly bored, gazing at the ceiling and abandoning any pretense of making the baskets for the servants. Well too bad, she thought, standing. She didn't suppose she would ever figure him out, and so she would just leave him to sulk in silence. "I'll go and get them," she said, looking back to Silvia and Rowland.

Sourly, Vaughan watched Lady Silvia, how she constantly cut glances at the reverend and deferred to him as they sat around the table making baskets up for the staff. Baskets! This was women's work, and he had done precious little but muck up one bow after another. Making the kissing balls was one thing—after all, what gentleman had not been recruited at some point by a hopeful lady into making kissing balls? But baskets of fripperies for the servants? And now, as they worked, Verity Allen was giving a lecture, almost, on life in the Colonies.

The young woman ignored him completely, taking from a cloth bag several pairs of the "moccasins" as she called them. Like carpet slippers, he thought, unconscious of how he was moving forward, more interested than he would have thought possible. He picked one up and fingered the leather. It was soft, softer than cowhide, certainly.

"It is doeskin," Verity said, in answer to his unvoiced question. "When the men have completed the hunt, the skin is stripped, the animal is gutted, and the meat is made into pemmican. That is, it is cut into strips and dried over a fire to smoke it, and then . . ."

Lady Silvia wrinkled her nose. "Dried over smoke?"

"Preserves it," Vaughan said absently. "So it can be eaten later. I say, what about these hides?" He noted the beadwork on the toe of one pair, very fine, all in brilliant reds and yellows and black in a stylized bird shape with wings outstretched.

"They are scraped; it leaves them very soft and pliable, fit for making these moccasins. The Indians use everything. The sinew of the deer is used to lash things together. The gut makes bowstrings and thread; bone makes needles and scrapers; antlers and horns make beads. Nothing goes to waste."

Lady Silvia, her eyes sparkling, asked, "Did you really know Indians?"

Verity nodded. "Good friends with some of them, women and men. Women are important; do most of the work for the tribe. Without the natives we would never have learned what natural foods can be eaten, like what we call wild rice, even though it isn't rice at all. And how to build a canoe." Her voice rose with enthusiasm, her hands moving as she described life in Upper Canada. "It is the best vehicle for travel because it is light and can be carried past rapids. I learned how to paddle before I was six. Not like a rowboat, you see; it takes balance and ability."

Vaughan gazed down at the moccasin in his hand and gave in. He was fascinated and had to confess he had questions. Questions only Verity Allen could answer. He hated to admit it, but there it was. "Miss Allen," he said, clearing his throat, "I cannot quite picture this 'canoe.' Would you describe it?"

"Yes, do," Lady Silvia said, a tiny smile on her bow lips.

"Well," Verity said, sitting down and drawing a piece of paper toward her, "where a rowboat is short and broad, a canoe is long and slim, so it cuts through the water. . . ."

The evening ended late, around the piano. Mrs. Stoure was a natural musician, not needing any sheet music at all to play the old favorites and Christmas songs by the dozen. As Lady Bournaud drowsily smiled on, everyone gathered, after drinking mulled wine and eating ginger cake, and sang.

Sir David had a very fine baritone, Beatrice remembered from a past Christmas so long ago now. As he began to sing, alone, "What Child Is This?" Beatrice surprised herself by moving closer and joining, her own soprano voice adding a counterpoint. His light blue eyes warmed and a smile drew up the corners of his mouth, even as she continued to sing. His arm stole around her shoulders, as if to draw her closer so they could blend more harmoniously, and the touch of his warm hand sent a chill down her back. She would have this to remember when he was gone, this night, as the wind howled outside and the warmth of good food and good fellowship set her heart aglow.

It was a moment in time to treasure, she thought, as she glanced around the parlor. The crimson saloon, so called because of the deep red walls and furnishings, glowed warm in the golden candlelight. Smiles wreathed every face, and as voices rose to join them in the song, it filled the high-ceilinged chamber with joy.

The song over, she started to draw away, but he said, "Stay, Miss Copland. We may need to harmonize again; one never knows."

She stayed in the protection of his arm, and had never felt so happy, nor so blessed.

Silvia and Verity sang a song together, and then the gathered company sang one all together. Beatrice noted how Silvia, emboldened by the wine she had imbibed, perhaps, moved closer to Rowland. His expression was tender, and he held her arm close to him, even threading his fingers through hers. She gazed up at him, her eyes shining with adoration.

Verity had likewise gravitated to Vaughan's side. He had slung a careless arm over her shoulders as they stood close to the piano to sing. But as the glow of candlelight burnished her high cheeks to pink, his gaze sharpened and settled on her lips.

"We are under the kissing ball," he said out loud, as the last song finished. He leaned down and kissed her lips, his expression, when he looked back up, bemused. Verity had her eyes closed and only opened them slowly.

"Yes, well," he said briskly, releasing Verity abruptly, "time for all the ladies to take the same punishment, I say." He kissed Beatrice's cheek, then his gaze settled on Lady Silvia, and flicked down to where her hands were clasped with the reverend's. Rowland let go of her and cleared his throat. Vaughan stepped forward and took the girl's shoulders in his hands, and pulled her close, setting his lips directly on hers with a forceful movement.

There was a hiss of withdrawn breath from somewhere. Beatrice rather thought it was from Verity.

"I think there has been enough reveling for one night," Lady Bournaud said sharply. As everyone had thought her asleep in her bath chair, most were somewhat startled. But she was awake, eyes glittering in the candlelight shed by the candelabra that sat on the piano.

Silvia had pulled away from Vaughan and scrubbed her lips with what could only be named insulting vigor.

Lady Bournaud had not missed the exchanges of looks, Beatrice thought. She gazed steadily at Verity and beckoned her closer. "Your mother was wrong about you, my child," she said. "Fanny says you are wild and have no accomplishments, but I think she just misunderstood you. I was listening to your fascinating stories about your challenging country. You are a new breed, my dear, a Canadian." She held out her hand.

"Thank you, my lady," Verity whispered, her voice thick with unshed tears, as she took the old woman's hand in hers.

"And now it is time to retire," Lady Bournaud said sternly, releasing the girl and glancing around at the company. "Tomorrow is a long day, so off to bed with you all."

Sixteen

Clouds lay thickly on the horizon above Harn Moor, gathering like gloomy messengers of trouble to come, and yet there was a brilliant belt of blue above them. Verity frowned up at the sky. At home she would know just how to interpret the sky, whether snow was coming or if the good weather would hold awhile yet. She strode into the stable. A ride would not hurt, for no weather could come upon her fast enough, in such open country, that she would not have time to start back.

"Bobby, I will ride"—she looked around the gloomy stable and finally saw Vaughan's big stallion snorting and puffing, anxious for exercise and not likely to see any that day— "him," she said, pointing to his stall.

"Ah, no yer don't," Bobby, the wiry thirteen-year-old stableboy, said. "'Is lardship would 'ave me knickers if I was to let yer 'ave yer way wiv Bolt. 'E comes 'round ev'ry evenin' to check on 'im."

"But Bolt and I are old friends, are we not?" Verity said, opening the stall door and allowing the stallion to whicker gently in her ear and search her hands for sugar.

Bobby, wide-eyed, said, "'E does like you, don't 'e? Never seen 'im act like that fer anyone, not even 'is lardship. An' I hates like hell to take 'im into the pen; he sets up such a almighty fuss, 'e do. Bolt, not his lardship, I mean."

"Which is why," Verity said, deciding in a rush to take the responsibility away from the boy, "Lord Vaughan asked me

especially to exercise the lad. How is that?" She led him from
the stall.

"Zat true?"

"It is completely true," Verity said, one hand behind her
back and her fingers crossed against the bouncer she had just
told. She would be back before anyone knew she had even
taken Bolt out. If there was one thing in the world she knew
she could depend on, it was her horsemanship. Not that she
had ever ridden such a prime bit of blood and bone, but a nag
was a nag. She reached up and rubbed the horse's velvety
nose. This was a morning when she needed a real hard ride to
rid her of the pain of the night before. Everything had seemed
to go so well, and then . . .

She turned her mind away from it. Forget about the knav-
ish varlet! Lord Jacob Vaughan was not worth the time and
energy it took to think of him. "I am riding Bolt," she repeated, glaring at the stableboy.

Bobby shrugged. "Then on yer 'ead be it," he said.

So, he was only half fooled, Verity thought, grabbing a
worn groom's saddle. He had turned his back and was
whistling unconcernedly while she saddled Bolt and led him
to the mounting block. The stallion acted up some as she
mounted, sidling and tossing his head.

"Settle down!" she commanded, and he instantly obeyed.
"Do not try to play off your pretty tricks on me, sir," she said,
patting his neck. "Now we understand who is master," she
finished, with some satisfaction. He would act out no more of
his dramas. High-strung as he was, she had an understanding
of him; they respected each other.

Bobby came forward as she exited, and she waved as she
trotted past. He was hollering something after her, something
about snow, but she could not hear him. Whatever it was
could wait. She cantered out into the uneven sunlight to find
Silvia strolling along the path above, on the terrace. She
slowed her mount.

"Verity," Silvia called, waving one pink-gloved hand.
"Where are you going? It is Christmas Eve!"

"Just going for a ride," Verity called, restraining Bolt, who was impatient as she tried to keep him still. "He is too fresh. I have to run him."

"But Verity, is that not Lord Vaughan's—"

"Yes. But what he does not know will not hurt him," Verity called. "Tell no one where I am! Promise me!"

Silvia frowned.

Bolt sidled some more. "Your word of honor as my friend, Silvia!"

Silvia reluctantly nodded. "All right, but do not be gone too long," she called, cupping her hands around her mouth, her words coming out on puffs of frosty steam. "I want to talk to you about something."

"All right," Verity said, feeling the stallion's sides heaving under her knees. Talking was the last thing she wanted to do, especially after the episode the previous night, but Silvia had been kind, and she would listen. She dug her knees in and Bolt set off at a run. "I'll be back in a couple of hours!" she called over her shoulder. "Do not wait luncheon for me."

It was glorious. Bolt was the most responsive mount she had ever ridden, and it was like a dream. This was the England she could not have imagined in all of her mother's stories. Her mother, raised in the rarefied atmosphere of privilege and wealth, had never ridden anything more than a "lady mount," a horse suitably mild for a ride in Hyde Park along Rotten Row. *This* was riding! This was the wild impetuous galloping of her father's stories. She loved Canada and her home there, but the only horse they had ever been able to afford had to double, or rather triple, as mount, carriage horse, and work horse, pulling the plow that tilled their acreage.

She galloped to the top of Harn Moor and gazed out over the land. One side of the slope, beyond Chateau Bournaud, led down to Harnthwaite, the village she and the others had been down to a couple of times. The village was set on the banks of a silvery stream, glinting through the bare branches of the trees that lined it. A beam of sunlight played across the old gold color of the dead grass down the moor and the stone fences that wound in undulating lines, crossing and bisecting.

The other slope led to . . . She turned Bolt and took in a deep breath of astonishment. It was as if the world opened up beyond the moor. There, in the distance, was a round lake, and then a broad plain, and then, rising majestically, an even higher moor, dark and forbidding, snow clinging to the lofty peak. Dread Moor. Sir David had spoken of its forbidding heights. There were copses of forest and silvery gills fed the lake. She felt like she could see the whole world. There was nothing in her part of Canada to compare, and she felt dizzyingly alone. She looked back over her shoulder at Harnthwaite and safety. There was the manse, beyond it the village, and the silver stream that wound through. The road hugged the moorside.

But just for a brief time she wanted to be alone and free. It was a once-in-a-lifetime opportunity. And given the choice, adventure beckoned.

"What do you think, Bolt?" she said. He tossed his head.

"I agree. Let's go. We'll explore for just one hour and then start back. Let's mark our spot. . . ." She glanced around. She was on the top of Harn Moor, but it was a barren place. She saw a rocky outcropping that looked like a face, with a couple of dark caves for eyes. "That is our mark," she said out loud. "It looks like two eyes, with a nose under it, that heavy boulder that juts out. We're off then. We'll be back in early afternoon and Lord High-and-Mighty Vaughan will never know. It will be our secret."

She kicked at Bolt, and he gathered his strength under him and started off with the quick leap that had given him his name.

"Weather is about to change," Lady Bournaud said fretfully.

"I think you are right, my lady." Chappell wheeled her chair out on the terrace, having bundled her up well against the chill.

"I know I am right," she snapped peevishly.

Chappell stopped and took a seat on a bench in front of her. He took her hands in his and chafed them. "Another minute or two and we are going to go back in. I will not risk Miss Copland's wrath by letting you get a chill."

"Ah, so you fear her anger more than mine?"

Her gray eyes were wintry, but he knew her too well to miss the twinkle. "Hers has unknown consequences, my lady. Yours I know is all bluster."

"Pish tush! She is as mild as milk."

"I do not think she can be. She has survived things we know nothing about, I think, and with her honor intact, if I am correct."

"Honor, perhaps," Lady Bournaud brooded. "But something is bothering her, and has for years. Curiosity eats me up, I will admit, but my secrets are my own, too, and I cannot feel easy invading her privacy."

"Even though you confiscated a private poem?"

"Ah, but that was left in a public part of the house. Not my fault if she got careless." She shook a crooked finger at him, then frowned as a snowflake touched it. "It is starting," she said, gazing up.

As they had been talking, the dark clouds, charcoal on the underside and heavily laden, had mounted up, scudding against each other until they were piled high on the moor. Snowflakes drifted lazily in pretty patterns, but neither of them was fooled. They had both spent too many years in the moors not to know that a Yorkshire snowstorm could quickly turn lethal.

"Time to take you in, my lady. It looks like we will have snow for Christmas after all. And lots of it, if I am not mistaken."

The copse was lovely, dark and green, mysterious like the woods back home, Verity thought, walking Bolt through the thickly wooded grove. The firs were fragrant, but the air was becoming bitterly cold, and she thought a snowflake had drifted onto her nose a few minutes ago. Perhaps it was time to go home. She had no idea if she had exceeded her promised two hours, but it was no matter. In such open country she could not get into trouble. From anywhere she would be able to see the top of Harn Moor. She had a good sense of direction and impeccable skills at finding her way in any wilderness. It had been a necessity at home. And here it was so much easier to see one's way! Impossible to get lost.

She sighed deeply as snowflakes drifted in between the deep and dark conifers. She grabbed one branch and pulled some needles off, lifting them to her nose. Fragrant with pine scent. Like home. Bolt whickered and tossed his head.

"All right. I know. We will head back now. You deserve some mash or oats after this marvelous outing, my boy, and I shall see that you get it. I will likely miss luncheon, but will scrounge the kitchen for some bread and cheese."

She led him out of the copse, hoping they were going out the way they had come in, for the trees might block their view if they were not on the right side. There was daylight, she thought, peering through the woods as the snow thickened. She supposed she had better hurry. It was getting heavier even as she walked.

They broke out of the copse only to find that they were on the side facing the round lake and distant Dread Moor. They would need to walk . . . hmmm . . .west some, she thought, trying to think where they were situated as if she were looking at their position from above, at the top of Harn Moor. West. Unfortunately, the sun would be close to directly above right now, even though it was, of course, in the southern sky. But she could tell her direction in reference to it still, she thought, if she could only determine where it was!

But even as she started shading her eyes from the snow, trying to decide where the sun was in relation to her, she found that impossible, so thickly was the snow coming down and so heavy the cloud cover. The ground was already coated with a blanket of white. Bolt tossed his head, uneasy in the wind that had sprung up, blowing the snow sideways almost.

She grabbed the saddle and struggled up onto the tall horse, thinking that she had better decide soon which way to go. If Bolt was a local horse . . . But he wasn't, and he would not know his way back to the chateau even if she gave him his head.

Luncheon was a subdued affair. Beatrice was wondering where Miss Allen was, but did not want to alarm anyone, so she said nothing. If the girl had gone walking, though, and gotten lost . . . She shivered. Another half hour and she would start asking the staff. She already knew that Sir David had not seen her, nor had Lady Bournaud.

But it was nothing. It was not the first day the girl had not appeared for lunch. Twice before she had disappeared, only to be found in the stables in one case, and up in the attic in the second. The girl was an incorrigible explorer, with a zest for discovery and a restless nature. She would turn up later, hungry as a wolf cub and with sparkling eyes and dust in her hair.

And so Beatrice kept the conversation going.

"After luncheon," she said, glancing around the table, "I would like the company together in the kitchen for the stir-ring of the pudding. Cook has decreed that she will now be putting it in its bag for steaming on the morrow, so those who want to make a wish should follow me after we are done here."

"I would not miss it," Lady Silvia said brightly, glancing around the table.

"I will join you, my lady," Vaughan said. "I am sure the reverend would find that silly and superstitious, though, right Rowland?"

Beatrice watched the interplay uneasily. The previous night had ended so peacefully . . . almost. But then Vaughan had given Lady Silvia that long kiss under the mistletoe. It had been the work of a moment, but Beatrice had not missed Verity's stricken expression.

She had felt like shaking the baron. How could the man not see that Miss Allen was in the throes of infatuation for him? Or was he so used to it it didn't matter?

Rowland paused in the act of scooping up a stray bit of roast duck on his fork. "On the contrary, Vaughan, I like the old customs and do not consider them superstition. I will be there, happily making my wish along with you all."

Lady Silvia cast him a warm glance. Beatrice sighed, and Chappell caught her gaze, smiling at her with such warmth that she knew she was going to turn beet red. She had not blushed in fifteen years, but all of a sudden, just because David Chappell was in her life again, she was acting like the green girl she had been when first they met. Infatuation seemed to be in the air like the grippe, and she not immune.

She turned away. "Good. We shall all stir the pudding and make our wishes, then." All except Verity Allen.

As luncheon ended, she herded Vaughan, Lady Silvia, and Rowland into the kitchen. Chappell trailed behind them.

"You do not have to participate, sir," she said.

He put on a deliberately hurt expression. "Shall I have to tell Lady Bournaud that I was excluded?"

She rolled her eyes at his teasing smile, and they gathered by the stove where Cook, red-faced and smelling just a little of the brandy that went into the pudding, greeted them with smiles and winks. "We are here, ready to stir and wish," Beatrice said.

"Ladies first, I propose," Chappell said.

Lady Silvia stepped up to the stove, one of the new-style cookers, and grabbed the wooden spoon that stuck up out of the thickening, spicy mixture. She glanced at Rowland, who watched her intently, and closed her eyes, giving a quick stir of the pot and then stepping away.

"Now what did the loveliest lady in the household wish for?" Vaughan said.

"That is a secret." She was pink cheeked as she moved back to stand by Rowland.

"Now you, Miss Copland," Chappell said, taking her arm and guiding her forward.

"Oh, I hadn't intended . . ."

"But you will anyway," he said. "We are missing some of the company—Miss Allen, Mrs. Stoure—and so you must take part."

It wasn't hard to make a wish, Beatrice thought. She remembered as a child wishing for something so hard and wanting it so badly it was like a tangible taste in her mouth, that desire. One year it was a silver brush set. Another year, when she was older, it was to be allowed to stay up for the adult party her frivolous, social mother always held on Christmas Eve. Neither had come true.

This time, her wish was just as unlikely to be granted. She glanced at Sir David, thinking as she took the spoon that she would like for nothing more than his forgiveness. That, and a clean conscience. They went hand in hand, she thought. She stirred, and then stepped away from the pot.

"Now, Rowland, how shall we decide who goes next?" Vaughan stared steadily at the reverend.

"You should go next, my lord," Rowland said quietly.

Vaughan stepped forward and pinched the cook's bright red cheeks. She laughed gustily and threw her apron over her head in her confusion. Then the baron took the spoon and said, "My wish can so easily be granted by a female in this room at this very minute. I wish . . . I wish . . . that Cook shall add more brandy to this pudding."

Beatrice couldn't help but laugh. It was said with such a droll tone, and she knew he had intended to make it sound like something else.

Rowland laughed with the others and stepped forward. "Well said, Vaughan. And now me." He glanced around at each one of them, his look lingering longest on Lady Silvia, who pinked under his gaze. He took the spoon in hand and skillfully stirred it around the edge of the pot. He closed his eyes for one second, and then stepped away from the stove.

"And that is done. I think we should allow Cook to get back to her chores now. I am sure she shall take your wish under advisement, Lord Vaughan," Beatrice said.

Vaughan winked at the flushed cook, who watched him walk toward the door with dazzled eyes. "I hope so. Nothing better than a really good Christmas pudding. And mind I don't find the bachelor's button," he commanded, waving his finger back at the flustered woman before disappearing out the door.

Beatrice made a quick excuse and slipped away from the others, determined to ask the upstairs maid when last she had seen Miss Allen. She was not worried about the girl, but she did want to be sure of her whereabouts. If she was playing a prank or deliberately staying away after the hurt she suffered the night before, Beatrice wanted to have a talk with her about gentlemen of Vaughan's stamp. She would search the barn and stables herself, if necessary, to find her. The snow was now coming down thick and fast outside of the window in that sudden onset of wintry weather that was prevalent in the moors. At least she knew the child would not be foolish enough to be out in this. She shivered as she passed a window, unable to see even the hedge on the terrace, everything was so closed in with white.

Drat the girl, anyway!

Verity felt her toes numb bit by bit, the lack of sensation creeping from her big toe to the rest, and then up her foot. And still she could not find her way. She thought she was on the right track, going up moor to the top of Harn, only to realize that she had gotten twisted around and was climbing another nearby hill instead. When she reached the top she was farther from Harn Moor than when she had started, and closer to Dread Moor.

"Where am I, Bolt?" she mumbled, pushing a hank of lank hair out of her eyes and trying to peer through the blizzard. Her hands were soaked through her gloves, and she twisted them together, trying to warm them. Another few minutes and they would be numb, too. Snow coated her and was even finding a way to blow up her skirt. But mostly she felt awful for Bolt, who shivered, wet and exposed to the elements.

"All right," she said. "It must be in that direction, and I know it is so, because . . . Well, I hope it is so. If not, we shall have to take cover, and there is precious little cover out here for a lad of your size, my boy." She patted the horse's neck and urged him downhill again, keeping her bearings firmly set so she would not get turned around again. Afternoon was wearing on, and night closed in early this time of year. She must find her way.

"I do not know where she is, Sir David," Beatrice said, anxiously pacing in the library, stopping to glare out the window every few seconds.

"I wondered why she was not at luncheon. That girl usually likes to eat. I have seen her tuck away more, even, than Vaughan."

"It would not be so strange if it were just that, for she has missed luncheon before when she was exploring the grounds or the house. And after last night . . ."

The knight, sitting at his ease in a chair by the desk, nodded. "But?"

"But I have looked everywhere, asked everyone. She has disappeared! And then I thought, perhaps, as a lark, she accompanied the carriage when it went to Squire Fellow's for Mrs. Stoure's baggage, but no. It is back, and John and Alfred, the driver and groom, have not seen her all day. I cannot find Bobby, the stableboy, or I would ask him."

"Miss Copland," Chappell said, rising and interrupting the woman's pacing. "Beatrice!" He took her hands, and she looked up at him, startled. He rested back against the desk, retaining her hands in his own. "She is somewhere. Maybe she fell asleep somewhere odd. The girl does not think like other people. Perhaps she fell asleep up in the stable loft, or in one of the other outbuildings."

"Do you think so?"

He felt her hands tremble and knew then that she was truly concerned. Putting his arm over her shoulders, he walked with her to the library door. "It seems like a logical explanation to me. I will summon John and Alfred, and we will go through every outbuilding."

"Thank you, Sir David."

"Can you not just call me David? I promise to not ask you to shorten it to its inelegant diminutive, as my lady does, calling me Davey as if I were still in short pants." That did it, brought a smile to her quivering lips.

"David," she said.

Gently, he thought. Bit by bit he was gaining ground. He squeezed her hands. "Together we shall find her, and scold her thoroughly for giving you such a scare."

But she was not in any of the outbuildings. Nor was she asleep in the attic, the wine cellar, nor the pantry. Nor the chapel, the belfry, and not even the goat shed or the storage compartment of the carriage.

Sir David was now truly concerned. Where had the silly chit gone?

The company gathered in the gold saloon, minus Lady Bournaud, whom all agreed to spare from worry for the time being. Frowning, Chappell surveyed the gathering, his gaze finally settling on Lady Silvia. Her face was pale, and her eyes were glittering. When their gazes met, she burst into tears, and Rowland put his arm over her shoulders and bent his head to her.

She murmured something.

Rowland did not appear to hear her, but instead of repeat-

Lady Silvia broke down into tears. "I should have told someone. I should have said something."

Rowland sat on the sofa next to her and patted her shoulder ineffectually as she sobbed.

"Stubble it, Vaughan," Sir David said. He caught the girl's hand in his and said kindly, "My lady, it is Miss Allen who made the choice, not you. It was perhaps not a good choice, but it was hers to make. You did not ask to be taken into confidence, nor to be made a partner in any deception. All you did was keep your word. The rest is her own responsibility." He looked up and it was to see Beatrice's eyes on him, wide and fixed.

He frowned, wondering what it was in her eyes that was different somehow, but he did not have time to think about it. He stood, brushing off his knees.

"We must go out for her. She could be somewhere quite close."

Seventeen

Her thoughts racing, Beatrice went about the business of helping put together a search party. She had the groom and driver outfit them, and Bobby, the stableboy, would not hear of being left out. He was devastated by Verity's disappearance, and vowed he would help find her or die trying.

But even as she made sure the men had lanterns and ropes—God forbid they should need to use them—and extra clothing, she was pondering Sir David's words. Her own responsibility. Yes, Verity was responsible for the chances she took, even the foolhardy ones, and Silvia's silence or failure to reveal her disastrous plans did not make her a part of them.

Oh, but her own part in Melanie's last journey was more active, was it not? And still inexcusable. Or was it youthful folly, all of it? When the awful present was over, and Verity safe again, then she would tell Sir David all and let him be the judge. It was time to surrender her burden.

Right now, every thought, every prayer, every hope, must be bent on finding Verity safe and bringing her back. As the men trudged into the snowy gloom, she sent a prayer with them.

"Come back safely," she whispered. "And with that foolish, darling girl in tow."

The hours ticked by slowly. She and Lady Silvia sat holding hands for an hour or more, unable to talk, each twisted in their own miserable thoughts.

Then Lady Silvia spoke. "You know, I saw her when we were in London during the last Season."

"Really?" Beatrice was caught by surprise, though she knew instantly the girl was speaking of Verity.

"Yes. She made quite a stir, though I do not believe she knows it. She is so beautiful in a different way. One of my beaux, a Colonel Johnson, was quite taken with her, but most of the gentlemen were afraid of her. She is . . . intense, wild, and the gentlemen did not seem to know how to understand that. I wanted to meet her, to be friends with her. She looked so jolly, and yet so sad on occasion, and lonely. But my mother . . ." Her voice trailed off. There was no need to say that the daughter of the Earl and Countess of Crofton must be careful about unsuitable acquaintances if she was to marry properly. She would have been carefully guarded against any taint from the outré Colonial girl.

Silence fell again. Tidwell came into the room and cleared his throat. "Will you be wanting dinner, ma'am? Lady Bournaud is having a tray in her room with Mrs. Stoure, but then she expects to gather with everyone in the crimson parlor. . . ."

"Oh, I had forgotten. . . ." Beatrice was stricken with guilt. How could she forget her employer, and that the woman would not know what had befallen Miss Allen? To tell her or not to tell her; what was best?

"I'll come with you to talk to her," Lady Silvia said, standing and patting down her rumpled skirts.

"Are you sure?"

"Yes," she said. "It will give me something . . . someone to think of other than Verity. It will be a kindness if you allow me to."

Beatrice was glad of the company, and grateful for the streak of practicality in Lady Silvia. As flighty as she seemed, she was a levelheaded and pragmatic young woman.

Hand in hand they went up the stairs to break the news to Lady Bournaud.

* * *

Hours passed. It was dark, and still the snow came down. Lady Bournaud and Mrs. Stoure played a desultory game of piquet while Silvia and Beatrice pretended to sew. Just as the clock struck seven, Beatrice was the first to hear the door in the great hall creak open, and she raced out of the red saloon with Silvia directly behind her. The gentlemen straggled in the front door and collapsed, exhausted, wet, and covered in snow.

"Tidwell! Call Sir David's valet and two of the footmen. We must get the gentlemen's wet outer garments off and help them close to the fire. And hot drinks. Hurry!" Beatrice raced to David's side and knelt by him while Lady Silvia joined the two younger men.

"We couldn't find her," David gasped. He pushed himself up to his feet with Beatrice's help.

"You couldn't find her," she repeated, feeling the horror settling into her very bones. Involuntarily, her gaze went to the windows that flanked the big front doors. Snow howled past and helpless tears rolled down her cheeks as she thought about the girl outside in such a storm.

"We found Bolt, though," Vaughan said. "That's m'stallion. He was wandering just on this side of Harn Moor." He was panting, his face creased in lines of worry as he shed his greatcoat and the sodden woolen jacket underneath. Sir David's valet and Charles, the footman, took their wet clothes as another footman opened up the saloon door.

They could hear Lady Bournaud's querulous voice from the red saloon. "What's going on? Have they found the girl? Where is she?"

David shared a look with Beatrice. "I shall have to tell her."

"I know. She is not as strong as she seems anymore."

The warning was unnecessary. "I know." He took Beatrice's arm and squeezed it to his body, passing one hand over his soaking hair. "Come with me."

Together they went into the saloon and crossed to where Lady Bournaud, sitting at a table with Mrs. Stoure, a pleasant-faced widow of sixty, awaited them. Her watery eyes were red rimmed and worried, and Beatrice felt a clutch of fear at what this news might do to her.

But she had underestimated the old woman. David sat near her and told of their search. "We sent Bobby home with the horse when we found it and searched some more. But I have a feeling the horse had made it a good way toward home, and that we wasted hours looking near where we found Bolt."

"Can she have found shelter?" Lady Bournaud, wrapped in layers of shawls by a fretful Mrs. Stoure, shrugged one off.

David pondered that, running through his mind his childhood knowledge of the area. Lord Vaughan approached, separating himself from the group by the fire, leaving Lady Silvia and Rowland alone. He crouched by the knight, his handsome face ruddy in the fire's glow. "Chappell, I wondered if there was a spot somewhere that Miss Allen could have sheltered in?"

Chappell frowned down at his hands, red and raw from the cold. "Lady Bournaud was just asking the same question." He looked up at his mentor. "Do you remember, my lady, those caves on the other side of Harn Moor? I used to go up and stay overnight sometimes."

Rowland and Lady Silvia joined them, unable to stay out of the discussion when both were so very worried about Verity. "I remember that," Rowland said, his face lighting up with expression. "When I was here that summer I explored them. The one is not deep, but the other goes back and down about thirty feet or more. But Miss Allen would not have known about it."

Tidwell and Charles, the footman, brought in trays of food in place of the dinner the men had missed; they laid the trays on a table near the fire. Sausage-stuffed pastries and mulled wine, cakes and biscuits and coffee; the steam rose in fragrant waves as covers were removed. But Vaughan looked at it all with a twisted mouth.

"I can't eat," he said. "I can't stop thinking about Verity, out there, cold, freezing. . . ." He stared off out the window and silence fell over the group.

"Do you think she might be in one of those caves?" Silvia asked, her voice thick with tears.

"I don't know," David said. "She has not had the chance to explore in good weather, so she would not know about them, and how likely is it that she would have stumbled on them in this weather?"

There was general indecision. Should they go back out when the wind was still howling and the snow still falling? Would that not be foolhardy when they only just made it back to safety? After all, they could not help Verity if they ended up lost themselves, Lady Bournaud pointed out.

Not one of the men wanted to admit defeat, but what was practical?

"Have something to eat, and then decide," Beatrice, feeling her stomach clench at the thought of David out there again, searching in that awful storm. And yet poor Verity . . .

David nodded. "If we do go out again, we will need every ounce of strength we can muster. So eat, gentlemen . . . and ladies. Eat and then we shall decide."

Vaughan, his stomach twisted, could not bear to even smell the food. He took some of the mulled wine, but then separated himself from the group by the fire, retreating to the window. He stared out at the black night, brooding as he stared at the drifting flakes that tapped at the window and sipped the warming brew.

She was out there, alone and vulnerable, shivering, cold, wet . . . frightened. He hammered his fist on the wall, remembering the night before, how she had looked up at him with an expression of—was it longing?—as they had sung together. So what demon had prompted him to try that juvenile trick with Lady Silvia under the mistletoe, and right in front of Verity, too? Verity. She was unlike any girl he had ever met. Too smart. Too energetic. Blazing with restless vigor.

Not a comfortable chit at all. Not a woman one could master. She would run roughshod over a lesser man, but someone like himself, he would be up to the challenge of a girl like Verity.

Was that what frightened him? Life with her would be different from anything he had ever imagined. New territory, marriage to her would be. She would expect more of him. And did that explain his unconscionable behavior toward her, when he had realized early that she had a weakness for him? He had never been deliberately cruel to a woman in his life, but he had hurt her the night before; he had seen it in her eyes when he kissed Lady Silvia the way he had. He had wanted to run after Verity and apologize, oddly enough. He had been a cavalier bastard. It was uncomfortable, this new self-knowledge, but he would face the truth. He wanted time with Verity, time to decide what he felt, and how to handle it. Time to apologize. Time.

He glanced back at the company, comfortably gathered around Lady Bournaud. Then he looked back out the window. The snow had almost stopped, and a faint glimmer of the moon shone out from behind a cloud. She was out there while they were comfortably ensconced by the fire, and he could not bear it another minute. After one long look, he did not hesitate a moment longer, but slipped from the room and down to the kitchen.

"I don't know about the rest of you, but I cannot bear to think of her out there, and us not doing a single thing." The reverend glanced around at the huddled group.

Chappell nodded at what Rowland was saying. The young reverend was right; they should wait no longer. He looked up and said, "Vaughan, what think you of starting out—where did the fellow go? I thought he was mad to go out again?"

"He was by the window before," Rowland said, standing and stretching his legs.

"Tidwell, have you seen Lord Vaughan?" Beatrice asked.

The butler stepped forward. "I last saw him as he left this

room, miss. Perhaps he was going upstairs to change his clothing."

"Have him summoned. The gentlemen are going to go out to look for Miss Allen again."

"Very well, miss." He signaled to Charles and murmured something, and the footman left the room.

There was silence.

"Vaughan has the right idea," Rowland said. "We should change out of our wet attire if we are to go out again."

The gentlemen agreed to meet in the red saloon in a half hour and departed to change into dryer clothing. When they gathered again, though, Vaughan was still not to be found. Charles, the footman, raced into the room at that moment in an uncharacteristic fluster. He whispered and handed something to Tidwell, who paled.

"What is it?" Beatrice asked, clutching her hands together.

"Miss Copland, Charles says that he has been told by Cook that Lord Vaughan and Bobby went out over an hour ago, bent on searching for Miss Verity alone. He left this message." The butler handed the note to the companion.

She read it once through, and then looked up at the group who stared at her, eyes alike in the anxiety they held. "It reads, 'Weather better; I will find her and bring her home. Do not follow. I know what I am doing.' And that is all it says. It is signed, 'Vaughan.'"

"The fool," Chappell whispered, glancing anxiously out the window. "He thought the storm had stopped. If he were a Yorkshireman he would know that that lull only meant the storm was preparing to strike again, harder. More deadly."

It had remained starlit for only half an hour. As Bobby had predicted as they set out, the wind was howling again and the snow driven sideways, directly into their faces. The lantern sputtered wetly, and Vaughan was sure it was going to go out any minute. They had taken horses the first time, but there was no way any horse could make it through this wind and weather, not up moor. They were better on foot.

Bobby knew the way to the caves, he insisted. Vaughan was not going to take anyone when he left the house, but the boy would not be left behind, and simply followed the baron even when ordered back. So they were a team, clambering up the moor together through the knee-deep drifts of snow. A distance that should have only taken a half hour was going to take much longer.

And the boy was so small. He was wiry and smart, but small for his age. Vaughan looked back at him struggling. Bobby would never go back, not even if ordered. There was only one thing to do.

Above the howling wind, Vaughan shouted, "You're holding me back, boy. I would make much better time if you weren't so damned slow!"

His thin face twisted in a grimace, the stable hand planted his feet in a snowdrift and braced himself against the ferocity of the wind, which raced down the moor faster than a stallion could gallop and battered his small body. "I carn't go no faster, me lard. Carn't help it."

"Then go back, damn you, or I shall never find Verity! And I will blame you, see if I don't." It was hard, bitterly hard, to hurt the boy that way. He saw it in the way the lad's mouth twisted down.

And then a knowing light came into Bobby's gray eyes, squinted against the blustery gale. "You just be tryin' to pertect me!" he shouted.

Damn. Sternly, Vaughan glared at him. "Do not think me so damned noble; I am not. Just ask your precious Miss Allen when we find her. Nevertheless, my boy, no matter what you think, it is true. If I spend all my time worrying about you, then I shall not move as fast as I can alone. You can serve me best by taking back word to the others that I have crested the peak and am all right."

The boy stared at him for a moment, swaying in the wind, and then nodded sharply. "I be stubborn, me lard, but I be not an idiot. Yer right." He gave the baron directions, and then started back down the moor, helped by the wind. He stopped and looked back, though, before he had gotten more than a few paces. "Promise me, me lard, that you wull stop at the caves no matter if she be there or not."

"I'll promise you nothing, nodcock, but that I will not be foolish with my life."

And with that the boy had to be satisfied. He started off down the hill and Vaughan was able to go forward. The landscape was very similar to the night he had arrived, in much this same kind of storm. But now, with Bobby's guidance, he knew just where he was. And if Verity was in that cave, he would find her. It was a rather dim hope, but it was all he had to hold on to.

"M-Mr. Rowland," Silvia said, her teeth chattering together.

He drew her closer to the fire and seated her on a brocade sofa. "Come, my lady, you are chilled. Let me fetch you another shawl or a blanket." He pulled her merino shawl more tightly around her.

"I shall be all right. But . . . will Verity?" She watched his eyes, waiting for the censure she felt she deserved. As her new friend had wandered, getting caught in the blizzard, she had slept away the afternoon. But Mr. Rowland would tell her the truth; she was sure of it. If any part of the blame were hers, she felt he would help her see where her guilt lay. He had ever been gentle, but he was honest, too, and she valued that as much as any other single trait in a person. There was so little honesty in society.

"We must trust in our Maker, my lady, and keep Miss Allen in our thoughts and prayers this night."

She turned to him, staring deeply into his dark eyes. It had not escaped her attention that he had not really answered. Not one of them could say if she would be found alive. "I know you will tell me the truth, sir. I blame myself for this. If only I had said something earlier, or told

Lord Vaughan that she was taking his horse. If this is my fault I want to know."

Rowland smiled down at her and joined her on the sofa by the fire. He took her frigid hands in his and held them between his own, warming them. "There is no guilt in your actions," he said gently. "And this is not a time to be thinking such things, anyway. This night is about keeping our focus on Verity, and asking God to help Lord Vaughan in his search."

Her expression calmed, and he felt a surge of gratitude and humility. He could say it now to himself. He was in love with her. No matter how young or how unsuitable she seemed, he was in love. Nothing would ever come of it, for there were still the same obstacles in their way. He was a reverend of adequate but not brilliant birth. He had no connections, nor any money to make up for his humble birth.

She was the precious daughter of the Earl of Crofton. And though remarkably untouched and unaffected by her noble birth, she would still never be his. But he could give her comfort this night. And truth.

"Perhaps it would have been for the best if you had broken faith with her," he continued. "But it was not something you could ever have known. And I honor your friendship to her, and your desire to do the right thing by her."

"Thank you, Mr. Rowland," she said.

"All we can do this night is wait and pray." He slid his arm around her on the sofa and she moved into his embrace. He looked down at her, at the dark shadows under her eyes and the tears that trembled on her lashes. He would keep her from hurt if he could, but if that was impossible, he would be there to comfort her if tragedy struck.

Blast the snow! And blast the girl for wandering around in it like an idiot! Vaughan struggled through another drift, feeling his toes numb and his fingers become stiff. Damn and blast and hell!

He pushed through yet another drift—there were bare spots between the drifts, thank God, scoured so by the persistent wind—and saw a darkening ahead, like . . . like the mouth of a cave! Was that it? Was he close? He pushed on, knowing somewhere inside of himself that this was his last spurt of energy. No matter what he found in this cave, he would have to stop and rest, at least for a while. He carried blankets and food in a canvas sack slung over his back, and he might have to camp here for the night. If he didn't freeze to death first.

The wind battered him. It was the sound that amazed him most. He had never heard wind truly howl before. He struggled up to the darkened opening, but to his disappointment, it was merely a depression in the rocky outcropping that burst through the moor here and there. But now that he was here, was that not another darkened spot ahead?

Vaughan struggled on. Finally a cavern yawned ahead. He stumbled and fell forward, and struggled back to his feet, pushing on and finding the mouth of a dark cave ahead. His lantern sputtered and the flame dimmed. Blast! Was it going to go out?

He forced himself onward, into the cave, and walked up a rocky slope as the snow thinned and the wind abated in the protected depths. His boots slipped on the rock, but he surged forward, eager now for the protection of the cave almost as much as he was eager to find out if Verity was there. It seemed too much to hope for that she would be.

He raised the lantern, the sputtering having steadied now as the wind was no longer a factor, and saw something white floating in the darkness, and then . . .

"Who is it? Who is there?"

"Verity?" Vaughan shouted, unable to believe his own ears. Or eyes. There she was, limping forward, her ugly brown coat wrapped around her securely.

"Vaughan? Good God, I can't believe it is you! You are the last person I would have expected to find here."

Sweeping over him was wave after wave, first of relief,

then gratitude, then some indefinable emotion he had never really experienced before, with a final roiling breaker of fury. He put his lantern on the rocky floor, strode forward, grabbed her in his arms and shouted, "How could you have been such a blistering, blasted idiot as to go out in unfamiliar country on an unfamiliar mount in unpredictable weather?"

Then he lowered his face to hers and kissed her.

When he came up for air it was to find her glaring at him. "You needn't shout, you know! How is Bolt? Did anyone find him? Is he all right?" Then she wrapped her arms around his neck and kissed him back.

"He is all right, no thanks to you, you bacon-brained, caper-witted blubberhead." This time the kiss was softer, longer, and when he released her from it he was panting.

"You needn't be rude, you pompous ass," she said. And her kiss this time was no less passionate, but more knowledgeable, deeper, and full of yearning.

There was silence finally, as the kiss inevitably ended.

"Are you cold?" he asked.

"Not at all," she panted, gazing up at him in the dim light shed by the lantern. "Quite warm now, for some reason."

"Me, too. Let's go and sit down. You were limping, and I want to know why."

Chappell paced the library floor. Bobby had long since arrived back at the mansion and made his report. Vaughan, gallant idiot that he was, was close to the cave, and that was the last hope of finding Miss Allen before daybreak, they had decided as a group. But for Chappell that knowledge did not mean that he would be easy, nor that he would sleep.

It was Christmas. The hall clock was chiming the hour, and he decided he deserved a brandy, for it was all that would keep him warm this evening, he was convinced.

There was brandy in the red saloon, sure to be deserted at

this late hour. That was good because he was in no mood to meet anyone. He strode down the hall and opened the well-oiled door, finding that there was still a fire in the hearth and the brandy was on a side table near the fire. Might as well make himself comfortable there.

And then he heard weeping.

He quietly approached the hearth to find Beatrice slumped on the brocade sofa, her head in her arms over a cushion, her shoulders shaking with the sobs that racked her.

"Beatrice, what is wrong?" He sat on the sofa and pulled her into his arms.

She pulled away from him and scooted to the other end of the sofa.

He tried to ignore the pain that shot through him at her continued rejection. "What is it?" he asked again.

"That poor girl," Beatrice said, wiping her eyes with the back of her hand and sniffling. "Will she be found? Do you think she is all right?"

"She likely is. She is a clever and resourceful young lady; not at all the usual sort."

"You mean she is not heedless and flighty," Beatrice said, her voice dark with bitterness.

"Oh, she is heedless." He chuckled, but there was no mirth in the sound. "Aren't most young people? But it is a condition we recover from and go on to change if we are lucky and are given the chance."

"Yes, change," Beatrice said, staring into the flames. "Like I did."

David moved imperceptibly closer to her. It was the first reference she had voluntarily made to her own life. He moved closer still and tried to take her into his arms again, finding he needed that more than brandy.

She pushed at his arms. "I do not need comforting. I shall be all right."

"Perhaps it is comfort that I need," he said.

She gazed steadily at him, and then moved into his arms. He enclosed her, feeling a budding of hope swell and open, bursting into flower before he could quell it. He gained courage from that one simple movement. Something had changed with the night.

"Now," he said quietly, leaning back, holding her, "we must speak of something else, or we shall fret ourselves into illness. Tell me why you have gone around for a month with sadness in your beautiful eyes and a burden in your heart? I feel that it has something to do with me, and yet I do not know how that could be."

After a long pause she sighed. "All right," she said, gazing up at him with fathomless blue eyes, the reflection of flames dancing there.

She reached up and touched his hair, smoothing the silvered temples and touching the corners of his eyes. He felt her soft form cradled against him and knew that this night was somehow going to change everything.

"I suppose the time has come," she said softly, "to tell you everything."

Eighteen

Now that the moment had arrived, Beatrice felt a surge of courage. One way or another, her secret would be revealed. If he despised her, then it was how it must be.

She twisted away from him. She could not lay in his arms at her ease with the story she would tell. She must see his eyes. If they turned frosty . . .

But she would tell him no matter what.

"Long ago, when you were merely an aide in the government and Alexander was just born, do you remember a girl, a friend of your wife's by the name of Betty Gordon?"

He frowned and stared into the fire for a moment. "Mmm, yes. I think so. She was a flighty chit, all eyes and hair?"

Beatrice chuckled, but without humor. "Yes, she was flighty. And worse. She was vain, and silly, and obstinate. And her head was turned easily by praise."

Chappell's expression darkened. "Ah, yes, I do remember her."

Beatrice felt a chill steal through her heart. He remembered. She could see that he remembered why he had cause to despise Betty Gordon.

"Betty was flattered by the attention of Melanie Chappell, who was everything she was not: sophisticated, lovely, sought after. So when Melanie became her friend, it seemed too much happiness for one girl."

Beatrice went on, telling the story, for the moment, as if it was as it felt, that it had happened to another person.

They had become good friends, Melanie and Betty. They had a lot in common, though neither of them recognized it at the time. Melanie enjoyed the hero worship of the young, green girl, and Betty enjoyed the society into which Melanie introduced her.

Good company. *Fast* company.

Lord Oliphant's friends were high *ton* and very fast. He seemed to waver between the two girls, but settled on a flirtation with Melanie Chappell, the lovely—and lonely—young matron. With the experience of years, it was clear that Oliphant had chosen Melanie because, as a married woman, there was no danger of entrapment. The viscount was a wily fox, and had been close to a trap or two in his time.

He was a known rake and man-about-town, but he swore to Melanie that he was in love with her, desperately in love. She was the love of his life and he could not exist without her. And so they started an affair, though in public Betty allowed her name to be linked with his to throw the gossips off course.

And she did more. When Melanie asked her to lie for her, at first she was reluctant, but then she witnessed what should have been a private quarrel between Melanie and her husband, when he said things Betty thought were cruel. Though now, looking back, it was clear that it was a private argument; people often say things in the heat of the moment that are not kind. And he had plenty of provocation.

And so she did lie so that Melanie could sneak away and meet her lover-to-be. Just that once, Betty said. She allowed Melanie to tell her husband that she was staying overnight with Betty at her aunt's home. It worked, and Melanie raved about the lovemaking with her beau, telling Betty things an innocent girl should never have been told.

And then she asked again. Betty said no at first; it made her uneasy. But she was cajoled and flattered and wheedled into it again and again as December faded listlessly toward Christmas. Lord Oliphant's friends made a fuss over her, but she knew if she did not please Melanie and her beau, that company would be withdrawn and she would go back go being the nonentity she was before. That seemed a fate worse than death, by that time, to be cast back into the oblivion through which she had suffered for most of her one Season, her one shot at life in glamorous London.

But finally Melanie asked her something she was not willing to do. The young woman wanted to go to his lordship's country house for a week, and asked Betty to lie for her, to say they were going to visit her parents in the country. She said no. After all, David would know as soon as he saw Betty in town that it was not the truth. She couldn't hide away for a week, could she?

But Melanie kept plaguing her, wheedling her with the promise that when Betty's visit to her aunt finally came to an end, she could come to stay with Melanie in the new year.

Betty, silly girl that she was, was in the throes of infatuation. . . .But that had little to do with her decision really, and was not necessary to mention. In truth, she was beginning to realize that she must attract someone soon to marry, or she would be a spinster and would have to go home to her father's house, where penury threatened and life was dull.

Melanie had a lot more friends who would be flooding back into town in the spring, for the Season. Lots of eligible young men, and now that they were such good friends, she would be introduced to a whole new circle of people.

The lure was dangled in front of her, and it was irresistible.

Finally she said yes. She would do it. And so, by prearrangement, in front of David Chappell, she asked Melanie if she could please, *please* come down to Dorset with her to stay, just for a week.

Melanie turned to her husband.

"What about our son?" he asked.

"Alexander is too young to care if his mother goes for a week's visit. Am I to have no life of my own?" Melanie replied. Besides, he had his wet nurse and a nanny. What more could *she* do?

She could stay home and start acting like a proper wife and mother, Chappell said, pointedly and coldly.

And that was when Melanie flew into a rage the likes of which Betty had never seen. It clearly startled David Chappell, too, and by the end of it he would have agreed to anything just to calm her. And so Melanie won. She left the next day, Boxing Day, with her paramour.

It was an awful time for Betty, who began to understand more of what her friend was really like. Melanie Chappell did not really intend to end things with Oliphant; that was quite clear. And Betty would never be able to stay in the Chappell household. Not with Melanie the way she was.

Betty hid away in her aunt's house, but Oliphant's friends visited, and with sly hints it became obvious that they thought that she might be a highflier, too. Was she open to some fun?

It was degrading and horrible, and Betty was humiliated. When she rejected one of Oliphant's close friends, the gentleman said that if she was waiting for Oliphant, it would not be long. The viscount was going to have his fun with Melanie that week, but he would be releasing her after that. The "friend" expected to have his own go soon at Melanie Chappell, as Oliphant had promised to pass her on. And then the fellow made filthy suggestions that frightened Betty, sending her up to her room to hide from any more company. She longed to go back a few days, to release herself from the hideous jam she was in now.

And then two days after Boxing Day there was a pounding at the door. It frightened the maids, and Betty, afraid her aunt would have an apoplectic fit, raced to the door to answer it herself. It was David Chappell, drunk and demanding to know where his wife was. He had heard a wild tale of his wife, and a carriage accident up Northampton way, but had rejected it soundly, saying Melanie was at Dorset.

A carriage accident . . . Betty tried to sort out what the intoxicated man was saying, but he was ranting and raving,

making no sense whatever. At her door, in the confusion,
came another visitor, another one of Oliphant's friends. Not
one of the ones who had been so disgusting toward her, but
one of the few who were respectable. Betty had never noticed
him because he was a homely fellow, and she was very certain, in her youthful folly, that no one could love a homely
man.

White faced, the fellow delivered the message that yes,
there had been a terrible carriage accident, and Melanie
Chappell was dead. Oliphant was unharmed.

David Chappell, his worst fears realized, went quite mad
with grief. Drunk and angry, he railed at Betty, accused her
of all manner of things, some unjust. But some very accurate.

The simple truth was, if Betty had stood her ground and refused to lie for Melanie, David Chappell would not have lost
his wife and Alexander Chappell would not have lost his
mother. Betty Gordon never got over that guilt, and carried
the taint her whole life.

"Even to this day," Beatrice said, gazing steadily, sadly,
at David. He had not tried to take her in his arms again, and
she knew all hope of that was dead. She longed to reach
out and smooth the lines that creased the corners of his eyes
and smooth back the silver wings at his temples. She had
been so in love with him as a girl, so absolutely infatuated
with his good looks, charismatic manner, and intrinsic mag-
netism.

Meeting him twenty years later, she found she had not only
underestimated him, she had failed to see the deeper attributes he carried, his rectitude, his intelligence and kindness.
He was looking at her now, she realized, meeting his gaze as
calmly as she could. His eyes were searching.

"You are Betty Gordon," he said. It was not a question, but
a statement.

She nodded. "When I began looking for employment I
took my mother's maiden name, Copland. I was so ashamed
after that . . . that day. Poor Melanie! And poor you and
Alexander!" She covered her face. Even after twenty years it

still hurt. She took a deep breath and sat up straighter. "I went home, but it was only a couple of years later that my parents lost all their money and our home. I took a job as a governess at first, and that lasted another couple of years, but then . . . something happened, and I was . . . I was let go. By then both my parents were dead, and I lived alone for a time, on the money I had saved."

"But it was gone when you came up to Yorkshire for the job with Lady Bournaud," Chappell said, watching her face.

"Yes."

"In fact, it had been gone for some time," he said, hazarding a guess. His eyes never left her face. He was trying to trace in her eyes and on her face the silly, willful remnants of the girl he had known as Miss Betty Gordon. But try as he might, he could not recall what that child looked like, or her expression, nor even her voice.

She licked her lips and said, "Yes, it had been gone for a while. I was . . . unable to find another position until a kind relative sent my name to Lady Bournaud."

He waited. The dying embers in the fireplace burst into a last show of flames, crackling and dancing, the golden glow adding color to her pale skin. He reached out and touched her cheek, frowning when he saw her chin quiver. "How could you think yourself guilty for Melanie's misadventure?" His voice was barely audible in the quiet saloon.

"If it had not been for my weakness, she would not have been able to go with Oliphant. She would have had no excuse. And for all the times before, her—her infidelity—"

"Was not your fault," he said sternly, cupping her cheek and wiping the tear trail with his thumb. "Was not your fault," he repeated more quietly. "My dear, I understand so much more now about that time. Let me share it with you."

She nodded, closing her eyes against his gentle hand.

"I started as a lowly assistant to an assistant to a diplomat. And I was only acceptable in that position because I had gone to Cambridge, and I had only gone to Cambridge because of Lady Bournaud's kindness. I had much to repay, but it was not with money that my debt would be recompensed. I was driven to succeed."

It was a thrilling time, and he really should never have married, but Melanie had enchanted him, and it seemed that if he did not snatch her up, she would not—*could* not—wait. And so they had married before he really had time or money. And marriage and a child coming had driven him to work even harder.

But Melanie, young and frivolous, pretty and thoughtless, what had she known of ambition? At first she had been petulant at his frequent absences from home. Then wheedling, then whining, and then sulking. After the birth of Alexander her desire for his company had been at an end, and she had just cried all the time, hopelessly and helplessly.

"If only I had tried to be more understanding," he said, gazing absently down at his hand. He had taken Beatrice's in his and was threading his fingers between hers. "But I was impatient and hard. We turned away from each other in those months. I had my work still. But Melanie had nothing. I think when she looked at Alexander, poor babe, all she saw was the reason I had turned away from her. She didn't understand—and I didn't help her understand—that I thought I was doing the right thing for our family by working so hard."

"I remember," Beatrice said. "She called your job your mistress."

He nodded. "It might as well have been. And so, my dear, with or without you, the end would have been the same. She was lonely and hurt, and she turned to another man to give her what I could not. Oh, I may have blamed you at the time, but not for long, and not now. She would have found a way to be with Oliphant."

"But if I had not given her that excuse at that particular time, she would not have been in the carriage. . . ."

"Stop blaming yourself! There are a hundred and one variables that took her to that spot at that time. If Oliphant had not lived in Northampton, if I had not stopped fighting her about her departure, if, if, *if*!"

"You have forgiven Melanie?"

"Long ago. But only recently I forgave myself, for I carried that blame, too, for long years. A very wise woman told me that I was afraid to let go of the burden of guilt, for it kept me from loving again and risking that pain."

"A woman . . ."

"A woman who loved me," he said gently, but would not explain further. "Only since she has been gone have I understood what she meant. That was when I began the journey to forgiveness of my own part in that terrible tragedy. How much less responsibility did you, just a girl, bear in that awful accident? You were silly, you were frivolous, but you were blameless."

She sighed deeply. "I hope in time I come to believe that."

"Believe it," he said, stroking her hair. "You have clung to guilt for too long. Let go of it. Now, will you come back to my arms? I find comfort in holding you."

The present sadness came back to her then, and her breath caught in her throat. "David, do you think she is all right? Verity? I couldn't bear it if she is not. She is so full of life and love. . . ."

"She is a determined young woman used to surviving the elements. I have confidence in her abilities."

She turned her face up to his as he took her into his arms. The skin under his chin was soft, not taut as it had been in his youth. His hair was silvered and there were lines creasing his face, but he had never been more dear to her. The burden of her life seemed almost self-indulgent now. That guilt, that blame that she had carried around in her heart had been a way of insulating herself, she thought, against truly living, just as he said of himself. There had been men, good men, who had wanted to love her. But she had carried that blame as a taint and had rejected any tender feelings.

She reached up and stroked his hair, and when he gazed

down at her and lowered his mouth, she did not shy away.
The kiss lingered, gently, hovering at first just above her
lips, just on the borderline of touch. His breath caressed
her, then his whispered words, her name on his lips, over
and over.

And then the touch of his mouth, tender, giving comfort,
demanding nothing. She was helpless against the flood of
tears that coursed down her cheeks as he held her close and
kissed her lingeringly.

For David Chappell it was the last stage. His heart, rent almost in two at one time, had been healed over the years
except for one small open wound. But now it was knit together and whole, the pain finally and irrevocably gone.
Together, wound in each other's arms, they found blissful
peace and sleep. Tidwell, as he came to check the fire, found
them thus, and, old romantic that he was, tiptoed out of the
room and sternly admonished the rest of the staff that no one
was to disturb the red saloon that night.

The lantern had long ago gone out. After those first desperate kisses, cross words had separated them. They sat now,
in the absolute darkness, close but not touching.

"Just what did you think you were doing taking Bolt out in
that weather?" Vaughan said finally. His voice, tight and
angry, echoed in the stony depths of the cavern.

"It wasn't like that when I went out. Do you think I am an
idiot?" Verity, responding with equal vigor, sounded con-
temptuous even to herself.

"Yes!"

"Well, I am not!"

Silence again. Verity burned at the unfair accusation of
carelessness leveled against her, but a natural sense of justice
came to the fore, and she said, more quietly, "I am sorry for
taking Bolt out without your permission."

"I should think you would be sorry," Vaughan said, his
voice sounding huffy and pompous.

"Well, you needn't be an ass about it."

"I beg your pardon?"

"I said, you needn't be an ass about it!"

"I heard you the first time, I just cannot believe that any young lady would use a word like that!"

"I am not like the young ladies of your acquaintance."

"You could not be more right," he muttered.

She felt lonely in the dark, even though she could feel him, hear him breathe, just inches away from her. She shivered. Now she was feeling cold.

"Are you cold?"

"No!"

"Well, you do not need to snap at me about it."

"I am not." Miserably, she tucked her freezing hands under her arms and hugged herself. When he had first come, she had been experiencing a moment of terror so profound that seeing him had released the floodgates and she had practically thrown herself into his arms. Just what a conceited popinjay of a Bond Street fribble needed. He was just like all of the other men she had met in London during her disastrous Season. All buckram wadding and cotton wool for brains.

But he *had* come to get her. And that was after he knew Bolt was safe, so it wasn't for his horse's sake. Though she would not put it past him to come all this way through the ferocious storm just to rail at her about her insanity. Well, she had been insane. She admitted it to herself. She had broken the first and second rules her father had hammered into her brain as a child when she had wandered off alone and gotten lost.

Her papa had scolded her—out of love, she now knew—and told her that she must never go into unfamiliar territory without someone else as a companion, and second, she must never, *ever* forget to respect nature. She could have seen this storm coming. She should not have lost herself in that wood, wandering around like a dazed moonling with no sense of direction.

She sniffled, wiping her nose with her sleeve, glad now that the lantern was out.

"Are you crying?" His voice was hesitant.

"Of course not. I am not some sniveling coward afraid of the dark."

"I did not say you were. Why must you make everything a fight?"

"I don't do that . . . do I?"

"Yes. You are not a comfortable female to be around."

"I suppose Lady Silvia is!"

"As a matter of fact, yes. She listens to a gentleman when he speaks, doesn't interrupt him with a snowball to the head. And she makes a man feel that he could offer her some protection, or—"

"Good God, have you listened to yourself?" Verity hooted, her vigorous shout coming back to her again and again in the cave. "She doesn't want or need your protection, idiot. She doesn't give a fig about you. Can't you see she is mad for Rowland?"

"That dull dog?"

Verity laughed. "Not my taste, but there it is. She likes him."

There was silence for a moment, and then Vaughan said, "So you do not find the broody reverend to your liking?"

"Never did like the studious sort. Don't care much for books, unless they are about horses. Not one much for religion, either, though I agree it is all very well on a Sunday. Leaves you feeling peaceful and calm for the week. I don't often feel peaceful and calm."

She was startled to feel his leg against hers as he moved closer to her.

"Are you cold?" he asked again. "I only ask because I thought I felt you shivering."

Her instinct was to deny it, but instead, she surprised herself by saying, "I am a bit. I got awfully wet out there, and I can't seem to get warm, though I was when you first came."

"You mean when I did this?"

His lips were warm and firm, and his arm around her shoulders was strong and comforting. No buckram wadding there, she thought, as she felt that peculiar warmth start in her toes and work up.

"Yes," she sighed.

"I . . . I brought some food and a blanket. Don't know why I didn't think of that until this moment, but . . . well, got distracted."

"Food?"

He chuckled, a warm sound even in the frigid darkness. She thought that she could listen to that sound for a long time and not be tired of it.

They shared pork pie and cheese, with some bread, followed by some wine. It was a Christmas Eve feast as she had never before eaten. Then Vaughan unrolled the blanket and pulled it around Verity's shoulders.

"Vaughan, why did you come to get me?" she asked, in a small voice.

"Couldn't rest knowing you were out here alone, cold. Couldn't just go to sleep." His tone was gruff. He pulled her to his shoulder and said, "Why don't you close your eyes and try to catch a nap?"

She lifted her face and found the warm pulse point at the base of his neck and kissed it, feeling exceptionally bold in the darkness. His breathing was raspy, she noted, as her arms stole about his waist, her fingers creeping across his taut belly as she moved closer to him. This time, when his lips found hers, the kiss was different, longer, harder, leaving her breathless.

The next kiss lingered, and her whole body quivered when she felt him doing ticklish things with his tongue. Ticklish, but rather pleasant. Her hands found their way under his coat, and it seemed he must be as cold as she had been, for he was shivering, the muscles in his stomach quivering as she ran her fingers over them.

"Vaughan, we must find some way to keep warm," she said.

"I think I know of a way," he said, his voice gruff and his breath tickling her ear.

Every sense was heightened with the darkness, and she could feel the lightest touch of his lips on her ear. "Good," she said. "Wouldn't want to get chilled."

He slid off the rock onto the floor of the cavern and pulled her onto his lap, wrapping them both tightly in the heavy blanket. "Just trust me," he said. "I will keep you warm tonight."

"I trust you," she said.

Nineteen

Christmas morning, a time for miracles.

Sunlight peeking over the looming fells glinted off the icy crust of snow making it sparkle like a bed of diamonds.

But the household slept.

Beatrice stretched, and in the foggy haze between sleep and wakefulness, realized that something was . . . not precisely wrong, but different about this day. Christmas. Yes, it was Christmas, but there was something else. Another body, close to hers. A male body.

She opened her eyes to the sight of the ceiling of the red saloon, and as she turned her head, she realized that she was fully reclined on the brocade sofa with Sir David Chappell sprawled almost on top of her. He looked younger in sleep, his face relaxed into softness, no harsh lines or grim expression. She touched his face, the softened jawline blurred with whiskers, the slack mouth. This would be what she would see if she could have been so fortunate as to marry him.

Fruitless speculation. She laid her palm flat on his cheek and kissed his forehead, closing her eyes for just a second and letting the feel of the weight of his body imprint itself on her memory. From this Christmas season she would have this to remember. She shifted, and he groaned, pressing himself to her in ways that made her body flood with heat. Some instinctive part of her longed to press back, to shift and let him fully recline on her supine body.

And then the full force of memory flooded back to her. Verity Allen was missing, and Lord Vaughan, too. She pushed him gently aside and scrambled to her feet, staggering as one leg was numb. "David," she said softly, bending over him and touching his face.

His eyes opened and he smiled sleepily. "Thought that was a dream, you and me," he said, reaching up and pulling her down for a kiss.

She surrendered for just a moment, but then pulled away from him and stood, smoothing down her hair. "We have to find Verity," she said.

Fully awake, he launched himself to his feet and rubbed his jawline, the faint hint of whiskers a gray shadow on his chin. "You're right, of course, Beatrice. I shall summon the men."

"I want to go, too. I know these moors after ten years of living here."

"You can do no more than I can, my dear," he said, reaching out and caressing her face. "I was a child in these hills, and a child learns everything there is to know about the land."

And of course his good sense won the day. He would expend all of his energy worrying about how she was doing if she did accompany the men, and it would be for naught. With just murmured greetings of "Happy Christmas to you" and "All the joy of the day," Rowland and Chappell were soon in heavy coats, grimly going on a mission. Silvia and Beatrice accompanied them to the door, and they threw it open on the dazzling sight of snow that blanketed the hedges and bushes and trees with a glittering blanket.

As their eyes adjusted, though, they saw a much more welcome sight, one that caused such jubilation among them, such shouting and shrieking, that the bramblings flew up in a panicked rush from their berry foraging in the hawthorn.

Lord Vaughan, staggering slightly under his burden, carried Miss Verity Allen up the drive, finally making his way to the shoveled part of the limestone gravel.

* * *

Lady Bournaud, struggling against the exhaustion that threatened to overwhelm her after a night of terrors that she would never admit to anyone, the fear of a lifetime of recrimination over the death of her cousin's daughter, Verity Allen, was calmer than she would have thought possible. The news that Verity and Vaughan were home and in fine fettle had mended much of her discomfort.

Rowland had been with her and they had prayed together, thanking a beneficent Lord for the girl's safe return, but now she was summoning her strength for a meeting she had a feeling would be difficult. The tap at the door, then, was not a surprise.

"Come in."

Vaughan, handsome and cheerful, looking far too rested after a night spent in a dark, frigid cave—ah, for the resilience of youth, was Lady Bournaud's fleeting thought—entered. "Happy Christmas, my lady," he said, coming over to the bed and leaning down to kiss her proffered cheek.

"And to you," she said, indicating that he was to pull a chair close. "I assume you have breakfasted?"

"Yes, and bathed and shaved and changed."

"I thought I detected the scent of bay rum on your cheek. That was François's favorite, too."

Vaughan sat and crossed his legs, entirely at his ease.

"Where are the others?"

"Rowland went out to the chapel with Lady Silvia, and Chappell and Miss Copland are still at the breakfast table, looking rather rugged, I might add. Something going on there between them?"

"I most sincerely hope so. Now," she said, fixing her most stern expression on her face, "we are all extremely grateful for your heroic effort in saving Miss Allen's life last night and this morning."

He shrugged. "She would have been just fine," he admitted. "She was not only not frightened; I think she was rather enjoying her adventure. Once she knew Bolt had taken no harm, she was disgustingly cheerful."

"You sound like you admire her odd behavior."

"I do."

"Good. It makes what I am about to say more easy." She cleared her throat. "The fact remains that I am, at present, Verity's guardian. Though four-and-twenty, she is an unmarried young lady of good reputation. It is known, though, throughout the household that you and she spent the night together in a lonely cave with no chaperon."

He laughed out loud. "No chaperon! Suppose I should have made poor young Bobby struggle on, then."

"This is not the time for levity! Do you have any idea what I am getting at? I consider you, from this moment, honor bound and engaged to Miss Verity Allen."

"Do you now? And am I allowed no say in this?"

"Regrettably, no. I know what we had spoken of, and that Lady Silvia is much to be preferred over the Colonial chit, but there it is. You have inadvertently compromised her, and marriage is the solution. I owe it to the girl and to her mother."

"All right, then." Vaughan stood and bowed. "Shall we announce it at luncheon?"

Taken aback, Lady Bournaud gazed up at him, silent for a moment. "You mean you do not object?"

He shrugged. "Life with Verity will never be boring."

She squinted up at him. "Just what did take place in that dark cave last night?"

"If anything *had* happened d'you think I would say a word? I am a gentleman. As far as anyone will ever know we spent th'night chastely speaking of . . . flower arranging."

Lady Bournaud made a rude noise and waved her hand in dismissal. "Get out, rogue. If we are to make an announcement at luncheon I intend to be there."

He bowed. "My lady. I shall leave you to your ablutions. Just don't make yourself too beautiful or I shall have second thoughts about marriage to Verity."

"Devil," she said with a chuckle as he closed the door behind him. "Those two will lead each other a merry dance, I have no doubt."

Vaughan, whistling, plucked a holly sprig from one of the decorations on a side table and went in search of his bride-to-be. Verity would not have been his choice. She was as unlike the young ladies he had thought of as marriageable as . . . Well, he could not think of an adequate comparison. But the night had been interesting and had revealed to him things about her that would make marriage an endless voyage of discovery. He knew things about her now that she did not even know about herself, he would wager.

He opened doors around the great hall, looking in the red saloon, the music room, the gold saloon, and finally, the library, where he would least expect to find her. And there she was, looking out the window, the curtain drawn back with one hand. She heard the door and turned.

She looked very handsome, rigged out in her best dress, no doubt, a dull gold gown of simple lines and severe cut. It suited her as no frivolity in frothy lace ever would. He would delight in dressing her after they were married. And undressing her.

Especially that.

Keeping his mind firmly on the task at hand, he approached her, enjoying the glow in her blue-green, tantalizing eyes under dark arched eyebrows. She was beautiful really, though she needed some professional help with the cut and style of her hair.

"How are you recovering from our adventure?"

She shrugged and turned back to the window. "I am all right, I guess."

He sauntered across the floor, much less at his ease than he no doubt looked. When it came down to it, this was damnably difficult, being the one thing he had never done. He perched on the edge of the wide window ledge and looked up at Verity, trying to get used to the idea that this was the face he would see across from him each morning and under him each night. "Glad to hear it," he said. "That you have taken no harm."

"I am a tough bird," she said with a faint smile.

He reached up and tucked the holly behind her ear. "Now you are decked." How to do this? He took one of her hands in his and cleared his throat. Then he glanced out the window, the view being of the snowy garden. "Verity . . ."

She pulled her hand away. "I suppose we should go join the others. It is almost luncheon, and it is Christmas Day, after all. Aren't we supposed to be making merry, or something?"

"Verity, wait! We have to marry!"

It was not at all what he had intended to say, but at least it got her attention. She had been turning to go toward the door, but she stopped and turned back, gazing at him, her blue-green eyes wide. "What?"

"Lady Bournaud thinks . . ." No, that was not a good start. Damn, but this was difficult. "I think we had better get married, my dear."

"Why?"

Her bald question left him speechless for a moment. "Well, for one thing, I have compromised you." Again, not what he had intended to say, but if she insisted on acting unlike a normal young lady, then she would get an abnormal proposal.

"Compromised me?" she echoed.

"Yes." He stood, strode toward her, and took her hand. "Let me do this right. Every girl should have a proper proposal to remember." He knelt. "Miss Allen, would you do me the inestimable honor of agreeing to be my wife?"

She snatched her hand away. "No!"

"What?"

"I said 'no'!"

"Why?"

"Because I don't want to."

"Why?"

"Oh, for . . ." She made an impatient noise and left the room.

Vaughan stayed stupidly knelt on one knee in the dim library for a full minute before he recovered his wits. She had refused him. He ought to be happy. Ought to be doing a caper across the floor. The girl he had never intended to marry had refused him.

Instead, he felt like he had one Christmas morning at the age of eight, when a toy drum he had very much wanted had been snatched from his hand and broken in two by his irritated father. Bereft. All the joy of the day gone in one stroke.

He stood. But he would shake off that feeling. It was just that he had thought his future was settled, and had looked forward to getting on with things, and now he had to start all over to find a suitable wife. That had to be all it was.

Verity, shivering, bolted up to her room and locked herself in.

Coward. Coward! She paced, limping still, castigating herself for the cowardice that would not let her admit to herself that what she wanted most in the world was to accept his horrid proposal of marriage.

Or was that just her baser instincts longing to explore the revelations of the previous night? For Vaughan really had the most amazing way with his hands and his lips and tongue. It made her warm just to remember places his hands had been. She had not had to worry about being cold all night, that was for sure.

She slumped down on the bed. No, the one thing she had always been certain about was that she was not suited to marriage. Suffering the London Season had only stiffened that resolve. She never wanted to go back there, never wanted to suffer the humiliation of being the awkward girl on the sidelines, the one no one wanted to dance with. It was grim and horribly boring.

No, this being "compromised" was a welcome twist, really, if she could just look at it in that light. For now, if that was so and her reputation was really ruined, then she could go home, back to Canada. She took a deep, calming breath. Home.

She stood, patting down the gold skirts of her dress and putting up one hand to smooth her hair. And there was that holly sprig Vaughan had put there. She pulled it out and stared at it, touching the points of the glossy green leaves. She had done him a favor by rejecting him. He was even now likely rejoicing.

Sighing, she heard the butler ring the chime that meant luncheon was served, and she slowly exited her room and went down to the dining room. Everyone was gathered already, and eager, expectant faces greeted her. Lady Silvia, her sweet face wreathed in a smile, came toward her and surprised Verity by catching her to her bosom in a tight embrace.

"Congratulations, my dear friend! I am so happy for you!"

"What?" Verity stared stupidly around the room, her survey ending with Lady Bournaud's smiling face.

"I took the liberty of telling them your good news, child," she said from her position at the head of the table.

"Good news?"

Vaughan, just arrived at the doorway, said, with a sardonic grin, "Sorry folks. Should have waited, you know. Should've waited for the official word. The lady has said no."

"Verity looks miserable." Lady Silvia, under the guise of her cards, whispered across to Rowland.

He slanted a glance over to where the young lady in question was sitting, playing cards with Lady Bournaud, Mrs. Stoure, and Mr. Chappell. "How can you say that?" he asked, as Verity's voice rang out in a loud laugh.

She shook her head, her lips primmed into a firm line, and watched for a moment longer. "Look," she said. "Her knuckles are white, she is holding her cards so tightly. And her movements are jerky and inelegant. She keeps looking over to Vaughan, and he does not even seem to notice."

"My lady," Rowland said softly, "even if it is true, it is none of our affair."

"Well, it is just too bad of him, I say, not to marry her."

"She rejected him!"

"I can just imagine how the lout asked her. He is a very careless fellow, and for all his town polish does not seem to have the slightest idea what others are thinking or feeling."

"Ladies are unfathomable to most of us poor males," Rowland said. "And I think Miss Allen is every bit as inscrutable in her way as any lady. I pity Vaughan."

Lady Silvia threw down her cards with an exclamation of disgust, tossed Rowland an exasperated look, and walked over to join Beatrice.

What had he said? Rowland stared after her. Their fragile connection of the night before seemed to have evaporated. Troubled, he looked ahead to the days to come. He would be leaving very soon after Christmas. He wanted to visit his aunt Cordelia, and then in January he was to go to Loughton to take over his new parish duties. The challenges ahead had been all he thought of before coming to Yorkshire, but now they rarely entered his mind. It was not right, and if he was made of sterner stuff he would be able to conquer this ungovernable passion for Lady Silvia.

But now, when he did think of Loughton and the quaint cottage the parish provided for him, he saw it all with Lady Silvia in the picture, at the low stone fence, by the comfortable kitchen hearth, in the garden, in the attic bedro—his face flaming uncomfortably, he tried to rid himself of the sensual images that tortured him at night. It was not for her body that he had fallen in love with her, and yet just the touch of her slender fingers, or the merest brush of her form as she passed by, left him breathless.

He needed advice on how to rid himself of these inappropriate thoughts and feelings. But surely no one would understand. He was in the throes of a completely unbefitting infatuation. If he was at all Methodistic he would think the devil was tormenting him, but he subscribed to no such beliefs, and could only reason that lifelong abstinence from physical liaisons other men took for granted had left him vulnerable. He would prevail.

And Lady Silvia would find someone more suitable to wed. The thought stung, but he welcomed the pain as an antidote to his sensual desires.

The afternoon dwindled into evening, and dinner was served. Lady Bournaud, looking tired but calm, surveyed the company, her eyes lingering on each one. Things had not turned out at all as she had planned. Her own physical strength was less than she had calculated, and she had not been as interfering nor as intrusive as she had expected.

In the end she had decided that there was no way to prod people into relationships they had no taste for. Verity Allen, the silly chit, was passing up a match the likes of which many a London mother would swoon over. Vaughan was handsome, plump in the pocket, and not an unpleasing pup, certainly. And Verity was miserable. It was plain by her stiff manner and determined avoidance of Vaughan, who had a damnably sardonic expression fixed on his face.

And there had been no announcement from either Beatrice or Davey about the state of their dalliance. Was it love? Something had changed in the last twenty-four hours, but no one had thought to take a poor, ill old lady into their confidence. She almost snickered to herself. Should she play that card, the pity card? No. If there was something between them they would tell her soon.

Strangely, the most pleasure she had came from the one relationship that was not progressing. She had trusted to Mark's good sense, even though anyone with eyes could see Lady Silvia fancied him. But Mark knew his place. He would never overstep the bounds of good taste and propriety.

Pity they both looked so miserable.

This was not how folks should look at Christmas. She

clapped her hands. Everyone looked up from their meals, the last remove being all that was left.

"It has been a delightful Christmas season for me," she said without preamble. "I thank you all for making an old woman's last Christmas—"

There was an outbreak of voices, but she put up one hand. "I don't know the workings of fate, of course, but I just have a feeling. I won't say it again," she said, glancing over and seeing tears start in Beatrice's eyes. "You must know that death means something different to everyone, and to me it means joining François at long last. When my time comes, I will go willingly. But I did not start out to talk of things such as that. I was thanking you all for indulging me. And I was about to say that the Christmas pudding is all that remains of the feast."

Tidwell, trusting no one else with the burden, brought in the large pudding and waited a moment as a footman touched a lit taper to it. It blazed up, and the guests burst into applause.

"Thank you, Tidwell. As always, you have the instincts of a Haymarket stage manager. You and the other staff are now to consider yourselves on holiday. Make merry, but don't break the crockery."

He bowed and exited, and Beatrice, as prearranged, took over serving the pudding, slicing it neatly and passing a sauce boat with the rich hard sauce in it.

"Be careful of your teeth," she said. "As Cook has put in the traditional charms and, she assures me, a few more."

Beatrice took her own place, and each person dug into the spiced pudding, the rich sauce dripping down off forks and coating the dark treat to brandy-flavored excess. The first person to get a token was the reverend.

Rowland carefully removed the glinting piece from his portion and held it up. "Sixpence."

Vaughan snorted. "And are you likely to become rich at your chosen profession?"

"No," Rowland said, smiling. He put the sixpence to the

side of his plate. "I cannot imagine any eventuality that would bring me a fortune of any kind."

"Ow," Verity Allen cried, and picked from her mouth the silver thimble. "Well, that's appropriate, anyway," she said. "I am not likely to ever marry."

"Too prickly," Vaughan said. "Though what a thimble has to do with you and spinsterhood, I do not know. Unlikely female to take up stitchery!"

"Maybe she will go home and meet a handsome woodsman and marry and have ten children," Lady Silvia said, shooting Vaughan a look of dislike. "I know what the thimble is supposed to mean, but if she did, would she not be more likely to have to sew?"

There was general laughter.

Chappell said, "Lady Silvia, I do believe you have hit on a truth. In this case, perhaps we should be interpreting what the tokens might mean to our true history and future?"

"Not fair," Vaughan said. "Tradition, and all that, you know. Besides," he said, holding up a coin. "I got another sixpence. I prefer to think my next Derby wager is going to come in and land me the big payoff."

Beatrice gazed blankly down at her plate.

"Miss Copland, you are quiet," Chappell said. "What have you found?" When she didn't answer, he leaned over the table. "Ah," he said with a knowing grin, "you have gotten the ring. Does that not mean an imminent marriage?"

"So, Beatrice, are you going to be leaving me?" Lady Bournaud chuckled.

Mrs. Stoure, usually silent except when sitting with her friend, spoke up. "If she does, you know I shall bear you company, my lady."

Beatrice looked up. "What have the rest of you got?" she asked, her eyes bright.

"I, like Verity, have got a thimble," Lady Bournaud said. "Lord knows, I would not know what to do with a husband at my age, so this is an enormous relief."

There was general laughter, as it was discovered that Mrs.

Stoure had another of the plentiful sixpences. Finally Chappell said, "We have not heard from Lady Silvia yet. What have you got, my lady?"

The girl frowned. "How odd. I do not remember ever finding this in a pudding before. This must be one of Cook's innovations."

"What is it?" Verity said, leaning over and peering past the enormous silver epergnes.

Lady Silvia held up the pretty silver piece. "It is a cross." She glanced at Rowland and colored. "A silver and amber cross, as if off a necklace."

It was later, and the company was gathered in the red saloon. Lady Silvia had fashioned for each lady, as a gift, a holly hair ornament. She had not omitted even Mrs. Stoure, who looked regal at the piano, with a spray of holly tied with gold ribbon in her silver and black hair.

Lady Bournaud, comfortable near the fire with a new scarlet lap robe knit by Beatrice over her legs, watched the company with sleepy eyes. They played at silver loo for a while, but then Sir David rose and stretched his legs.

"I do not know about the young people, but that heavy meal has made me sleepy. Therefore I suggest we all . . . dance!"

Beatrice felt treacherous heat rise in her cheeks. He had said there would be dancing, and he would instigate it himself, clearly. She watched him lean over and speak to Mrs. Stoure at the piano, and set to work with the gentlemen rolling back the heavy carpet from the broad open space between the fire grouping and the instrument.

Any tensions among the company seemed to have evaporated with Sir David's determined good cheer, and Rowland and Vaughan laughed together as they huffed and puffed to get the heavy carpet pushed to one side far enough and the furnishings safely stowed.

Mrs. Stoure struck up a cheery Sir Roger de Coverley, and

Rowland grabbed Beatrice's hand and took her into the line as Vaughan took Lady Silvia and Chappell paired with Verity. More enthusiastic than skilled, half the company was very good and half very bad, but no one watching would have cared which was which. Lady Bournaud had awoken from a very brief nap with the sounds of the merriment and she clapped happily.

It was an inspiration, and Sir David, with all the diplomatic skill of his considerable career, steered the company through a country dance, a mazurka, and finally named a waltz as a good way to catch their breaths. Somehow, no one apart from Sir David seemed to know how, Vaughan and Verity were paired, Lady Silvia was on Rowland's arm, and Sir David claimed Beatrice, bowing to her deeply.

"I told you there would be dancing, and that you would owe me a waltz," he said, his eyes sparkling with light from the candelabra.

This was the moment, he thought. All his life had been moving toward this, the one perfect night. After her confession of the previous night, and then sleeping and awakening with her in the red saloon, Chappell had been thinking of little else. Was it truly meant to be?

But he was sure. Beatrice Copland, née Gordon, would be his wife. He took her in his arms and they swept around the floor. She was not too sure of the waltz, as during her only Season it had not been danced yet. And she had had precious little opportunity in all the years since for lighthearted enjoyment.

He would change all that; he would take her to London and she would sparkle, her wit, intelligence, and grace making him proud of his new wife a hundred times a day.

"Are you enjoying yourself?" he asked softly.

She glanced around the room, at the couples and the candles and Lady Bournaud smiling on them all. "I am," she said. "Thank you for your part in all of this."

"Young people must always want to dance," he said. "I remember when I was twenty . . . But we did not have such a marvelous invention as this waltz then, nor even when you made your bow."

"No."

He led her, as they whirled, to a quieter corner just beyond Lady Bournaud's seat. Beatrice looked up at him with a question in her eyes, but when they stopped twirling, he answered it by pulling her closer and kissing her gently.

"My dear, I do not think I can imagine going on, going back to London and to work and life, and leaving you here."

She said nothing, her eyes wide and sparkling in the dim light from a wall sconce.

"Beatrice, my dear, I cannot imagine any part of my life without you anymore. Will you do me the honor of becoming my wife?" He didn't wait for an answer, but lowered his face to hers and pressing her lips, tasting her with hunger surging through him. This was the moment he had been waiting for.

Twenty

Beatrice tore herself away from Chappell and stood staring at him, shaking her head. Then, without another word she raced away; he could hear her footsteps in the hall and then up the staircase.

"What in heaven's name is wrong with her, Davey?"

Lady Bournaud's forceful words brought him back to where he was, standing gape mouthed and staring off at the doorway. "I don't know."

"Well, go after her!"

Chappell strode from the room, through the chilly great hall, and up the stairs, but as he approached Beatrice's suite, close to Lady Bournaud's room, he slowed. Had he mistaken what was between them? Was the kissing and closeness of the previous night just the emotional detritus left over from a lifetime of guilt for her? He could not think it was so, but why would she run from him when he only wanted to be with her?

He lingered by her door. If he had expected to hear a storm of tears or wailing, he would have been disappointed. There was no sound at all, and perhaps she was not even within, but had retreated to some other part of the house. In the end he was puzzled and left her door without knocking. But he could not return to the red saloon. He strode off down the hall toward the library and liquid solace.

* * *

Lady Bournaud, noting Verity's pale, drawn face, called an end to the Christmas festivities. Besides, Silvia and Rowland were getting entirely too close for her liking, and there was no reason to let that happen now. Lady Silvia must leave for her home heart-whole so she could make an eligible marriage with someone of her own station. And she would not have Rowland hurt, not if she could help it.

She could send them all off to bed, but she could not control their movements once there.

Lady Silvia, unable to sleep, stole to her door and opened it, looking down the dimly lit hallway both ways. Satisfied that there was no one to see her, she slipped out and tiptoed down the chilly hall, pausing before one door. She put her ear closer to it.

Weeping. Hmm. She would have thought this was Miss Copland's door, but a woman of the companion's age would surely not be crying. She shook her head and tiptoed further, stopping by a door directly beside the servant's staircase.

This was it, she was sure of it. She tapped on the door. A muffled voice said either "come in" or "go away," she could not tell which, but chose to interpret it as a summons. She opened the door and quietly slipped in, closing it behind her securely.

The room was so dark! There was only one taper lit, and it guttered fitfully on the table by the gloomy tester bed. Hesitantly, Silvia took one step forward, and then another. There was a figure sprawled across the bed, but no movement.

Making her way across the room, she approached the bed and whispered, "Are you awake?"

"Mmm," was the only answer, but it was enough.

Silvia climbed up on the edge of the bed and tucked her toes underneath her snowy nightrail. "We have to talk. We must make a plan. Neither one of us is happy, but I hope at least one of us can find that elusive goal. It is within your own hands to reach out and grab happiness, you know."

"What the devil are you talking about?" Verity Allen rose from her prone position and stared at Silvia.

"I am talking about the future!"

"My future," Verity said, "is going home, to Canada. Spring shall see me on a boat leaving Bristol."

Silvia, her lips primmed into a straight line, tried hard not to laugh at the sight before her. Verity had not changed from her dress, nor had she altered her hair. So her holly crown was askew, leaning drunkenly over one ear, and auburn tresses stuck out at odd angles. Finally, giggling, Silvia said, "You look a sight. Here," she continued, her competent fingers pulling the holly from its tangled nest. "Let's make you at least a little respectable."

Verity waited, glancing up at her new friend who knelt over her, making her tidy. "What brought you down here?"

"Told you," the younger girl said through a mouthful of hairpins that she was removing from the Christmasy hair ornament. "Time to figure things out between us."

Verity was silent. When Silvia was done, she tossed the holly ornament onto the table and sat back down on the bed, curling her toes back up under her nightrail.

Seeing how cold she was, Verity pushed a blanket over to her and threw it around her shoulders. "Don't want you to freeze," she said gruffly.

"Time for confessions," Silvia said, staring at Verity. "How do you feel about Lord Vaughan?"

The other girl shrugged.

"He asked you to marry him and you said no."

"Didn't ask; commanded! And only because I had been compromised. Sounded dreadful, like I had been spoiled or disfigured. That he must nobly save me from a fate worse than death." Verity put one hand to her forehead in a languishing pose, like a Gothic heroine, and fell back on the bed.

Silvia giggled and pulled the blanket around her shoulders. "No, truly though. It is just us. You can be honest."

"Don't know how I feel," Verity said, still lying on her back and staring up at the lofty heights of the ancient tester bed. It was a monstrosity from hundreds of years before, dark wood and carved.

"Yes, you do," Silvia said impatiently. "How does he make you feel?"

Sighing, Verity pushed herself up onto her elbow and stared at Silvia. "I like him when he is nice to me. He came all the way out alone to find me, only to spend the first five minutes yelling at me about what a fool I was."

"He must have been terribly worried. He gave the other men the slip and went out alone. I think that is noble."

"Idiotic, really. Wouldn't he have kicked up a fuss if I had done the same thing!"

"What did you do all night? What did you talk about?"

Verity sat up. "Didn't talk *all* night. We kissed for a great deal of it, you know."

Silvia, astonished, stared wide-eyed at Verity. "You kissed all night?"

"Vaughan said it was just to keep warm, you know. Didn't mean anything on his side." She sighed. "Though it was mighty pleasant, I thought. Made me feel . . . tingly. Prickly."

"He told you it was just to keep warm? You idiot, why would it keep either of you warm if you didn't . . . if he wasn't . . . well, if you didn't feel something for each other? Dolt."

"Are you saying . . . ?"

"I am. Both of you idiots are in love with each other, and neither of you willing to admit it. Stubborn dolts!"

Verity shook her head. "No. He favors girls like you. Pretty. Sweet natured."

Silvia stared at the lovely young woman in front of her. "You are far more beautiful than I am. Striking. You'll age well, where I shall look like an apple doll when I am old, all pudgy and wrinkly."

"Doesn't matter anyway. Even if we did love each other, marrying him would mean staying in England, and, not to be offensive, I don't think I could stand that."

Silvia was silent.

"What about you? You fancy the reverend, don't you?"

Tears threatened, but Silvia would not end their lovely Christmas Day with weeping. She sniffed them back. "I think I have fallen in love, and you know, I meant to be so sensible about love. I thought I could control it."

"But he's mad about you, too. It is quite plain."

"Do you really think so? He is so reticent, and I can't really tell how he feels."

"It's obvious. He maybe just needs a shove in the right direction."

"No, he'll never ask me to marry him. Nor will he ever tells me how he feels, if he does love me. There is no hope for us, you see, and he is too honorable to lead me into a declaration of love when both of us know it can never be."

"But why?"

"Verity, you have been here long enough to know the answer to that." Silvia drew her knees up and laid her head on them.

"Money?"

"Wealth, yes, but position, too. Mark is not titled, nor does he have anything but his pay as vicar. He has made it clear that when he weds it will be to a suitably industrious young lady. A squire's daughter, or a merchant's daughter."

"That makes no sense at all, when you both are mad about each other. You've got pots of money; what's stopping you from living on that?"

"It is only my money at my father's discretion," Silvia explained patiently. "My father can provide or withhold my dowry. Besides, Mark would never be able to live like that, viewed as a fortune hunter. And I could never ask him to."

Silence fell in the gloomy room.

Silvia spoke again. "Funny, you know, if I had fallen in love with Lord Vaughan and you with Mark, things would have been so simple."

"I don't believe that," Verity said. "Seems to me nothing about this love stuff is ever simple."

Lady Bournaud's room was comparatively bright, lit with a dozen candles and a blaze in the hearth. She would not sleep for hours yet, she knew from long experience. She had napped during the evening, her need for sleep now, at eighty, limited to short bursts.

Her elderly maid was much the same, which was useful in the middle of the night when one needed a tisane or a chat. She tried not to abuse that, though, as Partridge was willing but sometimes not able to get up and down the stairs as she used to.

This time, though, it had been a message the woman carried, and that just down the hall. A summons, really, not a message. There was a tap on the door, and Sir David entered without waiting for an answer.

"There you are, my boy," she said affectionately. Davey was the closest thing she had ever had to a child of her own, and she loved him dearly, thinking he was the brightest, the best, the smartest. Almost deserving of her darling Beatrice.

He kissed her cheek and sat on the edge of the bed, taking her hand in his.

"You're not dressed for bed yet," she said.

"I was working. I brought papers with me and more came by post. The business of our country never rests, my lady."

"Well, it is in good hands," she said, looking down at theirs, linked.

"You do me too much credit. I am still just a minor bureaucrat in a complex web."

"And that is why you were given a knighthood," she said with a scoffing tone.

"That year they were giving out knighthoods like sugarplums, my lady."

"You are too modest. But I did not call you here for idle chat. Did you find Beatrice?"

He frowned down at their linked hands. "I did not look for her."

"Why not?"

He sighed. "Much has happened between us that you do not know about, but suffice it to say, if she does not wish to marry me after what we have been to each other, then there is nothing further to say. I am too old to beg."

"Goose."

"Her or me?" he said, startled.

"Both of you. Plain as day you are meant to be together. Reason I tricked you into coming up here."

"I ought to be very angry with you about that, but I am not. Curiously enough, it has helped me make peace with the past. And I hope it has done the same for Beatrice."

"What do you mean?"

Chappell felt sure that Beatrice's story was safe with Lady Bournaud, and that it would help the old girl understand her reticent companion, even if nothing further ever happened between him and her. And so he explained everything.

"Poor girl," Lady Bournaud muttered, tears in her rheumy eyes. "I never knew. Strange the workings of fate. An elderly relative of your father's was how I first heard about Beatrice; I think I told you about that. I suppose that is how she met you those long-ago years in London; you and Melanie were on her list as contacts in the great city."

"Ah, yes, I had forgotten about that."

"But why? Why is she so guilt ridden?"

Chappell stared off at the hearth. "I have been thinking of it all day. You know her better than I. Does she not expect rather a lot of herself?"

"Always. Everything she does must be perfect, you know. Unfailingly kind to the staff. They answer to her now, not me, which suits both of us. One of the reasons, given your diplomatic position, I thought she would make you the ideal wife."

"Given all that, her past failure must loom like the great

blight of her life. It has likely affected everything since, made her this pursuer of perfection. All of that has changed in one night. It is a lot to take in."

"Do you love her?"

Chappell smiled down at his benefactress. "Cupid. Yes, I have fallen in love with her. But there is time. She is going nowhere."

"Good God, you are not twenty, you know!" Lady Bournaud struggled to sit up. "Don't let her push you away. She is just frightened. She has never been married, never had a beau, even since that long-ago Season. Her feelings are likely alarming in their intensity, for I have seen in her eyes that she loves you. It is an adjustment to begin to think of herself as a lover and wife, rather than colorless companion."

"Do you really think so?"

"Yes! I refused François the first time he asked me, you know. Scared to death, I was. Go to her. Find her tonight!"

"No, I am not going to burst into her bedchamber at one in the morning like some Gothic hero." He stood and kissed her hand. Her eyelids were heavy, and he blew out some of the candles, leaving only one to sputter, protected by a silver tray.

"Do what is right, Davey," she said. "Everything will work out."

The night sky was blanketed by brilliant stars scattered across the deep indigo. The air was so cold and still that every noise was sharp and crisp. Beatrice, cloaked heavily, made her way down the path, a stream of moonlight glistening on the snow ahead of her. Sleep was not coming this night. She felt like she would never sleep again.

Marriage. How could she even consider it? Melanie had been her friend, and David Melanie's husband. As a girl she had loved him before she should have, and she loved him still, but did she deserve to find happiness, even now, when she was beginning to believe that David was right and she had been too harsh on herself?

And yet marriage to David would bring her such great happiness.

Ah, and there it was. She was afraid of that. She had never dwelt in that state before and did not know what to expect. She had found peace, even contentment in service to Lady Bournaud, but happiness was another animal, she thought. Would happiness, so long deferred, last, or would it fade? She could not stand it if she found such joy, only to feel it slipping away from her again. Would she be doing him a disservice by marrying him? Was her duty, after such great kindness as she had known, with Lady Bournaud?

Her footsteps squeaked in the snow, crunching through the crusty ice in places where the snow was unbroken. The chapel was silent, the square Norman tower a blot against the starlit sky. She approached the building and pushed the huge oak doors open, surprised to see the altar at the end flanked by lit candles. A figure knelt by the altar, and she knew instantly who to expect. She was about to turn and exit, but he heard the door and stood, turning and smiling in the gloom.

"Please, Miss Copland, come in. Do not let me keep you from this awe-inspiring place by my presence. On this of all nights it is a wonderful place of peace." The young vicar's voice echoed in the sepulchral gloom, words lingering in the air like frost crystals.

She hesitated, but then started up the long aisle. "I have always loved this place above all. It seems to hold the history of this land in the very stone of its walls." The reverend, she noted, had placed an altar cloth on the altar, but he had not donned vestments.

He gazed up at the vaulted ceiling. "It makes me think of all the services that took place here, all the weddings and funeral services, communions, baptisms, christenings. All the pageantry of human life. Maybe one day it will be a living church again."

"It is possible. The St. Eustaces, who will inherit someday, have shown some interest in the chapel on their visits here." She stopped just short of the altar. "You spoke of this as a place of peace. Did you feel in need of that peace?" She moved forward and sat in a pew.

He looked troubled and glanced away. "This should be the happiest time of my life. I have the great good fortune of my own parish in the new year. Some men wait many more years than I. And yet . . ."

Beatrice felt a great sadness. She had thought that between two such young people as Lady Silvia and Mr. Rowland, both chaste and good, kind and admirable in spirit and behavior, that something would occur to bring them together, but it seemed that the world would intrude and make their love impossible. Lady Bournaud had been right in hoping that they did not fall in love.

"You will be happy again," she said, hoping her words were not as hollow as they sounded.

"Perhaps. And if not, happiness is not the only reason we live. But what about you, Miss Copland? Did you come here for peace? Do you need time alone?"

"No, I don't think my peace is to be found here. I have never thought that one building held the answers."

"True. Answers come from the heart."

She gazed at his handsome face, his cheeks red from the long, cold hours already spent in the chapel. "How odd for a vicar to say that. Are the answers not from above, then?"

"We were given hearts and minds to reason and trust and ponder."

"Then is there no hope of finding an answer outside of myself?"

"You are troubled in spirit," Rowland said. He took a seat in the pew across the aisle. He leaned on his knees and clasped his hands together, rubbing them for warmth. "I should not have made it seem that I do not believe in divine guidance. I am not sure where answers come from, but I do believe that if you ask for guidance it will come, whether it is from your own heart or the spirit world. Just ask. Whether you call it prayer or contemplation, you will find it in the stillness of your soul. And maybe a sign will come."

"Thank you, Mr. Rowland. I think perhaps you are right." She rose, pulling her cloak around her tightly. "My advice to you is to take your own advice. I hope you find your answers."

He smiled sadly. "I am not looking for answers. Unfortunately, I know the answers to my own problems. I am just finding the struggle to accept them long and difficult."

She was silent for a moment, but she could see he would say no more. "Good night, Mr. Rowland. Do not stay out here too long or you will get a chill."

Morning broke, sunlight glimmering, shimmering into Beatrice's room. She awoke refreshed, as if she had had eight hours sleep instead of just four or five. Stretching, her hand brushed the table at her bedside and something fell onto the bare floor, tap tap tapping as it bounced and rolled.

Rolled?

She jumped out of bed, feet freezing on the icy floor, and got down on her hands and knees, looking under the edge of her bed. Something glowed, faintly, against the wood floor. She scooped it toward her and jumped back up on the bed, holding her hand flat.

A ring.

Not just any ring, she found, peering closely at it. She turned it over and over, knowing what ring it was, but unwilling to believe it. She set it aside and got dressed.

Breakfast was casual. Only Cook was working, and one girl from the village. It was Boxing Day, a day for the servants, and it was strictly observed in the Bournaud household.

When David Chappell did not join the others at breakfast, Beatrice went in search of him and found him in the library, poring over papers on the desk, his glasses down on the end of his nose.

She closed the door behind her, holding one hand behind her back. He looked up, and his smile was warm when he saw her.

"Beatrice. How good to see you."

"Am I interrupting?" Her voice sounded giddy and breathless.

"It is a welcome interruption." He set aside his glasses and sat back.

She circled the desk, and he frowned, sensing something, perhaps.

"What do you have behind your back?"

"Something I found this morning." She held her hand out flat, and the gold circlet rested in the hollow of her palm.

He picked it up and looked it over, his expression blank at first, and then changing, his crystal-blue eyes widening.

"Do you recognize it?" she asked.

"I . . . it looks like . . ." He put his glasses back on and turned it to read the inside inscription. "It is! It is the ring I gave Melanie! How did you get it?"

Beatrice took it back, holding it up to the light. It was a simple gold band with a blue stone inset. "I didn't know that before," she said softly. "I should have known, I suppose. Why did she give it to me? It was a token of friendship, she said; she gave it to me the night she first . . . her first liaison with Oliphant. When I gave her her first alibi." She glanced at David's face, but there was no pained expression.

"I never knew where it was. When her body was brought back to bury, it was not on her finger," he said. "I thought it was lost or stolen."

"The inscription reads 'To My Only Love.' I didn't see that at first, and then I never knew what it meant, who the ring originally belonged to." Beatrice held it back out to him.

He didn't take it. He set aside his glasses again and looked into her eyes. "I don't want it. You may as well keep it, for she gave it to you."

Beatrice bit her lip. "David," she said, her voice shaking. She sank to her knees in front of him, and he, concerned, took her quivering hands between his, the ring enclosed in their four hands. "When I awoke this morning it was on the table beside my bed."

He was silent, waiting for more.

"It wasn't there when I went to sleep, David. And I did not go to sleep until, oh, after two this morning. Until after I visited the chapel and Mr. Rowland advised me to ask for guidance. What to do. About you."

"I don't believe in signs, my dear," he said gently, pulling her up and cradling her on his lap.

She looked down into his eyes. "I didn't expect a tangible sign, though, you see, just some knowledge in my heart. I . . . I love you."

"Beatrice!" He pulled her face down and kissed her mouth, gently, lingering over the kiss.

"But I was afraid. And unsure. And so I just asked for a sign. From above, from my own heart, from anywhere. I just want to know that I am not fooling myself with what I want so badly to do. I want to know it is right."

"And now?"

She watched his face. He didn't look overjoyed, and she moved to stand, but he held her waist.

"Don't go. I just . . . Beatrice, I do not believe in signs, and if you needed this . . ."

"It says 'To My Only Love.'" She held out the ring.

"I thought she was that," he said simply. "I was wrong."

She sighed. "That, you see, was what I was worried about, and didn't even know it. I was afraid that being older, we were both just grasping for happiness. That your only happiness had died with Melanie, and I was just a poor substitute."

"Never, my darling girl. I did not know what love was at

twenty-seven. I cared for Melanie, but if we had stayed married our love would have dwindled into bickering and coldness. I love you for who you are now, not for the silly girl you were, or the mistakes you made then. I love you now! Did I not say that last night? Did I not tell you how much you mean to me?"

She shook her head shyly.

"Dunderhead that I am. Likely why you, half asleep, took the ring from your jewel box last night and left it on your side table. You were worrying on it."

She ignored, for now, his assertion that she had done it herself. "So you did not put it on my side table?"

"Good God, how could I when I did not even know you had it? I had forgotten its existence before you showed it to me just now."

"True."

"Forget about it, my love," he said, pulling her down to nestle on his lap, her head in the curve of his neck. "May I ask you again now? And will you promise not to run away?"

"I promise."

"Miss Beatrice Copland, the only woman I have ever truly loved and ever will, will you marry me?"

A ray of sunshine touched the ring on the desk. A sign? Or just coincidence? Did it matter?

"I will marry you," she sighed.

After a suitable length of time, David murmured, "I suppose we ought to go tell the woman who planned all this."

"Mhmm," Beatrice whispered. She sat up. "I was so horrified when I figured out why she had invited you."

They stood together and started toward the library door. "You knew she was matchmaking?"

"I did finally. I was mortified. But it was so good to see you again. When you didn't recognize me, I thought we could get through the holidays and everything would be all right. But I didn't count on falling in love with you all over again."

Oh dear. Too late.

"All over again?" He stopped her and turned her around to face him before they could leave the library.

Her face flaming, she moved closer to him. "Oh, forget I said that."

"No. What did you mean?"

She reached up and touched his cheek. "I was wildly, unsuitably in love with you twenty years ago. That was partly why I felt so guilty over the whole affair. I felt like I had had some unconscious affect on events, just through my . . . my infatuation."

"My sweet Beatrice," he murmured. He pulled her close and held her to his heart. "I never knew."

"But I love you now for who you are *now*, not for who you were then."

"Good, because I am a much nicer fellow now."

"M-Hmm, yes. And even handsomer."

Twenty-one

Burning all night over Verity's refusal of his generous marriage proposal, Vaughan stalked out the garden door and down the long path toward the stable. He was going to get to the bottom of the whole affair. No girl who kissed like she did should stay unmarried. Silly Colonial chit. Did she think she was going to get a better offer? Not bloody likely.

He stomped into the dim confines of the stable and stamped the snow off his boots. Lady Silvia had implied that Verity was likely to be found in the stable at this time of day, and he was not going to wait any longer for her pleasure. He heard a murmuring, and moved toward it, finding it was coming from the stall where Bolt was kept.

He leaned against the doorway and watched. When she came around from the other side of the horse, curry comb in hand, she jumped, startled at his appearance. Bolt whinnied and stamped.

"There, boy," she said. Then she turned on Vaughan. "What do you mean, sneaking up on me like that?" she whispered, her cheeks pink with fury. She took a deep breath as Bolt shifted nervously. "Do you not know that horses, especially this one, are high-strung creatures? Need calm."

"Seems to me you care for his comfort much more than mine," he said, crossing his arms.

"You are right."

"You are engaged to me. Shouldn't be avoiding me."

"We are not engaged."

"We are," he said stubbornly. "Won't have it said that a Vaughan ran out on his responsibilities."

Her knuckles whitened on the comb, but she maintained her even stroking motion. "I am not your responsibility."

"But you are! You have been compromised and I should marry you!" Frustration boiled through his veins. He strode forward and jerked her hand away from the horse. Bolt shied, and Verity struck out at Vaughan and then stalked from the stable.

"Get away from me," she cried when he followed her.

His fists clenched, he watched in horror as tears came to her eyes. He hadn't meant to make her cry, hadn't wanted . . . He faced the awful truth. He had fallen in love with this idiot, but she didn't love him in return. But still she must marry him for her own sake. Had he known even when he sent Bobby back that she would be hopelessly compromised, and that marriage would be the only remedy?

Didn't matter. The only thing that mattered was that she see what must be, and that he would do his damnedest to make her happy. But how did one say that? What would do the trick?

Tears rolled down her pale cheeks.

"Damn it, Verity. What is wrong with you?" Hurt and rage boiled up. "Why don't you want to marry me? Don't you like me? Can't you love me, just a little?"

"I do like you," she cried, standing with her own fists clenched. Bolt stamped uneasily in his stall. "I like you more than you deserve, you pompous ass! I love you!"

"Then why the hell won't you marry me?"

"Augh!" She turned and stomped away, then whirled on her heel and strode back to face him again. "Because, you chucklehead, oddly enough, I want my husband to *love me back*!"

She whirled once again to flounce away, but he grabbed her arm and pulled her to him. He pinned her against the stall wall, as Bolt snorted and whinnied, and kissed her hard, with all the newly discovered emotion in his heart. "There, you maddening vixen," he said fiercely, releasing her. He stepped away, his whole body shaking. "I love you.

All right? I love you to distraction. It is driving me mad! All I want is for you to marry me. I'll do anything, go anywhere. Just marry me!"

"Blithering idiot! Why didn't you say so?" She whirled him around and pinned him against the stall, kissing him with a ferocity that equaled his own.

And then there was silence in the stall for a while. Bolt settled down finally, his nerves soothed by the murmuring and cooing coming from the other side of his stall wall.

Until the peace was shattered by an exclamation and Bobby's loud whistle. The boy capered off as the two scrambled to their feet, red faced.

"I think we had better go in and make the announcement, or you will be worse than compromised," Vaughan panted.

And for once Verity agreed with him.

And so there were two engagements to celebrate in the Bournaud household. The new year rolled in with most of the household merrily looking forward to new lives, new loves.

And then it was the day for some to leave.

"It is Epiphany," Beatrice said, clinging to David as they walked in the snowy garden during a mild spell.

"Would you like to marry here? In the chapel?"

"No," she said, looking up at him. "Lady Bournaud could never make it out there, and I want her to be comfortable. Do you object to marrying in the red saloon?"

"Of course not. It was where I first proposed, after all."

She chuckled. "And I ran away. I was so frightened." She leaned her cheek on his shoulder as they walked. "I hope my lady will be all right. I hate to leave her, and yet I cannot possibly stay here. I know that."

"No. My work is in London. Parliament will be back soon, and I have a lot of work to tie up before then. But she wants this for you; you know that. She planned it, after all."

"I know. And she has Mrs. Stoure now. I'm glad of that."

"And we will come up as often as possible. Maybe we can

even spend the summer up here. I would like to see that a proper memorial is put up over my father's grave. What do you think of that?"

"I would like that, David."

They rounded the corner to see the carriage being brought up to the door.

"Gracious," Beatrice said. "Vaughan is eager. I suppose he and Verity are ready to go."

Verity was accompanying Vaughan, in the company of a suitable chaperon, of course, to his parents' home. She was to be presented and the wedding planned. Beatrice and David went in through the front doors to find the hall a mass of confusion. Lady Bournaud, from her Bath chair, was directing things.

"No, Charles, Miss Allen will want that bag inside with her. It is the other bag that is to go on top with Lord Vaughan's things."

Vaughan, his face wreathed with smiles, strode into the hall and leaned down to peck Lady Bournaud on the cheek.

"Where is your bride-to-be, you rascal? Do not tell me that you two have quarreled and she is not coming?"

It was a joke about the volatile relationship the two shared, but their bickering had changed to teasing, now, and barbed words were accompanied by loving looks. It was not how Beatrice would like her marriage to be, but Verity seemed thrilled, and the pointed exchanges were always followed by whispers and laughter.

"No, she is upstairs with Silvia, saying good-bye."

"I see." Lady Bournaud's face betrayed her sadness over her one failure, and the ensuing heartache that was evident in the doomed love between the vicar and the earl's daughter. "Let them have their time," she said. "I am happy they have become such fast friends."

Upstairs, in Verity's gloomy room, even gloomier now that her cheerful scatter of cloak and boots and bonnets was not strewn over it, she looked around one last time. "I hope I haven't forgotten anything."

"If you have, I'll bring it with me. My home is not so far from Lord Vaughan's."

"Good," Verity said brightly. "Maybe you can visit me. I shall need a friend with only Vaughan's family around me."

"I am coming to the wedding, goose," Silvia said, stepping closer to her friend. She looked Verity over. There was no way to make the girl smart-looking with that awful coat and bonnet, but the radiance on her face more than made up for her attire. Silvia hoped Lord Norcross and his viscountess, Vaughan's parents, could look beyond her attire and into her heart, for there was no woman in the world who would make their son a better wife.

"I'm glad you are. I'll miss you."

The two girls hugged.

"I'll miss you too," Silvia whispered.

"Sil, I wish you, and Rowland—"

Silvia put up her hand. "Verity, please. There is no use. Mark and I . . . There is just no use. We have talked about it indirectly, circling around the issue. He is right, and I know he is. My father would disown me if I defied him to marry a humble vicar; Mark doesn't care about the money, but he would be horribly upset if I could not see my family anymore. He knows how much they mean to me."

"But you love him. And he loves you. Should be man enough to kidnap you or something," Verity said gloomily.

Silvia smiled, but her eyes were sad. "I understand him. He loves me too much to wrench me away from my family." She herded Verity toward the door. "You have to go, my dear friend. Vaughan will never forgive you if you make the cattle wait."

"I wouldn't forgive myself," Verity joked.

Down at the door, Verity hugged Lady Bournaud, then, in turn, Sir David and Beatrice. At the carriage, Rowland and Silvia, after tearful hugs and promises to write, stood and waved good-bye as Vaughan, Verity, and the dreaded chaperon rode off, with Bolt tethered to the back.

"My parents' carriage arrived yesterday. I am expected to leave today," Silvia said.

Rowland pulled her shawl around her shoulders and gazed down at her. Sadness threatened to overwhelm him, but he would not give way to it. "I do not think I shall be able to go to Verity and Vaughan's wedding, but he has promised to write me about it. He will let me know how you go along. He's a decent fellow, though I didn't much care for him at first."

"You mean when you were trying to push us together?" Silvia's voice was soft.

Rowland smiled. "Yes, my dear, when I was trying to push you together. Even then I suppose I knew he was a decent chap. Not good enough for you, but then no one is."

"You are."

"Silvia." It was a warning. Rowland took in a deep breath and let it out slowly.

"But I love you. I will always love you." Her voice was thick.

"Oh, my dear, and I—" He stopped. "I mustn't say it. It is wrong."

"You don't love me like I love you," Silvia cried, wrapping her arms around herself. "You can't, or you would fight for me! Elope with me, or . . . or something!"

Rowland took her by the shoulders and looked into her tearful eyes. He swallowed, and his lips worked as he fought to control himself. "I love you with every particle of my being," he said, his voice low and fierce. "Too much; I love you with parts of my heart that ought to be devoted to higher purposes, but even there, love for you has crept in. You are my waking and my sleeping, my dream and my purpose. If I can ever . . . But I cannot ask you to wait. Don't you see? I am not ambitious. I shall never be Bishop, nor anything grand. Or at least not for years and years. And you have told me enough that I know if we married without his consent, your father would cut you off from your family, from your brothers and sisters, your nieces and nephews . . . your mother. I know you too well to think that you would ever despise me for it, but I would hate myself. And I couldn't live with the pain of knowing the sorrow I had brought you."

"And I could not live with knowing I had caused *you* such pain, even inadvertently." She fell silent, but then gazed up at him again. "So this is good-bye," she said, unshed tears glimmering in her brown eyes.

He took her in his arms and held her close. "This is good-bye."

Inside, Beatrice stood in the window and watched, tears streaming down her cheeks.

Epilogue

Beatrice glanced at the date on the letter in her hands, trying to see past the tears that misted her eyes occasionally. "My love, I think this means that Mr. Rowland will be here today. He says that he is starting immediately and is taking the coach, so he should be here any time, do you not agree?"

David Chappell put one hand on his wife's shoulder and squeezed as he read the vicar's letter over her shoulder. They were in the library of Chateau Bournaud where almost a year before they had confessed their mutual love. It had been a year of change and happiness, and also great sadness.

The glorious Yorkshire summer had been spent here, with Chappell overseeing the placement of a suitable memorial to his father, and Beatrice spending time with her old friend and former employer. But she had known there would not be another Christmas for Lady Bournaud, and so the word that she was fading fast, when it reached them in London just the week before, had sent them scurrying north.

They had been in time. Lady Bournaud was still conscious, and when she did pass from the earthly realm to the next, it was holding Beatrice's hand and watched over by her beloved "Davey."

Deeply wounded by the passing of a woman who had become a second mother to her, Beatrice found consolation in her husband's arms. Together they found that an abiding love is a port in any storm and a safe harbor against life's turbulence. Following her ladyship's last instructions, they had sent out immediately a summons to all of the house-guests who were there the Christmas before, to return to Yorkshire.

Lord and Lady Vaughan were already there, having arrived that very morning, and Rowland and Lady Silvia were expected anytime. Mournful though the purpose was, Beatrice still looked forward to seeing them all one more time.

Rowland had spent the journey remembering his friend, Lady Bournaud. The letter from Lady Chappell, as the former Beatrice Copland must now be styled, had said only that Lady Bournaud's last wish was that he should preside over her interment. He supposed it was fitting, for the ceremony would take place in his beloved chapel on the Bournaud grounds.

It had been a year of discovery for him. He had taken up his preferment in Loughton, and tried to content himself with his duties and his plans. But thoughts of Lady Silvia were never far from his mind.

The party gathered at the chateau was the same as the year before, he found to his amazement, and yet what changes had taken place! Lady Vaughan, Verity to those who knew her best, was still vigorous and energetic, but she displayed a new confidence in herself and was dressed in elegant attire, selected almost entirely by her proud husband who seemed to love her more after six months of marriage than he had before it.

Sir David and Lady Chappell greeted him as an old friend, and after he was settled in his room, the same one as the previous year, he joined them in the red saloon.

To find that Lady Silvia was also there.

His heart thudded, but he maintained, or thought he did, his composure. She was as lovely as ever, but paler, more ethereal. Verity was arm in arm with her, and Silvia sagged against her, held up only by the strength of her friend. Pain seared his heart, and yet he did not regret his decision. There was no other choice for them, no way to be together *and* be happy. To wed her would be to tear her away from the bosom of her family, to destroy every hope of conciliation with her father. . . . It would have been selfish and stupid, and he hoped he was neither of those things.

He got through it somehow. They had tea, and after a time he even found he could breathe again, could look at her without growing dizzy. But she had not yet met his eyes. She was so young, so fragile. He longed to hold her to his heart, to protect her from the buffeting winds of life, but it was not his place.

Retreating to the library after the late meal in the saloon, he worked on his sermon for the service. It was not difficult. He need only speak from his heart, he had found over the last year. And especially in this instance, where he was speaking of a woman for whom he had nothing but love and respect. The challenge was in keeping it brief and not becoming effusive.

Tidwell, at the door, cleared his throat. "Sir, the solicitor is here, and he wishes to speak with you. May I show him in?"

"Certainly," Mark said, standing and moving around the desk to greet the man. What need he should have of him was not clear, but then maybe the fellow just wanted the library, the desk to work at. He started to shuffle his papers together.

"Mr. Mark Rowland?"

"Yes, that is I," Mark said. He shook the bony gentleman's large hand and said, "If you wish space to work, I can move out of here and take my papers to my room. Just one moment and I can give you the desk."

"Actually, sir, I wish to speak with you."

Puzzled, Mark indicated a chair across from the desk. "Please, have a seat then, Mr. . . ."

"Ballantine."

"Mr. Ballantine. Have a seat. What can I do for you, sir?"

"Lady Bournaud, before she died, asked that I inform you of your bequest in private, sir. Very specific she was."

"Bequest? I knew nothing of a bequest."

"Yes, well, she knew she was almost gone, her ladyship did. And somehow she knew she would be gone before Christmas. Not the first case of that kind of prescience I have seen."

Mark waited.

The man got out a paper and squinted at it. "Ah, here is the part. Have to make my way through the servants, you know, and the rest. Lady Chappell, et cetera. Now here is the part about you."

"Yes?"

"It is a conditional bequest. Frown on those, myself. Going to leave money, do so with no strings, you know. That is what I advise my clients. But Lady Bournaud was an obstreperous . . . Yes, well." He cleared his throat and squinted at the paper again.

Mark still waited. A little money would be welcome; he could not deny it. But what conditions would a woman like Lady Bournaud place on a bequest? Puzzling.

"Mr., ah, Mark Rowland . . . Here we are. Mhmm, mhmm." He mumbled through some words, and then said, "Here we are. 'I leave to Mark Rowland, Vicar of Loughton in Hampshire, apart from such furnishings as belong to Bournaud Chateau and such bequests as have been already made, all monetary amounts not heretofore accounted for within these pages, on the condition that he do marry within the twelve-month.'"

Mr. Ballantine rose and gathered his papers to leave.

"What . . . what does this mean? What money? And marry? I cannot marry. I have not money enough to marry, and there is only one girl . . . but I cannot!" Mark shook his head, trying to clear it.

Ballantine shrugged. "Told you, sir, I do not like conditional bequests. Urged her not to do it. But there you are. To receive your inheritance you must marry within the twelve-month or it will all go to the St. Eustaces. Hopping mad about it, they will be. But there is no challenging it. She was of sound mind when she made the will."

"I have no intention . . . no *ability* to marry." He would just have to forfeit the bequest. He could not marry, not loving Silvia as he did.

"Don't you?" Ballantine looked at the paper in his hand. "Let me tell you first what you will be passing up."

When he read the sum, Rowland thought he was joking. But he wasn't, Ballantine assured him; he never joked. The solicitor left, and Mark sat down, very carefully, in the chair. It was a lot of money. Enough to be worthy of one of the elevated titles.

But only if he wed. Only if . . .

"Mark?"

He looked up, not sure if minutes or hours had passed since the solicitor had left the room. It was Silvia, standing hesitantly at the door, one hand on the frame, who had spoken his name.

"Silvia, I . . ." He stood.

"How have you been?" she asked, stepping cautiously into the room, her eyes riveted on his face.

They stared at each other for a few minutes.

"I am all right. And you?"

"I . . . I suppose I am fine."

Banal as the words were, there was a depth of feeling trembling beneath them. Did she still love him as he loved her? He wanted to know, and yet was afraid of the answer. And then the meaning behind Lady Bournaud's bequest hit him in the stomach like a punch from Gentleman Jackson, sucking from him all ability to speak for a minute.

That was it. That was why the condition. Emboldened by Lady Bournaud's message from beyond the grave, he straightened. "How was London?"

"The Season? I did not go. I went from Verity and Vaughan's wedding directly to my aunt's in Bath and have been living there ever since."

"You didn't go to London in the spring?"

She tilted up her chin and looked him in the eye. "No. Lord Boxton asked me again to marry him and I said no. Papa refuses to see me."

The news infuriated him, and yet there was encouragement there. "I admire your refusal to yield in the face of such obduracy. It must be difficult for a young lady to withstand such pressure from her parents."

"It is not hard," Silvia said softly. "Lord Boxton is cruel. I could never love him. I could never marry a man I did not like, or at least respect." She stopped and looked away, her chin quivering. "And my heart is not my own to give."

His heart pounding now, longing to touch her, to take her in his arms, Mark kept himself separate from her, from his Silvia, his love. "What does your father demand of a suitor for your hand?"

"What do you mean?"

"Are they still set on a title? You are so lovely, so perfect, even a duke would be lucky, but do they . . ?" His courage deserted him.

"They wanted a title," she admitted. "But they despair of me now. My sister was recently married to a marquess, and all are so pleased with her. I think Papa would be satisfied with a competency for me." Sadly she met his eyes.

She knew he did not even have that, he thought.

He moved around the desk, toward her, closer, closing the distance between them but not daring yet to touch her, for his composure would crumble. "Silvia, do you still feel for me what you felt last January?"

Her eyes filled with water and her chin quivered again, her self-restraint fragile, tenuous. "Mark, how can you even ask? I told you then, and I will repeat it now. I will always love you."

He ached to hold her, to kiss her, to wipe the delicate shivering tears from her eyelashes and kiss her cheeks and lips. He was almost afraid of the need that pulsed through him, the desire to hold her to him, to have her for eternity. "Silvia, will you . . . would you consider marrying me?"

Eyes wide, her whole body trembling, she moved forward and put her hands on his shoulders. "Oh, Mark, I w-will, even if we have to wait forever! Even if we have to wait until we are old, I will promise to marry you."

"How would a Christmas wedding sound to you?"

"Christmas?" She frowned. "Of what year?"

"Of this year! Of this very year of our Lord eighteen hundred and seventeen." He laughed at the puzzlement on her pretty face. Taking her in his arms, he looked down into her brown eyes and said, "My dearest angel, I may not have a title, but if you will marry me, I will be a wealthy man, even, I think, by your parents' rigid standards!"

And then there was only delirium for a while. They kissed and hugged and touched and kissed some more. And Mark explained to her the news he had just received, the bequest, the strange condition, and what he thought it meant.

Silvia, crying in earnest now, said, "Bless her! Oh, bless her."

"Thank you, Lady Bournaud," Rowland said, gazing up at the ceiling. "Thank you, you scheming Christmas matchmaker." He lowered his face to Silvia once more, but the sound of hurrahs from the door made them both look up.

Two couples, Lord and Lady Vaughan and Sir David and Lady Chappell looked in from the doorway. They spilled in, and for a few minutes all that could be heard was the happy sound of congratulations, back-slapping, tears, cheers, and laughter. Tidwell, attracted by the clamor, was sent for champagne and invited to join the happy couples in a toast. A toast to a Christmas matchmaker.

"What do you think changed her mind?" Sir David asked his wife as they stood a ways away from the younger couples.

"Why? Do you think this was what Lady Bournaud had in mind when she added that bequest to her will? That it would allow Mark and Silvia to marry?"

He nodded. "I don't think there is any other way to interpret this." He held his wife close to his heart.

"I think you are right. I don't know what changed her mind, but when we spoke she said that she had a letter from Mark, and that he was different, sadder. It made her unhappy, to think that she had been any part of his sadness. This is her way of making up for what she saw as interference."

"Interference!" David snorted. "Without her interference I would not have you, my sweet wife!"

She hugged him, her arms around his waist. "I think Lady Bournaud is watching and smiling this very minute." She laid her head on her husband's chest and watched the two young couples toast their joy.

Stroking his wife's soft hair, Sir David chuckled. "Smiling? I know better than that. The old girl is up there doing a jig, and with François right alongside of her." With that, he found Beatrice's lips with his own and they lost themselves in their cherished and hard-won love.

ABOUT THE AUTHOR

Donna Simpson lives with her family in Canada. She is currently working on her next Zebra Regency romance, PAMELA'S SECOND SEASON, to be published in February 2003. Donna loves to hear from readers, and you may write to her c/o Zebra Books. Please include a self-addressed stamped envelope if you wish a reply.

Put a Little Romance in Your Life With
Constance O'Day-Flannery

__Bewitched $5.99US/$7.50CAN
  0-8217-6126-9

__The Gift $5.99US/$7.50CAN
  0-8217-5916-7

__Once in a Lifetime $5.99US/$7.50CAN
  0-8217-5918-3

__Time-Kept Promises $5.99US/$7.50CAN
  0-8217-5963-9

__Second Chances $5.99US/$7.50CAN
  0-8217-5917-5

More Zebra Regency Romances

BOOK YOUR PLACE ON OUR WEBSITE AND MAKE THE READING CONNECTION!

We've created a customized website just for our very special readers, where you can get the inside scoop on everything that's going on with Zebra, Pinnacle and Kensington books.

When you come online, you'll have the exciting opportunity to:

- View covers of upcoming books
- Read sample chapters
- Learn about our future publishing schedule (listed by publication month *and author*)
- Find out when your favorite authors will be visiting a city near you
- Search for and order backlist books from our online catalog
- Check out author bios and background information
- Send e-mail to your favorite authors
- Meet the Kensington staff online
- Join us in weekly chats with authors, readers and other guests
- Get writing guidelines
- AND MUCH MORE!

Visit our website at
http://www.kensingtonbooks.com